M000158586

ORDINARY

"It was a perfect balance of serious and sweet—and to top it off, it delivers everything it hints at!"

★ ★ ★ ★ ★

Feather Tone Reviews

"...fast-paced with thrilling action sequences and plenty of suspense..."

★ ★ ★ ★ ★

Literary Portals

PRAISE FOR

UNIQUE

"...loving this book as much, if not more than, the first book."

★ ★ ★ ★ ★

Feather Tone Reviews

"It's non stop action, from the start till the end. I feel like I didn't even blink till the last page."

★ ★ ★ ★ ★

Diary of a Wannabe Writer

MORE FROM STARR Z. DAVIES:

STONES: A STEAMPUNK MYSTERY

POWERS SERIES:
SUPERIOR (POWERS PREQUEL)
ORDINARY (POWERS BOOK 1)
UNIQUE (POWERS BOOK 2)
(EXTRA)ORDINARY (POWERS BOOK 3)

FRACTURED EMPIRE SAGA:
DAUGHTER OF THE YELLOW DRAGON (BOOK 1)
LORDS OF THE BLACK BANNER (BOOK 2)
MOTHER OF THE BLUE WOLF (BOOK 3)
EMPRESS OF THE JADE REALM (BOOK 4)

(EXTRA)
ORDINARY

Powers Book Three

STARR Z. DAVIES

PANGEA
BOOKS

Copyright © 2021 by Starr Z. Davies.

All rights reserved. No part of this publication may be reproduced, distributed or transmitted in any form or by any means, including photocopying, recording, or other electronic or mechanical methods, without the prior written permission of the publisher, except in the case of brief quotations embodied in critical reviews and certain other noncommercial uses permitted by copyright law. For permission requests, write to the publisher, addressed "Attention: Permissions Coordinator," at the address below.

Starr @ Pangea Books
PangeaBooks.online
www.starrzdavies.com

Publisher's Note: This is a work of fiction. Names, characters, places, and incidents are a product of the author's imagination. Locales and public names are sometimes used for atmospheric purposes. Any resemblance to actual people, living or dead, or to businesses, companies, events, institutions, or locales is completely coincidental.

Book Layout ©2021 Pangea Books

Cover Design by Fay Lane Graphics

(extra)Ordinary / Starr Z. Davies. -- 1st ed.

1] Survival Fiction 2] Superheroes 3] Post-apocolyptic 4] Coming of Age

ISBN 978-1-7363459-0-0

For Kharysma: Your stubborn will and sheer determination are an inspiration.

WARNING:
This book contains series spoilers.

This book is meant as a companion to the Powers Series. Some chapters overlap with events from the previous books. Please read *Ordinary (Powers Book One)* and *Unique (Powers Book Two)* before proceeding to avoid spoilers.

While every attempt to show these overlapping scenes from a different POV has been made, some parts will feel familiar (and sometimes strikingly so).

(EXTRA)ORDINARY | adjective | eck·straw·or·din·ary : beyond standard quality or rank, something exceptional; of a person with remarkable qualities or distinctive features

Part One

"CRIME CONTINUES TO INCREASE exponentially on the Eastern side of Elpis. Assault, arson, robbery, homicide. These crimes are spreading, and now the Department of Military Affairs and the Directorate are facing an even tougher challenge: a rogue group of radicals spreading anti-Directorate rumors. Now is the time for severe consequences for offenders."

~ Directorate Chief Seaduss
One Week Before Paragon Tower Bombing

1

I HAVE THIS REOCCURRING DREAM. I'M ATTACHED TO a table with tungsten straps all over my body. A shriek echoes off the stark white walls of the room and rings in my ears. Every time, I wonder the same thing, *What moron is making that racket?*

And then I realize it's me.

I scream as the metal straps cut into my skin, bending against the force of my struggling body. I scream as the doctors work together, holding me still enough to stab a needle in my arm, and fire burns through my body. I scream as the straps break free and I rush the tungsten door, buckling it against the frame upon collision. I scream a name I can never hear over the shrill sound of my own voice while I pound bloody fists against the door that continues to buckle but never breaks. I scream as they shoot me.

And then I never scream again.

2

THE ROOM IS WHITE FROM THE TILED FLOORS TO THE
seamless ceiling. Along one wall, a bay of mirrors casts the image
of an unfamiliar girl back at me. Her muscles are thick along the
shoulders and cable down her bare arms. Her clothing is stark, black,
like death. A fury burns in the copper eyes glaring at me.

Not a strange girl. Me. Bianca Pond.

Anxious and confused, I pull my long dark hair over one shoulder
and begin braiding it loosely as I investigate my situation.

The small, square room has no door. Only the single metal chair
and the wall of mirrors. Even the lights are recessed into the ceiling
so deep I cannot see where they are as if the ceiling itself glows with
light.

Anxiety presses against my chest and makes my vision swim.
Where am I? How do I get out? Maybe breaking the mirror will do the
trick. I ball my hands into fists at my sides and watch as the muscles
in my arms swell in size. Such strength! It pulses and hums in my
muscles, intoxicating in its primal power. I pull back a fist and slam it
into the mirror.

The mirror vibrates and my reflection quakes as the mirror
absorbs the impact, singing a dull song of mourning. But it doesn't
break. *It must be reinforced with Naturalist Power,* I think, surprised by the
sound of my voice in my head.

"Do you remember where you are?" a man says. His voice
emanates from all around me.

I tilt my head back to gaze at the ceiling and turn in a slow circle.

"Do you remember where you are?" he asks again. His voice carries the same inflection as before, as if the question is a recording.

I close my eyes, dig in my mind for memories, but can only grasp flashes. A funeral. Two caskets. Someone beside me with his arm draped over my shoulders. He has the same eyes as me. A squat, long government building with giant fluted columns and a balcony on the top floor. My finger pressed against a tablet.

I open my eyes slowly. "The Department of Military Affairs."

"Why are you here?" he asks.

"To protect the city and the citizens from acts of terror," I say. The words don't register with my mind, but they sound right as they slip past my lips. "So they don't lose their families to the radicals like I did."

Silence.

I turn to face the mirror again. Someone must be on the other side. "Why am I here?"

"To protect the citizens of Elpis from radicals," he says, spouting my answer back at me.

I shake my head. "No, I mean why am I *here*?" I wave toward the doorless room.

"You volunteered to be here."

Volunteered …

Again, the memory of pressing my finger to a tablet surface flashes through my mind, but it feels foreign, like it isn't mine. Despite the odd sensation, I *do* recall volunteering for a special DMA project. Radicals killed my parents, and the DMA offered me this chance … or someone did. A man, whose face I cannot quite grasp, extended me the opportunity to join this secret project with the promise that it would help me avenge the murder of Mom and Dad. It would make me stronger, faster, better.

Anger burns in my chest as I step toward the mirror again, examining the way my deltoid muscles are so defined, the increased size of my biceps. Clenching my fists again, the cabling of each muscle in my arms becomes more distinct. With this level of strength,

I could punch a fist through the giant fluted columns I recall from outside the Administration Building. I could crush a man's skull with a single blow.

I could exact my revenge on the radicals.

"I am ready," I say with confidence, simmering anger and hate burning in my voice.

"Not yet. First, we need to run you through some tests to assess the efficacy of your transition. Then you will be assigned to a unit and begin your training."

The metal chair disappears, replaced by a treadmill. I step back, but this is familiar. A simulation, perhaps.

"First, we will test your endurance and speed."

This test is unnecessary. I already know my capabilities, how fast I can run, and for how long. The knowledge is burned into my mind, as if pressed into my muscles by the sheer memory of having run it before. A desire to scoff and tell him I don't need to run rises in my throat, but I step on the treadmill as if it was a natural, given movement. My body betrays my thoughts.

And I run, my feet only grazing the treadmill as the speed of the belt keeps easy pace with me. Run until I can't run anymore, he says, and so I do without question even though I have plenty to ask. Once again, my body betrays my mind.

It's impossible to know how much time passes. The treadmill has no timer, no distance. No display. It's simply the belt, the rollers, and me. My breathing is evenly paced, matching the rhythmic whisper of my boots across the belt. Hunger burns in my stomach, yet I haven't even broken a sweat yet. I run for hours. How far have I gone? Miles? The longer I run, the more that hunger eats away at me until, at last, I hop off.

"Have you reached your limit?" the mysterious male voice asks the moment the belt of the treadmill stops whirring.

"I'm hungry."

"Have you reached your limit?" he repeats.

"Yes," I lie. I haven't reached my limit, but the hunger is

overwhelming, as if my insides are eating away at themselves.

"One seventy-seven in five fifty-four," he says, though I don't believe he is talking to me.

What does that even mean?

My stomach rolls painfully and I clench my gut. "I need food."

The treadmill vanishes. A small pedestal table appears in the corner of the room, piled with cooked fish and linguini noodles, along with a loaf of French bread. I sink into the single chair beside the table and dive into the meal, eating with a voracious hunger like I've never experienced before—or at least, I don't think I've ever experienced it before. Everything goes down so fast I don't taste any of it. They could have given it to me unflavored and I would not have noticed.

As I press the last piece of bread into the crumbs on the plate and wash everything down with my third glass of milk, the treadmill reappears.

"Again," he says.

With a full stomach, I am prepared for the next run.

As I run, my mind drifts to my parents. Mom, with her heart-shaped face so much like my own. I can remember her warmth, kindness, compassion, yet I can't seem to recall anything more specific. The same issue surfaces as I think about Dad. His presence is always strict, expectant, yet loving, and I remember that I have his eyes. But no specific memories will rise to the surface. Except for one.

My burning desire to avenge them. So as I run, I imagine their killers in front of me and it hastens my steps.

The rest of my day continues much the same. After running and eating three more times—the time getting longer, as well as the distance—a bed replaces everything in the room.

"Rest," he says. "We will begin again tomorrow."

I settle into the bed, wondering if they will require me to do nothing more than run again. The comforter is warm and soft, if a bit institutional white, and the pillow welcomes me. I drift off, thinking about what awaits.

3

THE NEXT THREE DAYS ARE COMPARABLE. DAY TWO, they test my lifting capacity. Day three, the force of my fists and feet. Day four, I watch videos of professional fighters in judo, MMA, boxing, and more, then have to mimic their fighting from memory.

On day five, I wake in a strange bedroom on a soft mattress. The surrounding room has walls in such a light shade of gray they almost appear white. A five-foot-long modern art canvas adds a brilliant rainbow of color to the space, and the throw rug on the floor has matching hues, though a unique pattern. A nightstand beside the bed holds only a clear glass tablet.

Frowning, I slip my bare feet out from under the sage down comforter and pad toward the door. The throw rug is soft as I pass over it and open the door to the narrow main living space.

I pause in the doorway, taking in the area. Like my room, the walls are light gray, with splashes of color on paintings, throw rugs, and furniture. The kitchen is compact, just off to the right, with two bar stools at one counter. Directly across from my door, another stands open, revealing a bedroom exactly like my own, and beside the kitchen, two more doors. One is open, revealing a small bathroom. The other is closed. It must be the exit. There are no windows anywhere. Where am I? Is this home? Why can't I remember home?

A girl perhaps two or three years older than me sits up from where she lounges on a blood-red sofa in the living room.

"You're awake!" she says, as if surprised ... as if I should recognize her. "They told me you were coming." She rises, placing her tablet on the sofa to approach me. "I'm excited to have a roommate."

"Roommate?" I ask, turning to her. "Do I know you?"

She pauses in front of me, a full head shorter with brilliant red hair in smooth layers to her shoulders. "Poly," she says, holding out a hand. "We haven't met yet, no."

I frown at her hand, taking it and shaking in a firm grip that causes her wince. My grasp is a touch too rough.

"Steele," I say, letting go of her hand. The name falls from my lips, but I don't recall it. I intended to tell her my actual name, Bianca, but cannot. "Where are we?"

Poly's smile falters, and she steps back. What is that about? "The DMA provided us with accommodations."

The Department of Military Affairs. The mission. To save the citizens of Elpis from terrorism. Understanding washes through me, even though I still don't recall any of it distinctly. My memory continues to feel disjointed.

"Are we in the same unit, then?" I ask, stepping to the fridge and deliberately opening the door to avoid accidentally breaking it with my Strength.

Fresh fruit, vegetables, and various meats and cheeses line the shelves. One full shelf holds dozens of cartons of milk.

"No," Poly says. Is she retreating further away? I hadn't caught when she took that initial step backward, but now she appears to be cautiously hedging away from me. "Everything you need to know should be on your tablet." Poly glances at the clock on the wall nearby. "Anyway, we should get ready. They will be here for us soon."

"Who?" I ask, but as I glance up from the fridge, she is already retreating into her room and closing the door.

Taking a carton of milk and an apple, I retire to my room. My thumb brushes over the skin of the apple and a peculiar sense of sadness envelops me. The sensation is absurd. Why should an apple cause so much sorrow? Yet I cannot deny the hollow notion, the desolation that accompanies it.

I set the apple down, impatient to cast off these new emotions, and pick up the tablet. The moment my finger contacts the screen, it lights up.

> B. Pond
> Call Sign: Steele
> Special Forces Unit 15
> Mission Log: 07:00 report for orientation & training
> Training Officer: Nevermore Poe
> Liaison Agent: Dr. Forrest Pond

I blink at the information rising from the surface. Forrest Pond. Coppery eyes like mine. A comforting arm. Rain and puddles and mud castles that melt into the ground. We share the same last name. Could he be the fragmented memory from the funeral?

My memories slip from my grasp like water through my fingers. The harder I struggle to maintain them, the more discouraging it is when they elude me. Yet some portion of them remains, just at the edge of my mind, like that thing you can sense behind you but never perceive.

Eager for a diversion, I explore the tablet for more information, but only the one report displays. With an exhale, I set the tablet down and study my room. I know this place, and yet I feel as if I've never been here before. Why is it so familiar, yet so utterly foreign? What has happened to me?

I volunteered to join the Special Forces in the DMA, I remind myself, and the conviction of that thought consoles me a little. I signed up for this. I belong here.

And today, I will start my formal training. Then, perhaps soon, I will hunt down the radicals and make them pay for what they have done to my parents.

4

POLY IS GONE BEFORE MY TRAINER ARRIVES TO ESCORT me ten levels down into the training facility. I'm uncertain if this is a reprieve or if I sincerely feel sorry that she isn't with us. The girl seemed apprehensive of me once she heard my name. Why?

Nevermore Poe, my training officer, turns out to be a boy only marginally older than me. As we ride the freight elevator down, his beady, bird-like eyes observe me. Between his jet black, slicked-back hair, the paleness of his face, and the manner with which he stares, he reminds me of a raven. He isn't Somatic like me—one of the Four Branches of Powers that enhances the body. The slim, frail shape of his frame makes that abundantly clear. It leaves me incredibly curious to learn what his Power is.

"Poly said you were coming for both of us," I say, soliciting conversation. "But she was already gone."

"She isn't in our unit," he says, and his voice slides over my skin like slime.

I nod as if this explanation makes perfect sense. It's likely trainers only work with their own units. Does that make Nevermore my superior? Just considering him my commanding officer makes my stomach bubble in revulsion. I have no compelling reason to hold such an intense reaction toward him. I don't even know Nevermore. But again my mind is pushing back against my emotions, rejecting any recollection of him while still seeking to warn me.

"You're uncomfortable with me," he says.

Can he read my mind? I wonder. If he can, that would make

Nevermore a Telepath, from the Psionic Branch of Powers that enhances the Powers of the mind.

The rim of his mouth curves up into a smirk. "Follow orders and you will have no reason to be uneasy around me."

We walk out of the freight elevator into an immense chamber. The stink of stone slams against me like we are in a cavern deep underground—like a superhero's lair hidden away from the world. The rock walls, floor, and ceiling are smooth and roughly thirty feet high, allowing ample area for practicing jumps or climbs. The training facility may have been nothing more than solid stone deep beneath the facility itself, but with the expert abilities of Naturalists—one of the Four Branches of Powers that can manipulate natural matter— they had molded the stone out into this enormous chamber.

Around the outlying rim of the training floor, which is as big as several football fields, if not wider, is a rubber running track. Other Special Forces officers like myself launch themselves over simulation platforms, scale a rock wall, practice firing at targets, or face off in roped sparring rings. A rope obstacle course with bridges and swinging ropes and climbing poles is currently unused, but I don't doubt these agents find a chance to practice on it. The sheer amount of training options seems unlimited. A weightlifting set in one part of the facility catches my attention. Hopefully, I will have time to challenge my limits with it.

Three levels up, a series of metal bridges crisscross the field, and men and women in white lab coats mill around. There are only a few of them engrossed in whatever data their tablets are reporting, operating with evident purpose.

Despite the massive area, only nine other agents are training. They work in groups of two that cluster close together. One pair runs past Nevermore and I after we stride over the track, but they hardly cast us a perfunctory glance. I could easily outrun both of them without batting an eye.

Poly is working on her aim with a boy about her height. He guides her arm into position. Perhaps he is her trainer.

Nevermore joins another boy my age beside one of the flat white simulation platforms. I immediately recognize his handsome, chiseled face as it cracks into a captivating smile when he looks at me.

"Happy to see you made it through to the other side," he says.

"Hound." I beam back, despite myself. *Hound?* That isn't his actual name, but I can't seem to recall what it is. My emotions are at odds with each other once more. I'm both delighted to see Hound, while also furious with him for reasons I can't determine. *The other side of what?* I wonder.

"You volunteered for an experiment that a lot of others did not complete," Nevermore says, and now I'm positive he can read my mind. "When you enlisted in the DMA Special Forces, you agreed to an experimental injection that would enhance your strength. The injection doesn't work for everybody, and they eliminate those who fail from the program. You passed the first phase."

I sweep my gaze over each of them. Hound is taller than I am and moderately well built, but I doubt he is Somatic. And I've already determined that Nevermore isn't.

"No, on both counts," Nevermore says. I wish he would quit reading my mind. "As you've already surmised, I'm a Psionic Telepath."

"Naturalist Hematology," Hound says, as if I will understand precisely what that means. I don't.

"He's a Bloodhound," Nevermore explains, "and can track anyone with a blood scent."

Hound. Now that makes sense. So I was correct. It isn't his name, just like Steele isn't mine. It's his call sign.

"You two know each other already," Nevermore says, "but periodically the injection can do strange things to the mind."

Hound grins again in that charming manner that causes my stomach to flip. "We went to high school together, and we were pretty close. I can fill you in later if you want."

That must be why he seems so familiar. And he must have done something that made me mad as well, which would explain why I feel so furious with him. Nevermore casts a disapproving glare at Hound but mentions nothing.

"Other units consist of four agents," I say. "Who are we missing?"

"Vortex." Hound rubs at his neck. "She had some trouble after her last dose, so they have her in for further tests right now. She should return in a day or two. It's pretty unusual for anyone to be gone longer."

Vortex. Another girl. "What is her Power?"

They both grin. "She can show you herself," Hound says. "But she is Divinic."

Divinics are the final of the Four Branches of Powers, with supernatural Powers such as reading auras or healing. I can't help but speculate what Vortex can manage.

"What dose?" I ask as the news finally seems to stick. I don't recall receiving any doses.

"It's your enhancement dose," Nevermore explains, scowling. "Part of Phase Two. You get one every night before bed. You take it before you go to sleep. It will help you rest as the enhancement does its thing. If you lose a dose, you will have to request a replacement using your tablet. Your request will be reviewed, but it's pretty unusual for them to provide a replacement, and without it your enhancement could have negative effects on your body. The scientists don't actually know what all it could involve, but degenerative diseases are a real risk. Don't miss your dose. Ever."

Have I already missed a dose? A flash of panic grips me, and I have to assure myself that the scientists wouldn't let that happen. Maybe they administered it to me and I just don't remember.

"What happens if I don't complete Phase Two?" I ask.

Nevermore shrugs. "Most of us are still in Phase Two." He crosses toward a sparring ring and Hound follows without prompting, leaving me to trail along behind them as if the discussion is over. "In the field," Nevermore begins as he assumes a position near the edge of the ring, "we will encounter quite a bit of resistance. If we face down large groups or strong Powers, we need to be ready to defend ourselves, and it requires more than just fists."

Did he just sneer at me? He probably longed for Somatic Power before his Telepathy emerged.

"We have to learn to act as a unit which means we need to understand each other's strengths and weaknesses," he continues. "To achieve that, we will fight using only our Powers. Hound, show her how it's done."

All the charm slides off Hound's face, supplanted by sheer determination and a resolute set of his chiseled jaw as he strides into the ring. I duck under the ropes to follow him.

Hound firms his stance, feet planted shoulder-width apart, hands at his sides. His fingers twitch, waiting.

I survey him, waiting as well, but he doesn't move. Am I expected to strike first? In seconds, I close the divide between us, but before I can pass halfway, extraordinary pressure captures my entire body and my muscles seize. Blood pumps thunderously in my skull, causing everything to blur. I blink to clear my vision, only to learn I'm lying on my back.

Hound stands over me, offering a hand to help me up. But this isn't over. I sweep a leg out to knock his feet from under him, and even as his back strikes the mat, I'm landing on top of him. Before I can pin him down, his Power presses against me. My back arches and my arms spread wide at my sides. He effortlessly uses a hand to shove me off him.

"No place for mistakes, Steele," Nevermore says nearby. His voice is dampened as if speaking through water. "Let's make this lesson clear."

Hound frowns as he climbs to his feet. My vision narrows around him as he raises a shuddering hand, the muscles in his arms twitching. He lifts my body helplessly off the ground. My feet dangle just inches from the mat and the magnitude of the pressure within me makes it seem as if my body is being stretched out.

"Fight back, Steele," Nevermore barks.

But I can't fight back. Control of my body is no longer my own, no matter how hard I struggle to concentrate. The muscles in my legs and arms strain at the uniform, causing the cloth to tighten like a vice around me. It only intensifies the sensation from Hound's Power like fire burning my blood or some invisible magnet repelling my cells from one another.

"Fight back!" Nevermore snaps. He thrusts a palm out toward me from outside the ring.

Suddenly, my skin feels like I've been plunged into an ice bath. The air punches out of my lungs. The training facility disappears, replaced by a desolate landscape. What is happening? We aren't on a simulation platform, yet I'm no longer where I should be!

In the distance, a ghostly form with indistinct features shrieks as lightning rains down on him. My chest aches. I struggle to move, but my body resists. There is no rational reason for the dread in my chest. More than anything else, I need to reach him, help him, save him. It's a compulsion driving me onward. My feet shuffle slowly forward as if I'm struggling against the weight of a wrecking ball. My target howls in torment so savagely that it rips at my soul.

I roar, tugging harder at the invisible force holding me back. Why do I care what happens to him so much?

By the time I reach him, my body aches like never before. Every part of me threatens to collapse. Stretching a trembling hand toward his charred flesh, I whirl him around only to be confronted by his back again. I turn him around repeatedly, but he possesses no front, no face. I howl in defeat and crumple to the ground.

The training facility returns in a flash, and I am on my knees in front of Hound weeping. The humiliation of it overpowers me. Great. My first day and I'm openly weeping in front of my team. As if to punctuate my humiliation further, Nevermore sneers. I bury my face in my hands to cover the sobs.

"Pathetic," Nevermore scoffs. "In the field, the radicals will employ every advantage they have against us, and you are remarkably weak. You have a long way to go, Steele."

"What did you do to her?" Hound asks, the curiosity in his tone as clear as a bell. He isn't perturbed or furious. He's intrigued.

"Take her back to her apartment," Nevermore orders. "Hopefully tomorrow she won't be as worthless." He squats beside me and leans close, whispering in my ear. "If you depend on your fists in the field, you won't last long. What a shame that would be."

I suck in breaths, battling for command of my emotions. What just happened? Who was that strange figure? Why did he matter so much to me that I would fight so hard to reach him?

Hound places an encouraging hand on my shoulder. "Come on. Let's get you back home."

Home. Is that what they call this place? Sniffling and briskly wiping away tears, I attempt standing with Hound's support, and his arm offers me some comfort. Despite my Super Strength, my entire body feels as if it has been crushed under a mountain. I can't recall the last time I felt so powerless. The burden was not physical, but emotional. If Nevermore aimed to get into my head and pick me apart, he succeeded.

§

Back in my apartment, Hound turns on the light and ushers me to the sofa. I sink into it with a thud that causes the sofa frame to object. Hound retreats to the kitchen, emerging a minute later with a carton of milk, a protein bar, and an apple.

"Food helps," he asserts. "These enhanced Powers can draw a load out of us. Our bodies burn calories faster, so we have to make sure we are eating whenever we have a chance."

I devour the protein bar, scarcely noticing the hints of peanut butter and cranberries, then guzzle the milk to wash it down.

Hound sinks onto the sofa and leans an arm on the back as he observes me eat with amusement.

"What about you?" I ask, mopping my arm across my mouth.

"Oh, it hits me, for sure. It'll be worse for you though. I manipulate other bodies. You manipulate your own, which means you will burn calories even faster."

I pluck up the apple, and that same sense of sadness washes over me as earlier that morning. I can't explain it, and I frown at the fruit as I brush a thumb over the red skin.

Hound cocks his head curiously. "You okay?"

"Nevermore doesn't like me much."

He snorts. "Nevermore doesn't like anyone. Maybe because he knows what we think of him."

That gets my attention, and I meet Hound's gaze, invited in by that charming smirk on his face and the way his blue eyes dance in delight.

"You don't like him?" I ask.

Hound sighs in a manner that implies something more dramatic than out of a desire to communicate any genuine emotion. "We are a unit. I don't have to like him. I only have to trust that when we are out there, he has my back. That's what counts."

I spin the apple in my hands. Images of that charred boy from training arises. I blink back unexpected tears. The boy had no front, no face. He was a little more than a charred body in gray scrubs. Yet a sense of familiarity teases at my mind, filling me with longing, fear, and despair. It makes no sense.

Hound's hand slips over mine. The touch sends a shiver down my spine. I react before thinking, jerking away and shoving him back hard enough to send him to the other end of the sofa. The wounded expression on his face immediately makes me regret my actions.

"I'm sorry," I mumble.

He rubs at his chest where my palm struck him, wincing marginally. "You really don't remember me at all?"

I want to remember everything, but the harder I try, the deeper the surrounding vacuum becomes. I shake my head.

His shoulders sag and he examines me as if he's seeking to decide whether I'm sincere. At last, he reaches his hands out to me, palms up, and waits.

What will happen if I take them? Curious, I set down the apple, edge closer, and slip my hands into his. They are warm and soft.

Hound releases a breath of relief and his thumb brushes over my hand. I expect he means the gesture to be endearing, or maybe to shake something loose in my memory, but all I desire is to pull away. It requires sheer willpower to wait patiently.

A sensation of tingling brushes my hands, then slowly travels up my arms as warmth flows through my entire body. He is using his Power on me. I want to recoil. I want to lean against him. His gaze remains locked on me, dragging me in deeper. My heart quickens.

"I can tell you how we know each other," he says, and the dulcet rhythm of his voice matches my breathing.

All I can offer is a nod.

The edge of his lips curls up in a slight, handsome grin. "We've known each other for six years. But not as Hound and Steele. We met in sixth year at homeroom and you loathed me." He chuckles as if that should be amusing when I find it anything but. "But by ninth year, we were practically inseparable. Bianca and Jimmy. The couple everyone else wanted to be."

Couple? We dated?

Tenderness relaxes his features, causing him to appear even more handsome than ever before. My breath catches, and suddenly I can believe that we were a couple. I can no longer tell if that tingling in my skin is from his Power or from within myself.

"In tenth year, we visited my parent's cabin on the lake together to celebrate your birthday." Hound—Jimmy—leans closer, and I am drawn toward him. An intoxicating sensation makes my head swim. "And that night ..." His fingers drift along my neck. I was not even aware that he had released my hand.

I swallow a lump in my throat. Realizing he is about to kiss me, I jerk away and jump to my feet.

The suddenness of it alarms him.

"I think you should go now," I say.

"Bianca, I'm sorry. I just ..." He rubs his neck. "I really miss you. I'm so happy to have you here."

All the yearning and headiness I experienced before, all the attraction, collapses. Was it even real, or just a trick of his Power? I shake my head, remembering feeling irritable with him before. "Maybe what you claim is true, but it doesn't feel right. I think it's best if you leave."

He balks. I couldn't care less if my words wounded him.

"Bianca—"

"Goodnight, Hound."

He rises and starts toward the door, but hesitates before opening it. "Just so you know, I asked for this unit so I could be with you."

He opens the door and slides out as Poly enters. She glances back over her shoulder to watch him leave. "So, are you two a thing? Because if not I wouldn't mind making a go at that myself."

I scoff and stalk to my room. "Be my guest," I snap, then slam the door hard enough to crack the frame.

The nerve of him, presuming we could just pick up whatever we might have had before! Just considering being with him sends a renewed surge of irritation through me. Yet, I cannot justify why.

5

A NIGHTMARE WAKES ME, BUT EVEN AS I WAKE, THE nightmare fades. I can't recall any of it distinctly. An overwhelming pang of hunger seizes my stomach. I shuffle out to the modest kitchen to dig out something to eat, rubbing my eyes. A faint light glowing from Poly's door catches my attention. What time is it? Why is she still awake?

After an exhale, I chew the precooked steak without bothering to slice it. I sink my teeth into the juicy flesh, tearing it off with an almost feral starvation.

The dose appeared on my nightstand before bed, and I injected it without a second thought. The blue liquid flowed through me when I depressed the plunger. Nevermore said the dose would assist my sleep. It produced no such results. Instead, I'm groggy and disoriented. The nightmare is gone altogether now, yet I feel the surge of adrenaline from powerful fear, and a profound sense of loss as if something valuable had been ripped away from me.

Eager to purge the nightmare for good, I pad barefoot toward Poly's door. Maybe she can keep me company or help interpret some of this.

Hushed voices emanate from within her room. I press my back to the wall beside the door, unclear why I'm nervous about being caught eavesdropping. Who would visit at this time anyhow? Unless Poly has a boy in her room.

"… deep denial," Poly says.

Her companion snorts. "Well, let's keep it that way," he says, and

I recognize Nevermore's tone instantly. "Our orders were clear, and you know what can happen if we fail him."

No. I'm not meant to hear this discussion. If there is a threat or risk if they fail whatever this order is, I don't want to be caught listening.

I creep back toward my room, careful not to bump anything or produce a noise. The steak in my hand makes my mouth water, but I don't dare take a bite and risk them hearing the squish of the meat. I close my door, allowing a crack open so I can hear or see when Nevermore leaves.

As I linger, I inhale the rest of the steak, then lick the savory meat and juice off my fingers. By the time I'm finished, Nevermore emerges from Poly's room. She trails alongside him. He appears more casual than he acted earlier in the day. The way he steps and carries himself reveals a cool, confident nature that contrasts with the rigidity and unforgiving edge he had around me. They arrive at the door, and he places a hand on her shoulder, then slides out.

Poly closes it behind him and peers over her shoulder toward my room.

I gasp and shuffle away from the door. Can she sense me watching? Does she know I overheard them?

Deciding to lean into the moment as Poly retrieves a drink, I open my door and stretch, pretending to have just woken.

She spins around and squeals. Maybe she didn't detect me after all.

"You scared me, Steele," she says, pressing a hand against her chest and squeezing her cup of water on the countertop.

"Sorry. I didn't intend to."

"Why are you awake?"

"Nightmares. And hunger." Not a lie in the slightest.

Poly studies me for a moment. She nods. "I can understand that. Have you, um, been up for long?"

"No." Also not a lie. "I thought I overheard another voice in here, though. Was someone else here?"

"No." Poly doesn't even blink as she lies to my face.

"Can I ask you something else?" I ask, snatching a carton of milk from the fridge.

"Um, sure…" She leans back against the counter, crossing her arms over her rather large chest and cupping her glass of water in one hand.

"Earlier, when I mentioned my name, you seemed … afraid of me. Why?"

Poly chews her lip and gazes into the glass of water as if it possesses her answer there floating on the surface. "You just … have a reputation."

I blink. What does that mean?

As if understanding my surprise, Poly sighs. "First, when you went through Phase One, you became a little … wild … as the enhancement worked its course. I overheard you took out ten guards on your own with only your hands and feet."

Ten guards? Why do I not remember that?

Poly takes a leisurely sip, then proceeds, unable to match my gaze. "And your brother, well … he sort of intimidates us. All of us."

"My … brother?" Coppery eyes like mine. A comforting arm over my shoulders. "Dr. Forrest Pond?" I ask, recalling the name from my tablet, and how it filled me with the same familiar emotion. Not to mention that we share the same last name. That couldn't be a coincidence.

Poly meets my gaze with a timid one of her own. No. Not timid. Scared. She is frightened of Forrest. Why? "You don't remember him," she says, bewildered.

I shake my head. "Not exactly. My memory is like water. I can't grasp more than sensations or emotions. Pieces come to me like reflections, but they ripple and dissipate just as swiftly. Have you met him?"

Poly nods.

"He looks like me, right?"

"Yes," she says deliberately.

"He is the sole person I seem to have any portion of memory of."

I lean against the counter on my elbows. "I want to see him."

Poly opens her mouth as if about to reveal something, but must change her mind because she snaps it shut again.

"Did you lose memories, too?" I ask, swapping the subject. For whatever reason, Forrest makes her uneasy. I don't need to force the subject now.

"Some. Not as much as you. I remember my family, but nothing good." She rubs at her neck and for a moment appears to retreat into some awful memory. "And I remember enlisting for this program, standing at the desk, and pressing my finger to the contract." For a flash, Poly frowns but quickly throws it off. "Anyway, they say that Phase One can affect everyone differently. Some people like Hound retained all of their memories, while others of us have more scattered pieces."

Or none at all. It barely seems fair that I should be the only one to remember practically nothing. Nothing but anger, sadness, and an appetite for vengeance.

"Hound said we used to date, or maybe we still did when I signed up," I say, tugging my hair over my shoulder and absentmindedly braiding it. "All I can remember about him is anger, disgust, and, on some level, attraction."

"Well, the attraction I can understand," Poly says with a smirk that lights up her face. "I think every girl in this place has tried flirting with him at some point. Not that any of us stand a chance. From what I gather, he is taken with you."

I tug on the braid in annoyance, then finish the last of the milk, smacking the empty carton down on the counter hard enough to force the plastic crumple.

Poly raises her eyebrows but gives not comment.

Even now, thinking about being with Hound fills me with inexplicable fury. It pulses through me, engaging the enhanced muscles as if readying for a confrontation. The sight of my swelling muscles must alarm her, because Poly's eyes become large.

"A lot of anger, evidently," she says, alluding to my previous remark. "You're honestly not interested?"

I shake my head. It's troublesome to even consider when thinking about being with him causes such a backlash.

"It will thrill the other girls to hear that," Poly says with a lilting laugh. She steps closer, settling her hand on my shoulder as Nevermore had done with her. "I should get some sleep. And so should you. I hear Nevermore can be pretty ruthless in training."

That is a grievous understatement.

"We can talk more tomorrow, Steele," Poly says as she drifts back to her room.

Hound has all of his memories from before, which clarifies why he could reveal so much about our time together. But how much of it is true?

6

THE FOLLOWING DAY, NEVERMORE ARRIVES TO USHER me to the training facility again. Before I can step through my door, he plants his hands against the sides of my head and glowers. For a moment, he squeezes my head in a vice. A headache develops, but almost immediately after he surrenders his grip, all the pressure and discomfort in my head melts away, leaving me refreshed. I blink in surprise.

"A modest gift," he says gruffly. "You obviously didn't sleep adequately. I need you at maximum strength today."

Nevermore is correct, of course. Even after returning to bed, I tossed and turned, flung between fits of anger toward Hound and profound grief that I can only guess is for my parents. To top matters off, I had some sort of hideous nightmare once I went back to bed. Now, as we travel down the freight elevator to the training facility, I can no longer recall what that nightmare was about. I remember it being dreadful, but nothing else comes to mind, as if all memory of the nightmare itself has wiped away.

Hound is already waiting for us, chatting with a black-haired girl who giggles at something he says and flips her hair back over her shoulder. Upon spotting me, Hound turns off his charm, and all but ignores the girl. His face lights up as he looks at me, and I can understand why all the girls find him gorgeous.

The girl peers our way, casts a vexed glance in my direction, and stands straighter upon noticing Nevermore.

"Feeling better, Vortex?" Nevermore asks as we join the two of them near a line of sparring dummies.

Vortex nods stiffly.

"Great. We have a vigorous schedule today. Steele needs to be properly broken in."

I barely contain my indignation. *What was yesterday, then?*

Vortex's dark eyes sweep me over as if weighing me, and she smirks. "I think I can manage that."

Nevermore crosses his skinny arms over his frail chest. "In the field, we will only be able to identify the basics of what any target's Power is capable of, and that will not include any unseen companions they may have with them. Steele, Vortex is your target. Arrest her before she reaches the safety of her companions on the other side of that rock wall." He points to the far side of the training facility. "Your target's known Power is Astrological Tracking."

An odd Power considering the arrogant smirk on Vortex's face. If she is a Divinic who can track anyone using the stars, and we are inside a starless building, her Power is utterly useless. *This should be simple.*

"Step one: isolate the target," Nevermore says.

Hound steps behind the line of sparring dummies. Somehow he disappears, as does Nevermore. They simply vanish out of sight like a mirage, shimmering then gone. How did they do that? Where are they?

Vortex clenches her fists at her sides and spins away from me, bolting around the track toward the rock wall.

I grin and dash after her, closing the distance easily. There is no way this girl can outrun me with my enhanced speed. The rock wall is too far away. She will never beat me to it. The gap between us shrinks, and when I'm close enough to reach out for her, an invisible force pinches my frame and jerks me onto my back. And I fall...

... And fall, tumbling through a void of perfect blackness. Tumbling without end, as if trapped in a nightmare.

At last, my back hits a mat hard enough for my dense body to press through the layers and crack the stone beneath. My vision swims for before I recognize the reinforced ceiling of the training facility above me. My heart hammers against my ribs, and I gasp for air.

"What…?"

Nevermore leans over me, sneering. "You didn't isolate the target." He seizes my hand and tugs me to my feet.

"But she was alone."

Nevermore releases my hand and rubs his own on his black pants like my touch has some sort of contagion. "How do you know?"

"I fell, like, forever. How?"

Vortex crosses her arms. "You assumed I couldn't control my Power without the stars visible. Can you control your muscles without seeing them?"

"Of course," I snap, annoyed by her manner. "But they're part of me."

The way she rolls her eyes makes me feel like a moron, but I don't understand why.

"So only Somatics have their Power as part of them?" she asks tersely.

A costly assumption. I have no idea how other Powers work, or what people need to connect them. I can only explain the Power within me. It makes sense, though, that a Divinic could pluck her Power from anywhere as long as she can discern the source—probably depending on how strong that Power is—like a Naturalist can manipulate the surrounding environment even if they cannot see it.

I shake my head. "Wait. I fell into *your* void. How?"

"You didn't isolate the target," Nevermore repeats, sounding more exasperated, as if I should understand. I wish I did.

"I was there, hiding," Hound says. "And when you drew close enough, I applied my Hematology to force you off your feet, and she dumped you into the void."

I spin to discover him standing close enough to my shoulder his breath ruffles my hair. I step away from him and that devilishly charming smile he bestows on me. Hound is dangerous.

"But you two literally disappeared," I say, unable to recall any

Invisibility Power.

Nevermore taps his head. "Telepathic projection."

He made me *think* they had disappeared?

"Again," Nevermore commands.

"With pleasure." Vortex takes off again, her black hair whipping behind her.

This time I offer her a head start. It won't matter. I can still catch her, but I have to be more cautious. I track her movements, then scour the training facility. She has about a half a mile before she reaches the rock wall. Nevermore warned that on the other side, she would have help and a chance to slip away. I have to cut off her path to freedom.

I dig my boots into the smooth concrete floor and grin as I launch after her. The gap closes more rapidly this time, perhaps because I already chased her so her pace is a hair slower. From the corner of my eyes, I seek Hound or Nevermore. They have disappeared again, but all eight of the other Special Forces agents are observing me and Vortex now.

As I run, I try to keep my eyes open for any traces of Nevermore or Hound. As the space between me and Vortex closes, a gunshot bangs off the facility walls, followed only a second later by a bullet ripping into my shoulder. The pain is sharp, piercing, burning, but I only stagger slightly off course.

A void opens to my left along the path where I'm veering. I catch my balance before dropping in and launch over the ten-foot void effortlessly, roll on my landing, and leap back up to my feet.

The gun fires again. This time the bullet clips my side right along the ribs before embedding in the wall ahead of me. My hands shake as I touch the blood trickling from my wound, and pain from the first bullet burns in my shoulder. Who is firing at me and why? They could kill me!

I flit between behind an obstacle course. The shots are coming from behind me, so this should remove their line of sight. Vortex glances over her shoulder at me, but my hesitation under gunfire has spurred her confidence.

The rock wall is close.

From my hiding place, I spot Hound beside the rock wall as he rolls his back along the stone and out of sight on the other side. He is waiting to help her there at the finish line. I have to cut her off.

I coil the muscles in my legs and crouch low after a breath to center myself, I thrust myself through the air toward the rock wall. The structure is solid, but if I can strike it right, I should be able to knock it over and block off Vortex from escape.

As I flip through the air over Vortex's head, she gasps and swings her hand out in front of me. In a controlled freefall, I can no longer direct myself as I plunge right into the void that snaps open in front of me.

Once more, I'm tumbling through an infinite expanse of black before I slam against the mat at Nevermore's feet. The floor trembles from the force and dust rains down from the ceiling.

He scowls at me, gripping a gun in his right hand. *It was him!*

"You shot me," I snap, holding a hand against the wound in my side. Not much blood flows from it, so it can't be more than a surface wound.

"Radicals will do that, too." Nevermore holsters the gun on his hip, appearing beyond irritated with me. Maybe he possesses a legitimate reason to be. So far, I haven't proven myself worth much in the field if they can so easily overpower me.

Hound crouches at my side and reaches for my injured shoulder.

I flinch back. After what transpired last night, he isn't about to touch me!

"Relax," Hound says coolly. "I'm gonna get it out."

Despite wanting to withdraw from his touch, I relax as his hands cup my bleeding shoulder. I expect it to hurt as the bullet slides out, but a curious tingling sensation floods my shoulder, followed by numbness. The bullet slides up and out of my skin as if guided to the surface by my blood. Hound catches it.

I gawk at him in astonishment and abhor myself for being impressed by this display of power. The skin of my shoulder pulls tighter, yet I'm only distantly aware of it with him so close, his gaze peering into the depths of my soul. My stomach flips and I draw back from him. *Stop using your Power on me!*

Hound does not indicate that he notices my discomfort as he holds up the bullet for me to see. The tip is perfectly flattened, as if it struck a solid wall and not soft flesh.

Vortex clears her throat and my face burns in embarrassment. Why was I angry with Hound earlier? I can't even remember.

"Again," Nevermore commands.

The rest of the day we repeat the same drill over and over until Vortex is dripping with perspiration and Hound appears ready to break Nevermore in half. Throughout the runs, I am shot several times—though never in the chest or head—or thrust headfirst into a vast hallucination where it's impossible to distinguish up from down, or I'm hoisted off the ground with no command over my limbs until I'm certain my body will tear apart.

Once, I snap my arm. Nevermore mercilessly resets it and insists it will heal with my Power. I don't believe him, but a few minutes later my arm is wholly normal. He breaks my leg during another run, with the same reset and healing results. I'm thrust into solid walls hard enough to bust my face and leave a permanent indentation in the wall, but in no time even those wounds heal.

The abuse is brutal and painful, and I battle to hold the tears at bay. I won't cry in front of the team. Not again. Instead, I employ that pain and anger as fuel for each of the next runs. They can beat me and break me and shoot me, but I refuse to quit. That's what Nevermore seems to crave. He wants me to give up. I won't allow him the satisfaction.

At long last, hours later, I tackle Vortex before her void can force me to tumble endlessly. I help her to her feet.

The grin Vortex gives me is unexpected. "Nice work," she whispers.

I can't explain why the praise makes me warm inside. Maybe because I devoted the entire day to trying to capture her. Maybe because someone on the team has finally showed me some form of compliment. Well, at least someone other than Hound.

"Get rest," Nevermore orders us. "Tomorrow will be tougher."

Harder than having my bones cracked and getting shot on numerous occasions? I almost gawk at the remark.

Vortex waits beside me. At first, I assume she is waiting for me to head back up to our apartments, but it swiftly becomes obvious she is expecting Hound to accompany her.

He looms nearby, his hands tight against his sides, rage blazing in his face.

"You coming, Hound?" Vortex asks in a silky, smooth voice.

"Go ahead," he says, the tension deep in his tone.

I spin away without a second thought and head toward the elevator.

Vortex shrugs as if Hound's decision doesn't matter, but her shoulders sag somewhat.

As the two of us cut across the training facility floor toward the freight elevator, I peer back over my shoulder to see Hound towering over Nevermore. I can only see the tense rise of Hound's shoulders and the unmitigated fury on Nevermore's face as the two quarrel.

"Come on," Vortex says, tugging on my arm as the elevator opens. "Leave them. Couple of Alpha males at work."

We travel up to the apartments in silence. My thoughts are consumed by Hound's displeasure and the evident disdain on Nevermore's face. We are supposed to be a team. Any fracture between them could jeopardize us in the field.

"What's up with the two of them?" I ask Vortex.

She peeks at me, her lips thinning in irritability. "Just a guard dog doing what he assumes is his duty." The words strike me as peculiar. I have no idea what that means, but the change in Vortex's attitude makes me wonder if it has something to do with me. I hope not.

The door opens and the two of us step out.

"I thought Nevermore was our commander," I say.

Vortex snorts. "Barely. He's our training officer, and he has a little more authority than we do, but not by much. Hound seems pretty close to equal with him in rank. We answer to our liaison officer."

Liaison officer, my brother. "Forrest."

Vortex grimaces. "Yes. Dr. Pond." She glances at me from the edge of her eyes. "You're his sister. We all know it."

I don't, I think to myself. Except that I do. I don't know how that's the sole thing I remember. "I don't understand why he hasn't been by to visit me."

"He doesn't work here." Vortex snorts. "Don't you remember anything at all? He's one of the top researchers at Paragon."

The name slams against my mind with sufficient pressure to punch all the strength out of my body. I stumble against the nearest wall moments before my knees give out. I nearly tumble to the tiled floor before Vortex slips her arm around my midriff and tugs me upright.

"An interesting reaction," she sputters. "You worked there too, you know. Security."

Tears well in my eyes, and I can't explain why.

"Oh." Vortex appears suddenly uncertain of herself. "Okay. We're crying now. Definitely didn't expect that."

I lean against Vortex as she steers me back to my apartment. Poly is there, and as the two of us barge in, she takes one glimpse at me and her face drops.

"What happened?" Poly asks, distressed and suddenly very flustered.

Vortex drops me on the sofa as Poly appears in front of me with a plate of meat and a carton of milk.

"Is she weak?" Poly asks. "Eating helps."

Vortex shrugs. "I mentioned her previous job at Paragon and she about fell over."

Something presses against my mind, bashing against it as if struggling to burst free of an invisible barrier that holds it back. Excruciating pain splits my head, driving out a moan. I squeeze back against the sofa. Something drips from my nose. I raise a quaking hand to wipe it away, only to smear blood on my hand.

"Get Nevermore and contact Dr. Pond now!" Poly snaps at Vortex.

Vortex streaks across the apartment, disappearing into one of her voids.

I wail as a high-pitch whistle sounds in my ears, but as I squeeze my hands to my ears, I realize the noise is in my head.

Poly presses a cold cloth against my forehead.

I close my eyes, sucking in breaths like a girl drowning.

7

BOOTS THUMP ACROSS THE FLOOR. BACK AND FORTH. Back and forth. A warm comforter brushes my chin as I angle my head against the pillow. Hound sits on the side of my bed and Nevermore paces the floor in front of him. Neither seems to notice I am awake.

"This isn't working," Hound whispers, brushing his hands together. "She needs isolation."

Nevermore shakes his head as he paces, tugging at the sleeves of his jacket. "No. It was working. But when Vortex mentioned Paragon, it must have triggered something. It worked. It's working again." He sounds like he seeks to persuade himself more than Hound.

Paragon. The name tickles at my mind, but there is something vacant in that space when I struggle to summon anything. Just another in a lengthy list of lost memories.

"Forrest is going to skin you alive, Terry," Hound hisses. "This isn't some dead-eyed regressor. This is his sister. After everything he went through to bring her this far." Hound shivers. "I've seen what he does when he thinks he's protecting her. So have you."

Nevermore freezes, his back rigid. Afraid they caught me awake, I snap my eyes shut and maintain steady breathing. What are they talking about? None of this makes sense.

"We need to find …" Hound trails off and the bed shifts, then he drops his voice to a whisper. "We need to find *him* before Forrest loses it."

"I don't like this any more than you do," Nevermore snaps. "But Forrest won't let us out there until she is ready."

Hound grunts. "She's not bait."

"She's all we have. You know better than me just how swiftly he runs to her. Forrest gets his man. We get the radicals. It's a win-win."

"The Project is on track," a strange man says. His voice is familiar and reassuring, but also chills my blood with the coldness of his tone. "Terry, go deal with Poly. She is climbing the walls right now. And when you finish with her, see to Vortex. I can't allow her to remember this."

Boots scuff the floor as Nevermore leaves.

"He's failing," Hound says tersely.

"He's not failing," the unknown man says. "He just requires the appropriate motivation. Thankfully, I know precisely what that is. You can go, Jimmy. Thank you for watching over her."

"Can't I stay a bit longer, Forrest?" Hound asks. The mattress shifts again as he rises. "I prefer to be with her when she wakes up."

My heart leaps and it takes all my willpower not to expose my surprise. Forrest. My brother, Forrest. He's here. I'm both delighted and intimidated.

"No. I'll be here," Forrest says. "I must speak with her alone."

"Well, at least let her know I was here," Hound says. "For appearances, if nothing else."

Hound leaves, and the door close behind him. A moment afterward, the mattress sags as Forrest sits where Hound had been. His hand falls over mine and squeezes gently. The touch is tender.

I wait for him to say something, like when people talk to a coma patient, but silence settles around us. His thumb brushes the top of my hand, but he doesn't move or talk.

What is going on? What is Nevermore failing? What happened to me they are all so concerned about? Am I the bait? And for whom? The only thing that has made sense is mention of stopping the radicals. That I'm on board with.

I struggle to recall what might have happened to me, but all that persists is the vicious training, then waking up in my bed. Something must have happened to me during training that has everyone worked up.

The sound of gentle tapping raises my interest and I crack my eyes open. Forrest perches beside me, holding one of my hands as he taps through data on my tablet. He must sense movement from me because he peers over. The lines of his face are serious, the cheekbones high. Piercing copper eyes gaze down at me. Eyes just like mine only sterner. I'm astonished to discover him in jeans and a collared shirt. It gives off an air of informality that somehow doesn't fit him. A smile cracks his stern face and he becomes warm, compassionate. The metamorphosis is distressing.

"Glad to see you awake," Forrest says, switching off the tablet and setting it on the nightstand. "You caused quite a panic."

I rub my head yet can't justify why. "What happened?"

"Training exercise gone wrong, but you're okay now." Forrest pats my arm. "It might help if you tell me what you remember."

If only. I strive to draw something back, but nothing arises. It's as if the memory of the exercise has sunk into one of Vortex's voids. What little I can recall, I tell him about the voids, the bullets, and broken bones. Forrest absorbs all of this with a tenderness that offers me comfort.

When I stop, he swings toward me and rotates a knee up onto the bed. "Bianca," he says, and his posture becomes more stooped as he averts his gaze to our hands, "do you remember why you are here?"

The hints in the slope of his shoulders, curved spine, and slumped face tell me explicitly what he refers to. Our parents.

I try to answer, but my throat closes off, driving me to swallow hard enough for him to hear. "Tell me what happened to them," I say, my voice gravelly and cracking.

Forrest's hand slides out of mine and he rubs both palms over his jeans. "The world is a treacherous place, and our parents ended up on the wrong end of the radicals. Things are getting hairy in Elpis, Bianca. You remember about regression?"

I provide a small nod. Regression from Powers is a rising threat to our way of life. Our Powers are what keep us alive.

"Regressors are becoming more violent, joining a group of radicals determined to break down our government. They don't seem to realize that we need this government and these Powers to endure. The world is still broken."

History lessons flood back to me. Non-Powered humans waging war on those with Powers. Atmos causing a chain reaction of a radioactive meltdown around the world with his Atmokinesis. Only people with Powers survived the fallout, applying their skills to sustain themselves; yet even with Powers, people still died alone. Elpis rose from the ashes at the meticulous hand of the Directorate, establishing a city that thrives on cooperation and depends on Powers. The world beyond Elpis is still a desolate wasteland, as far as anyone can tell. Now, regression threatens our very existence. Without our Powers, we will perish. Who would dare rise against the end of regression? Why?

Forrest scrubs his hands together—a habit, I've noticed—then examines them as he proceeds, "The night they bombed Paragon Tower, Dad approved a broadcast that this radical group did not appreciate. They assaulted the house on Dysart Lane and murdered our parents in their sleep." Grief catches his voice and it cracks.

Tears prick my own eyes. "That's why I signed up for this," I say, scarcely able to produce the words.

Forrest's head bobs as he continues to glare at his hands. "These radicals have torn our family apart, B. Which is precisely why I volunteered to be a liaison for Paragon Diagnostics in the Department of Military Affairs. I have to stop them."

I reach out and slide my hand into his. "*We* have to stop them."

His watery gaze meets mine, and the tears make his eyes gleam. "*We* have to stop them." He sucks in a breath and straightens, his jaw stiffening. "We have to stop *him*."

I blink. Another allusion to this unknown man.

"Who?" I ask.

Whoever it is, I will do everything in my Power to stop him. A terrible hunger for vengeance burns in my heart. Whoever Forrest is speaking of, he is responsible for the deaths of my parents. I will return that favor in kind.

Forrest sighs and pats my hand. "Later. Right now you need rest."

He leans forward and gives me a hug and kiss on the cheek. "I love you, B. If you remember anything, remember this. I will do everything I can to protect you; to protect us all."

The words warm me while also setting my misery at ease.

Forrest stands and nods to the foot of the bed. "I brought your favorite jacket. Thought you might like it when you aren't training."

I sit up and gaze at the jacket. An odd thing to bring me. Is that all I have left in this world, besides Forrest? As he departs, I reach down and pluck up the jacket, slipping it over my arms and flipping my hair out of the collar. It fits a touch loose, but when I clench my fists, the leather strains. A familiar odor of worn leather washes over me. Somehow, this simple jacket has made me feel more like … me.

Whoever that is.

After Forrest's departure, I devote the next hour to sitting up in bed, mindlessly fiddling with the tablet. Pieces of my childhood come back to me. Forrest and me at the creek where I broke my arm and he carried me home to Mom and Dad. Pink rain boots that nearly come up to my knees as I jump in puddles on the edge of the street, maybe only seven or eight years old. Mom yelling at me for dripping mud as I enter the house, the mud clinging to my clothes like I rolled around in it. The image of a mud castle sliding back in the ground as Forrest stands behind me with his arms crossed. He is hardly four years older than me, yet he acts much older as he informs me that Mom will punish me for certain this time.

And I remember Testing Day, where the effectiveness of our Powers is measured through a rather grueling test. My score was seven points below what I needed to be an athlete. I curled up on a cream-colored sofa with Hound—no, Jimmy—whose arms were folded tight around me while he offered reassurances that somehow rings hollow. My dreams were shattered by only seven points.

This memory has me on my feet. I peep out of my room into the main living space, but Poly isn't there. I tiptoe to the door and leave the apartment. Everyone lives along this hall, and I gaze up and down the hallway, wondering which of the twenty doors is his.

Only numbers mark the doors along the hallway. My apartment is 4. Slowly, I creep along the hallway, seeking to listen through doors for voices, but hear nothing. I could just try knocking, but I don't want to disturb anyone who might be resting by choosing the wrong door.

The hallway smells of industrial cleaner, as if someone recently washed the floors. Bright lights make the ceiling glow, yet I cannot spot the lights themselves. Behind me, the freight elevator hums with life as it reaches the floor. I twist to determine if Hound will emerge. Instead, Unit 12 exits, casting me a curious once-over as they each head to their apartments. I make a note of which doors they enter. Hound probably isn't in there. But then again, Poly isn't on my team and I share a space with her.

The door to Apartment 6 opens right beside my own, and Hound peers out at me. "Are you lost?"

"No. Yes. I …" Flattening out my black leggings, I march toward him as he tiptoes out and closes the door behind him. "How did you know—?"

Hound taps his nose. "My Power," he says, as if I should have foreseen that answer. And I should have.

I nod even though I realize his Bloodhound Power doesn't come from his nose, but a sense of who is nearby because of their blood. While I don't actually know how Hematology can sense blood, I know that he somehow does it.

"Everything okay?" he asks as I pause in front of him. His hand brushes my arm and delivers a flutter of butterflies through my stomach.

"I remember you."

Hound lifts his chin and his smile seems to suspend on his face. "Oh?"

His fingers tense ever so slightly against my arm. He is concerned about something, but withholds it behind a veil of charisma. Why?

"What do you remember?" he asks.

"Testing Day."

He nods slowly, as if this makes perfect sense. "That was a nasty day for you."

"But you were there."

Hound slides his hand up my arm until it cradles my cheek. "Always." He moves closer, and his eyes capture me. "That was the first time we kissed."

Realizing he is about to attempt kissing me again, I draw backward. His hand slips away, and he appears wounded by the withdrawal.

"If I had those feelings for you before," I say deliberately, "why do I constantly feel so irate with you? What happened to us?"

Time seems to stop as he retreats, powerless to match my demanding gaze. His entire body becomes rigid. Yes, something went awry, and it wasn't my fault. At this moment, Hound could claim anything, but it wouldn't make up for the certainty that our relationship broke over something he did wrong. He has no intention of explaining, either.

I draw another step backward toward my door. "Don't touch me like that again," I say, clamping my fists hard enough to make the leather jacket strain over my arms with a creak.

"Bianca, don't." Hound's gaze snaps up as he pleads. "I came here for you."

I continue retreating, shaking my head as the butterflies from a minute ago turn into a maelstrom of sloshing acid. My hand settles on the knob of my apartment door. "Did I ask you to?"

Hound hesitates before saying, "Yes."

"Too late." I twist the knob. "That took you a few seconds too long to answer, Hound."

"Bianca—"

"You can call me Steele," I snap, then slip into my apartment and lock the door behind me, pressing my back against it.

Either he is hoping to repair whatever he broke, or he is

withholding something much worse. Regardless, I cannot be certain of him anymore.

"You look like a demon just passed through you," Poly says.

I start, then press a hand against my pounding heart.

She provides a sincere smile and pours a cup of tea, edging closer. "Here. This always helps calm my nerves."

"Thanks," I say, accepting the steaming cup.

I stroll over and relax on the sofa. Poly joins me, gazing at me with intensely curious eyes. Her fingers rap on her thigh, but she never asks what I know she wants to ask. Eventually, I break down and explain to her what I remembered, and how Hound reacted in the hallway. We sit up for another hour breaking everything down into workable chunks, and Poly never once disagrees with my appraisal of him: that something about our history is missing, that I don't know what I can trust him with. Occasionally, my skin tingles like someone is running a hand over my back or arms, and I assume it's just my body still responding to the sense I received from Hound.

Our conversation moves to new subjects. Poly mentions a boy she likes, though she won't tell me his name—aside from reassurance that it isn't Hound. As she describes the way she feels around him, I can't help being a little envious. To have those sorts of butterflies and not have them produced by some sort of Hematology manipulation or suspicion that he is withholding something. Her face positively lights up as she talks about him.

By the end of the conversation, Poly is a friend—the only friend I have in this unfamiliar place, and the only one besides Forrest I'm comfortable around.

8

THE SAME NIGHTMARE PLAGUES MY SLEEP EVERY night. I'm strapped to a table, screaming, bleeding. Metal cuts my flesh as I bend and break it free. Each time, I startle awake as a gunshot echoes off the Power-reinforced walls. Sweat soaks the sheets and I have to shower to wash it off my skin.

After washing up, Poly initiates the same conversation with me, though each time the words are different. How did I sleep? She slept amazing. How am I feeling? I look a little pale. She can't wait for training for some reason or another. More about the boy. Honestly, the girl rambles so much I have a tough time caring about what she says. But she's friendly with me, something that no one else has bothered attempting.

One morning, I ask her about her name. "We all have call sign names connected to our Powers. But Poly is ... pretty ordinary."

She chews her lip, glances toward the door, then shrugs. "What can I say?" And that's where she leaves it. No explanation. Nothing. She leaves for the day, as if that answered my question. It didn't.

During training each day, Nevermore focuses on teamwork, abandoning the brutal lessons he forced me through in those first days with no mention of them. If it wasn't for the disapproving glares or the snide pointers thrown in my direction, I would have believed he forgot about the initial lessons altogether. But the bitterness in the little Telepath is targeted toward me. Maybe Forrest dressed him down about the broken bones. He certainly hadn't been pleased to hear about them that night. Nor the bullet wounds.

Instead, our group concentrates on developing each of our Powers and identifying inventive ways to make them function collectively. "The radicals like to band together like an unbreakable chain," Nevermore says one day, and the scorn he has for these radicals is evident in his tone. At least this, we can agree on. "If we can't stand together and discover ways to combine our Powers, they will overtake us even with our enhanced Powers."

Though he speaks to all of us, he scowls at me from the edge of his eyes. Nevermore doesn't like me at all, yet I have no notion why.

Hound only speaks to me during training, and his tone is remarkably professional. The tension he bears toward me is unmistakable, yet when we are working as a cohesive unit to use our Powers together he becomes all business, like he was designed for this purpose.

I suppose we all were, to some extent.

The first couple of days, he only talks to me when necessary for the job, and as we ride up the freight elevator as a unit, he never once even glances my way. When the doors open, he immediately walks out and says goodnight before disappearing into his apartment.

The distance doesn't bother me. We have to work together. It ends there.

On the second night, Vortex heaves out a dramatic sigh as Hound once again retires into the apartment, accompanied by Nevermore, who glares over his shoulder at me one last time.

"He despises me," I say.

"Are you kidding?" she says. "He's completely enamored with you, but he said you needed space, so he's giving it to you."

I'm speechless before realizing we aren't talking about the same person. "I mean Nevermore, not Hound."

"Oh." Vortex bites her lip as if realizing she said too much. She waves a dismissive hand. We pause in front of her door across the hall from me. "He hates everyone. Something about his past. He doesn't talk about it. Though he seems harder on you than on anyone else, I suppose." She shrugs as if it doesn't matter, and to her, it probably doesn't, but to me it does. "Nevermore doesn't like anyone. Maybe because he knows what we think of him. He can read our minds, after all."

Her words fill me with déjà vu. Have we had this conversation before?

"That couldn't have anything to do with his attitude," I say, intending it as a joke, though it doesn't quite sound that way.

Vortex cocks her head. She's undoubtedly a beautiful girl with a long, narrow face that accentuates her big eyes. "So there's nothing between you and Hound anymore?"

I shake my head, again sensing déjà vu. "It just … feels wrong."

She gnaws her lip again, then draws a deep breath and says, "So, if I, like, was interested, you wouldn't be mad?"

I shake my head. "Go for it."

Vortex glances at the door to Apartment 6 as if considering doing so at that moment. "Okay. If you don't care."

"I really don't."

She smiles, big, then nods and says goodnight before retreating into Apartment 3.

It doesn't take Vortex long. The very next day, she flirts endlessly with Hound, and he soaks it all up. Occasionally, I catch him scrutinizing me as if expecting me to blow up in a fit of jealousy. To my amazement, I actually *don't* care. While I can agree he's a terribly attractive boy, I have no interest in him. Some part of me expected to feel at least a little jealous—what with our history and all—but watching the two of them flirting with each other fills me with relief, even when Nevermore prods at me about it in his always-snide manner.

After training, we all ride up the elevator, and Hound brushes Vortex on the arm as they exit ahead of us. His gaze once more seeks some reaction from me.

I grant him nothing.

Not as he touches her back. Not as he brandishes his winning smile at her. Not even as he swings toward her door instead of his own and accompanies her in.

"That must sting," Nevermore says blandly, and instead of displaying any level of sympathy that might make him more human, he glares right through me with that obnoxious sneer on his face.

Why is Nevermore so bent on causing me pain? What did I ever do to him to make him despise me so much more than anyone else?

What I wouldn't give to obliterate that sneer off his face, right across a concrete wall. Road rash might even pretty up his ugly beak of a face.

This routine continues each night, and each morning Vortex feels the need to assure me that nothing serious happened between her and Hound, as if she's still concerned that I care. I don't, and after three days it annoys me that she constantly needs my endorsement.

Before training the next day, I open the fridge to retrieve the same food I eat every morning. I've learned that fueling my body with macronutrients at the start of the day helps diminish the overwhelming hunger from burning up my Power. I grab three egg and sausage sandwiches from the fridge, along with a carton of milk, leaning down to dig out a vine of grapes, then stand and close the door.

Someone waits on the other side, and I kick out instinctively, planting my foot firmly against their chest.

Poly yelps and skids across the floor on her back.

I recognize my mistake immediately and drop my food on the counter and dash over to help her.

"I'm sorry. You startled me!" I say, gripping her arm and hauling her to her feet.

Her hands are clammy. Poly's face is pale, and her eyes are red-rimmed. The appearance of her in this almost ghostlike state is absolutely frightening. Poly smooths out her black tank top over her matching leggings, and I note how severely her hands are shaking.

"I didn't mean to scare you," I say.

"You didn't," she says promptly, the pitch of her voice raised, gasping for breath. "I mean, you did, but that's not ..." She shakes her head as if she can't think of the rest of the words.

I attempt steadying her as she sways to the side. It isn't only her hands shaking. Poly's entire body shudders. Her eyes are wide with dread. Once again, she glances toward the door as she hugs herself.

"What's wrong, Poly?"

"So much. There's just—"

A thud in the hallway cuts her off, and her already-pale skin turns whiter. She looks ready to keel over.

"Poly," I say, seeking to reclaim her attention.

She licks her lips, then suddenly jumps toward me, seizing my arms. Her eyes are large and frenzied. "My full call sign is Polygraph." She says this as if it explains her behavior.

Polygraph. A lie detector. So she can detect when people lie to her?

Her grip tightens.

I almost pull away, and easily could, but something about her abject terror freezes me.

Poly's words tumble out of her mouth so hastily I have a tough time following her. "I'm here to observe you, Bianca. We need to talk. Tonight. They are lying to you. Everyone. Don't dose before bed. We will talk then."

A knock on the door makes me jump.

Poly swiftly releases her grip on me and darts back into her room.

Everyone is lying to me? About what? I've never been one for puzzles, preferring everything laid out for me. Poly's cryptic behavior this morning only serves to confound me further.

I gawk at Poly's closed door, unsure how to react. At another knock on the door, I jump and edge over to open it.

Nevermore waits rather impatiently in the hallway with his arms crossed and his mouth drawn in a thin line. "Took you long enough. Let's go."

My heart hammers against my ribs as we head to the training

facility. Nevermore can read minds. *They are lying to you. Everyone.* I distract myself from conversation or eye contact with him by scarfing down my breakfast as we go. I sense his eyes examining me. I can't distract my thoughts with food. Does he know what Poly said? She said everyone is lying to me, including Nevermore. But trust is vital to a unit. If I can't trust him, we are all doomed.

Nevermore remains utterly silent. He does not indicate that he knows what I can't shake from my mind.

We arrive and cross the training facility floor. Hound is leaning against one table with a casual ease that exudes confidence. Vortex stands in front of him closely. So intimately. He peeks over her shoulder at me and I swear I detect a hint of a smirk play over his lips.

"We may have our first assignment soon," Nevermore announces. "Which means we need to double down on training."

Hound groans.

Vortex heaves out a melodramatic sigh.

I simply drift into position to start. Perhaps a decent, vigorous training day will distract me.

9

TRUE TO HIS WORD, NEVERMORE RUNS US THROUGH
several brutal simulations. We are in an unstable, abandoned building
in the Eastern borough of Elpis. The boarded-up windows and
cracked foundation make me worry how my density will make the
building react under my weight as we chase a cluster of radicals.

They burst out into the street and drag the building down on our
heads as one of them produces a haze that splits the four of us apart.
Hound draws us all back together at the same moment Vortex opens
a void beneath our feet. We land on the other end of her void, but
a chunk of the building followed us, and I raise my arms in time
to catch it. The weight crushes me down to a knee. My shoulder
dislocates, but I hold on as the others escape to safety, then I toss
the heavy block of concrete aside. Nevermore crouches beside me,
snatching my dislocated arm and popping it back into place.

I don't scream. I barely even feel this degree of pain anymore.
Perhaps that was why he abused me so severely on my second day.
Maybe he prepared me for the pain to come. I should thank him.

At lunch, I seek Poly's unit, but it's nowhere to be found. The entire
unit has disappeared. I scan for them all day, only to be disappointed.

Our unit passes through another simulation. This time, the radicals
are Strongarms, like me—but not as enhanced as I am. I break bones
without a second thought, throw bodies through walls where Hound
finishes them off. I cannot see what he does from his position inside
the building, but the shriek the radicals release is piercing.

A group of aggressors surrounds the four of us while I carry the struggling form of our "target" over my shoulder. Nevermore clenches his fists, and his shoulders tighten. Then the radicals break into chaotic screams of pure horror and they scatter, swatting at nothing. One of them stumbles, and his knees buckle as he plunges forward.

I step carelessly over the lifeless body, barely sparing more than an offhand glimpse at his young dark face. That face—somewhat familiar—makes me nearly miss a step as my heart thumps against my rib cage and my pulse quickens in panic.

Get a grip on yourself, Bianca, I think. *It's a simulation. None of this is real. He isn't real.*

As the simulation completes and we step back into the training facility, I once more search for Poly. Unit 12 was on the training floor earlier, but they are long gone now. Only we remain.

Hound squats, mopping perspiration from his forehead with the hem of his shirt.

"I need to eat," he declares.

I nod in agreement.

Nevermore shakes his head, causing his raven black locks to drip sweat. He's always pale, but right now he appears ready to topple. "No. We have one more simulation to work through."

"That's sufficient for tonight, Nevermore," a familiar voice announces.

I spin around, stunned to see Forrest watching from a gangway overhead, scrolling through something on his tablet.

Hound stands, his back tense.

Vortex shrinks away.

Nevermore only presents what I expect as his perpetual scowl.

"The team needs rest," Forrest declares. "Tomorrow you have your first assignment. I need everyone in the conference room on the docking bay level at 0600 hours for briefing. Go straight to bed after you eat." He speaks as if we will all obey without question, and judging by the way the group murmurs acceptance of the command, he commands respect.

Forrest turns and strides along the gangway toward the elevator on his level. I head in the same direction, hoping to edge him off by calling it first. Really, I want to pursue him, to ask about Poly—but she cautioned me not to trust anyone. Does that extend to Forrest? No. Surely not him. He's my brother. He might be the sole person I can trust.

I open my mouth to call to him, but nothing comes out. *Everyone.* Poly's warning screams in my head.

The door closes on Forrest.

"You aren't even sweating," Vortex says as she joins me at the elevator. "It isn't fair."

I spin, heart jumping into my throat. "Another perk of Super Strength, I suppose." The words slide out, but my mind is elsewhere.

Nevermore studies me in a manner that makes my skin crawl. Thankfully, the door opens and we tread into the freight elevator to ride up.

Vortex bounces on her toes. "So. Tomorrow. Our first team mission."

Hound watches the numbers climb to our floor.

"Just remember," Nevermore says, "the radicals will say and do anything to turn us, and some citizens will defend them. It's dangerous out there. We could die."

"Quite a ray of sunshine," I mutter. Maybe if I could remember more of the world outside of this facility and the simulations, I might feel better prepared.

We step out of the elevator on the apartment level, and what greets us is hardly encouraging.

One boy from Unit 14—Poly's unit—sobs against the shoulder of his teammate. Out of twelve agents, myself included, ten of us are packed into the hallway. The atmosphere is grim, reminiscent of the hazy memory I have of my parent's funeral. My footsteps are heavy as I exit the elevator at the back of our group. My gut churns as I shuffle along beside Vortex.

"What happened, Levi?" Hound asks one boy from Unit 14.

Levi—a boy with dark hair cut tight to his skull and thick eyebrows to match the severity of his grief-stricken face—rubs at his teammate's back. "We left on a mission today. We …" His voice hitches and he lets out a shuddering breath. "We lost half the team."

The news turns my stomach to stone and my gaze sweeps the corridor again. Everyone loiters out here except for one boy from Unit 14 whose name I don't know … and Poly. I don't have to ask to identify who is missing.

We need to talk. Tonight. It can't be a coincidence that Poly died on the same day she came to me frightened, spouting about lies and truth. And if this mission was so dangerous for Unit 14, what will happen to us when we go out tomorrow? I'm not ready for this.

Hardly anyone glances my way as the sniffles and sobs rake against my ears, heightened by my paranoia. As I open my door, Hound's hand settles on my arm.

"Maybe you shouldn't be alone right now," he says.

I peer at him, at the worry in his eyes. Beside him, Vortex is nodding.

Everyone.

"I'll be fine." The words are hollow, not my own.

"No." Nevermore joins them. "That's a transparent lie." He's reading my mind.

Go away!

Nevermore shakes his head. "He's right. Why don't you stay with Vortex tonight?"

Had I not been already observing her from the corner of my eyes, I would have missed that momentary consternation at Nevermore's invitation. Vortex doesn't want me in her apartment, even if she doesn't want me to be alone. The subtle widening of her eyes swiftly passes, and she provides a charitable smile instead.

"Yeah. I have an extra room right now."

I fumble for something to say, anything to get me out of this and be left alone in my apartment.

"Or I can stay with you," Hound offers, prompting a vexing glare from Vortex. "If you prefer."

Unable to figure out of an excuse out of this, I accept Vortex's offer. Not only do I have no desire to spend the night with Hound, but I also don't want to upset Vortex the night before our first mission.

Despite my absence of hunger, Vortex insists I pack my stomach before bed. Going hungry overnight right before a mission will only harm the team. An hour after lying in bed awake, Vortex tiptoes in.

"Hey, you still awake?" she asks as if she doesn't already realize the answer.

"Yeah."

Vortex perches on the edge of the bed and her gaze wanders to the dose still resting on my nightstand. I didn't take it.

"I can help if you need it?" she offers.

Don't dose. Poly's warning makes me wonder why she demanded I skip. It isn't as if the dose has improved my sleep like Nevermore said it would. But what exactly does it do?

"You can't skip, Steele," she says, then rubs at her arm. No claws at it. "It's dangerous skipping doses. Nevermore told you, didn't he?"

I nod. Skipping could lead to degenerative diseases, to which there is presently no established cure. Is skipping on an impulse of Poly's paranoia worth the risk?

Why was Vortex out of the unit when I first reported? What happened to her? I want to ask, but I'm afraid all I will hear are lies. Even if Vortex tells me the truth, I will likely still suspect her of lying.

"Sure. Then I can help with yours," I say. "After all, we all have to dose, right?"

Vortex shakes her head. "I took mine just before I came in."

Something screams at the back of my head, instructing me to think, to see problems from a unique angle, to think outside the box. The voice is familiar, yet also not.

Vortex won't leave until she knows I've taken my dose and I can't run or hide, so I hold out my arm absently.

With great care, she retrieves the needle from the nightstand and unstoppers the tip. The blue fluid reflects in the lights. Vortex doesn't meet my gaze as she presses her fingers to my arm to stretch the skin. Is she shaking? The way she administers this dose is not with the practiced efficiency of someone who has done this a hundred times herself. She bites her lip, takes deliberate aim, and even seems to second-guess just moments before piercing my skin.

I should stop her, but before I can speak up, the needle slips in. I hardly feel it at all. Then the blue liquid slides into my veins.

The moment it's done, she disposes of the used dose needle and leaves me alone.

I glare at the ceiling, speculating about the dose, Vortex's ill-concealed apprehension, and Poly's warning. Everything about this place feels false.

Poly's death was no accident.

Part Two

"NO ONE EVER ACHIEVED ANYTHING OF significance by playing it safe. To ensure our existence in opposition to the radical agenda, we must fight fire with fire. That is what Proposition 9 will prepare us for: security at any cost. We owe it to our city, our citizens, and our very survival."

~ Directorate Chief Seaduss
After the Bombing of Paragon Tower

10

I'M SCREAMING. BLOOD TRICKLES FROM SELF-INFLICTED
wounds as I struggle to escape. An injection. Buckled tungsten. Shouting
commands. A gunshot, then the impression of a presence looming over me,
whispering reassurances as calm spreads over my body. I relax, blinking at the
blood. How did that happen? I spin in the pure-white room, unable to distinguish
the floor beneath my bare feet from the surrounding walls. An endless sea of white
and my muscles relax with a sense of serenity. Euphoria.

An alarm chimes on my tablet and I stretch in bed, yawning
languidly. Such a peaceful sleep. I brush my hand over the soft, earthy-
brown blanket covering over me. It takes a second to recognize I'm
not in my bed. Where am I? And why? I sit up in bed, examining the
room. It looks sort of like mine, but in a different array of colors and
everything is flipped on the wrong side of the room. I kick my feet
out from under the blanket and pad toward the door, easing it open.

Vortex exits the bathroom to my left, wrapped in a towel with her
hair dripping in stringy clumps. I'm in her apartment? Why?

"Morning, Princess," she teases.

I frown. The apartment is the same as mine, yet different as well.

"You were having nightmares and came over here," she explains.
"We talked for a little while, but you didn't want to go back to your
room and be alone, so you crashed in the spare room." She shrugs as
if it's totally logical.

I twist in the doorway and peer back into the bedroom. A change
of clothes awaits on the armchair, along with some of my bathroom

supplies.

"Shower up," Vortex sings as she heads toward her own room. "We meet in an hour for our briefing."

Right. The mission. I gather my things and head to the bathroom, closing the door and locking it behind me.

The bathroom is humid, and steam covers the mirror. It's like a warm hug, and I slip out of my clothes and shower. The citrus scent of my shampoo is familiar, comforting. I breathe it in as the soap rinses away. The heat of the water amplifies the smell, and it almost feels like an escape from this place. Yet reality is ever present, creeping through the cracks of escapism. My mind strays to what lays ahead. Excitement pulses through me. Our first mission. A chance to prove myself, at last, to Nevermore and the rest of the team. I won't fail as I have done in training. I can't.

I dress in Special Forces uniform—this one designed to hug my legs and arms without straining when I test my enhanced muscles. The material is smooth and flexible. Everything is so … black. The leggings and shirt, with matching boots. I pull my hair back in a ponytail so it won't get in my way while we are away on the mission.

Vortex waits in the living room on a dark gray sofa. We step out of her apartment to join Nevermore and Hound, who wait in the hallway.

With nothing more than his usual grimace, Nevermore leads the way to the freight elevator, but instead of going down ten floors as we do for training, we ride up.

The briefing room is in a long hallway of windowed offices. At the far end of the hallway, a set of double doors remains closed tight.

An imposing slab of a man—clearly a Somatic—with a face as grim as stone waits in the briefing room. The tag on his chest reads *General S. Sims*.

As my team files in, Sims stands at attention on the far side of the oval table—the only thing occupying the militant space aside from a few chairs around it. His hands are clasped behind his back and his stony face stares straight ahead. He strikes quite an image in his officer's attire.

Forrest sits at the table near General Sims.

The four of us stand behind chairs across from Sims, waiting for him to grant permission to sit. He doesn't.

"So this is the famous Unit 15," General Sims says, his voice gravely in a way that merely accentuates his face. "I look forward to watching you in action. Your Paragon Liaison officer has been quite optimistic about your potential." He nods once toward Forrest, who is engaged in something on his tablet.

Unit 12 enters the room and joins us around the table without a comment.

General Sims nods as if satisfied.

"Yesterday, despite the catastrophic results of the mission, Unit 14 managed to arrest a radical," Sims says.

What happened to Unit 14?

"The intel we extracted from him was quite enlightening," Sims continues. "We have learned that the radicals call themselves the Protectorate, and that they are living in a place they call The Shield. The location, sadly, has remained a mystery, but we do know it is outside of Elpis."

Vortex gasps, and I barely contain my own shock. How could anyone survive outside the city? The world beyond the city limits is a barren, radioactive wasteland.

"We also know that their numbers are significantly vaster than we assumed," Sims continues. "Hundreds, if not more."

Everyone in the room shifts ever so slightly at this news. At the rate the DMA has been progressing, even with our help, taking down such an operation will take months, if not longer.

"Dr. Pond," Sims says, staring at Forrest expectantly.

Forrest nods. "We suspect the radicals are contacting an informant by the name of Elpida Theus. You may recognize her from the news. Recent intel says that she has been conspiring with a group of radicals, providing them sensitive information while employing her Power to Influence others against the Directorate in secret."

He swipes his hand over the tablet into the air and an image of a woman in her early thirties with perfectly managed golden hair hangs in the air with the words:

CASS SCALE RANK: 91
POWER: PSIONIC INFLUENCE

The smile on her face is warm, welcoming, reassuring. I know this woman, yet I can't place why. Maybe I saw her on the news, as Forrest suggested.

"She can apply her Influence masterfully," Forrest continues. "Unit 14 attempted retrieval of the target yesterday, and Theus persuaded two agents to turn against each other. They killed each other. The mission was a tragic failure."

Unit 14 lost half the team? Why have I not learned about this before? How do we defend ourselves against someone who can turn us against each other? I peek at the others for some sign of surprise, but they are attentive and don't seem alarmed at all by this development. The news that we could easily be tricked into killing each other makes my stomach churn. I don't want to die, and I don't want to kill anyone on my team.

Nevermore glances at me, and the corner of his mouth curls up marginally.

I gulp down the knot in my throat.

"Make no mistake," Forrest continues, and for a moment I am sure he glances as me as if searching for some reaction to the news about Unit 14, "Theus will not come easily. She knows we are hunting her now and will attempt to slip into the arms of the Protectorate before her arrest. You will retrieve the target and bring her to the DMA for questioning."

I'm dragged into her warm and kind and confident eyes.

"Nevermore will plant an extra barrier of protection on your minds that will prevent Theus from exerting her Influence," Forrest says.

As he mentions this, Nevermore puffs out his chest, proud of himself.

Forrest doesn't seem to notice as he moves on. "Just remember you cannot trust anything she says. Theus is a masterful liar and will do everything in her Power to cast shadows of doubt in your mind. Intel reports that, after Unit 14's failure to capture Theus, she fled her home. We suspect she is currently hiding in this safehouse either to distribute further intelligence or awaiting extraction. DMA troopers will hem in the area for backup support, out of sight in case she attempts fleeing. They are instructed to fire on sight without hesitation if she escapes you."

Forrest taps the tablet again, then pushes a button on the table and a 3D grid of part of the eastern borough of Pax rises off the table's surface. Run-down houses and apartment buildings line the neglected streets alongside squat businesses with barred windows. I survey the map and attempt committing it to memory.

"The radicals will meet Theus here." Forrest taps the 3D map and one house turns red. "A known safehouse for this Protectorate. Both units will function together on this mission. We have no idea how many radicals will be there."

"It's vital that these radicals have no idea you are in the area," General Sims adds. "Wait for them to enter the safehouse before closing in. With any luck, one of their leaders will be on this mission." He peers at Forrest, who appears peeved at the reference.

What was that look for?

"If we can secure just one of their leaders, we could finally locate their position and end this." Sims reaches under the table and hauls a long metal crate up onto the surface with ease of a powerful Somatic.

Forrest taps at his tablet a few times.

The crate beeps and the General opens the lid, revealing exactly eight handguns.

Why do we need guns with our enhanced Powers?

"Paragon has developed these weapons to help finish the radicals," Sims explains as everyone crowds tight to the table to study the guns.

"The bullets are meant to incapacitate the targets, not kill them. However, a head or heart shot will be lethal. I cannot underscore enough how crucial it is that you secure as many of these radicals alive as possible. Do not aim for the head or chest. Even a shot to the arm or leg will be adequate for the bullets to do their job."

I glance at the others around the table. The other unit doesn't look the slightest bit perturbed about this firearm.

In fact, Stretch extends his arm to unnatural length to pick one up, grinning at the gun. Hound gazes at the handguns with fierce curiosity. Nevermore sneers as if eager to shoot the radicals. Vortex looks impressed, caressing the steel handle.

I would rather not resort to gun use, but I suppose the judgment is unfair considering I can run faster than anyone else and punch hard enough to knock people out with a single blow.

As everyone else is captivated with the handguns, I want to know more about the mission. "Sir," I say to General Sims, "What do we know about the radical targets?"

Forrest grimaces. "Nothing. We are reasonably certain there will be at least four and we hope that one of the leaders is among them, but we don't know who they are or what their Powers are. You will all be entering that house blind."

My stomach drops. Without knowing what Powers we are up against, the eight of us are vulnerable to anything.

But so are the targets, I remind myself. *And at least we have the element of surprise.*

"Ivy will barricade the windows and doors," Forrest says.

Ivy preens at the mention of her name. I've seen her around before, but never engaged in conversation with the girl. She's just another in the list of girls who make covetous eyes at Hound, along with the other girl in her unit, Dyspnea, who is all limbs.

Forrest doesn't notice Ivy's reaction or doesn't care. "Ivy's poisonous leaves will hinder anyone who slips away through a window or door. Dyspnea will deoxygenate anyone inside. Stretch will cover emergency exits. We cannot repeat this enough. You must arrest as many of these radicals as possible by any means necessary, short of killing them. We can heal them if necessary, but we can't bring them back from the dead." His gaze flicks to me momentarily.

Actually, I feel multiple sets of eyes shift to me, but when I check the room, no one is looking at me. It's an odd phenomenon.

General Sims leans his fists against the table, and his hard gaze meets each of us. "Prepare yourselves. With any luck, this arrest will lead us right to their Shield where we have a chance to finish this group permanently. You leave immediately."

As he shifts away from the table and marches toward the door, everyone eagerly grabs a gun, studying the safety, testing the grip, and appearing as if they understand precisely how to handle the gun. I pluck up the last one. The metal is chilly in my palm. The notion of shooting someone doesn't settle easily with me, despite the training.

Then I remember my parents, and my grasp on the gun tenses as I stare down the sight.

These radicals killed my parents.

Now, I have a chance for payback.

11

THE DOCKING BAY IS A BROAD AREA WITH HIGH ceilings. The space reminds me of an old parking garage, with a gradual slope winding to upper levels. The air around us smells of oil and rubber like a mechanic's shop, and I repel the urge to gag. What a dreadful stink. Our unit marches up the ramp and passes armored trucks with fat wheels charging beside each other. DMA trucks.

Forrest leads the way, with Unit 12 on his heels and Nevermore and Vortex close behind. Hound trails along at the rear of the group with me, matching my stride. He continues to glimpse at me from the corner of his eyes, as if watching for something or waiting for some reaction out of me. I don't show him anything as we ascend a ramp up to the next level. What is he expecting me to do?

Boxy black DMA air shuttles line either side of the vast space at the top of ramp, charging for their next mission with doors securely closed. They must be vehicles for the Special Forces units like ours. At the far end of the bay, the big doors are sealed against the outside world.

Forrest taps a button on his tablet and a door glides open on the side of a windowless shuttle. He stops outside the open door and hardly spares more than a glance in my direction as his gaze fixes on whatever his tablet is reporting. Forrest absently motions us inside.

I stride forward first, impatient to get this underway.

The interior of the shuttle is roomier than I expected. Seats line either side of the space, with harnesses to strap us securely in place. I choose a seat as Vortex settles beside me. In the shuttle's front is a reinforced cage containing various weapons and tactical equipment. Hound and Nevermore open the door after it clicks unlocked at a touch of Forrest's finger to his tablet. Hound hands out bulletproof vests.

Without being told, I strap the vest on. The extra load won't slow me down.

Forrest closes the door to the shuttle after he clambers in. Once both units are all vested and harnessed in, the shuttle lurches into motion as it lifts from the ground.

Nevermore unfastens his harness, cracks his neck side to side, then crouches in front of Hound, planting his hands against Hound's temples. For a moment, Hound pales and gasps for air, then his eyes widen. It all passes so quick, and by the time Nevermore releases his grip, Hound appears confident and at peace. What did Nevermore just do?

He repeats the process with Vortex and the agents of Unit 12, much to the same result, before he crouches in front of me. Something about him placing hands against my head or interfering with my mind doesn't settle well with me, and I flinch away from his touch.

"This isn't optional, Steele," Forrest says so coldly it sends a shudder down my spine. "Let him place the barrier or hang back from the mission."

I gulp down the dread and doubt, compelled to obey Forrest, to make him proud of me. I have to prove myself valuable to Forrest if no one else, so as Nevermore reaches out again, I clutch the harness and brace myself for whatever happens next.

The grasp is solid, but Nevermore's touch is surprisingly soft. His black eyes penetrate mine, and the set of his jaw firms. Suddenly, I'm plunged into an icy river that expands from my skull like brain-freeze all the way down my spine and out to my fingers and toes. I inhale in sharp breaths as my lungs collapse. His gaze never flinches, and I'm dragged into the depths like pools of Vortex's voids, spilling into a complete deficiency of emotion. The impression settles over me like a net, fusing first with my mind, then into my bones. When he surrenders his hold, I no longer feel anything but a notion of commitment to the mission.

We touch down two blocks from our targeted location. Forrest remains with the shuttle as the eight of us march toward the row of troopers hiding in the evening shadows casting from the houses lining the empty street. Their uniforms are similar to ours, but bulkier, and they wear helmets that mask their faces with black visors. The sight of us causes some disturbance among them. The troopers ease back to provide us space to cross through, all heads turning along with us. I can't see their eyes, but I sense them watching us all the same.

Many of the home windows are boarded up or have bars over them. Porches sag on sinking foundations as tin roofs threaten to slide off rotting wooden posts. Not a soul is in sight, with the exception of the troopers hunkered down against the houses, their eyes engaged on the shacks across the cracked road. Is this section of Elpis abandoned?

A breeze brings with it the stench of rancid food and refuse from the trash bags piled along either side of the street. The aroma is pungent enough that, were it not for the void of emotion Nevermore graced me with, I would have choked or wretched on the street. Clearly plumbing in this part of town is in serious disrepair, which also means disease could easily spread here. How could people live like this? Do they?

Unit 12 breaks off and heads down another street. The four of us halt in unison and take a knee in the gloom of a porch across the street. No one speaks. We don't have to. Somehow, we all know what the other is thinking like a bond between the four of us.

Steele, you remain in position here in case anyone escapes, Nevermore says. For someone who isn't a commanding agent, he sure as hell acts like one. I would love to give Nevermore the benefit of my doubts, but the guy always makes me uneasy. *You can resent it all you want, but you are the fastest among all of us. You will be our sole chance of catching runners.*

I despise how right he is. No one can outrun me.

Hound will cover the back, Nevermore continues. *Vortex will take up position near the front door to open voids to trap any runners. I will keep watch there.* He shoots his gaze to the house next door, at one of the second-story windows.

Hound doesn't move a muscle, his face a mask of focus, yet I sense a ball of excitement seeping from him. My own emotions have sunk into a void, unreachable.

The perfect stillness of our huddled forms accompanied by the way we rise in unison draws the gazes of troopers once more, as if we are one and not four. I can hardly imagine what that must look like to them.

The others split off at a sprint in unison.

Streetlights cast a ghostly yellow glow on the cracked, pothole-filled pavement as I assume position in the shadows of a house across the street from our target. The fact that I'm placed on watch duty chaffs at my skin. I'm undoubtedly the strongest fighter among all eight of us enhanced Special Forces agents. Watching the house reeks of DMA trooper work, and it isn't why I enlisted. Arguing with Nevermore is hopeless, though. He knows what I will say before I say it.

Nevermore disappears into the desert house next door and Hound melts around the corner. I try to spot Nevermore in the second-story window but, somehow, he has merged into the darkness completely. I understand what will happen, what they require of me: Unit 12 will invade the house to capture the targets. Hound blocks the rear exit. Vortex the front. My role is to chase down anyone who escapes Ivy's vines, as well as Hound or Vortex. Nevermore will apply his Telepathy to maintain communication between us—an untraceable communications channel. *Unless they have a Telepath inside,* I think to myself.

Steady yourself, Steele, Nevermore says.

I clamp my jaw.

The streets of the Pax borough of Elpis are silent at night, perhaps because there are dozens of DMA troopers crawling the neighborhood. Or it could simply be because this borough of the city is the most crime-infested part of town. I taste refuse and decaying garbage with every measured inhale. The earlier we finish, the sooner I can escape of this place and shower away the rot.

A quartet of shadows crouch beside a dead bush near the path to the front door. Vines climb the walls of the narrow, two-story house. I watch in fascination as the leaves of three sprout along the boarded windows on the first floor, then the second. It spreads around the front of the house, encompassing everything as if consuming the home like green flames until only patches of the faded and cracked siding show through the black-green leaves. Only the door remains untouched.

Unit 12 lops toward the door simultaneously, then they disappear into the house. Why am I left outside to stand by when I could be much more useful inside? It's as if Forrest is trying to keep me as far from trouble as possible. Does he not trust me? I grind my teeth and listen for warnings from inside the house.

The instant Unit 12 enters the house, hollers and explosive booms erupt from within. Leaves shake loose and tumble from the vines, though not nearly enough to make escape safe. The ground beneath my feet continues to shudder, but all the explosive roar and shouts from within the house cease so entirely that, if it wasn't for the slight howl of the wind between houses around me, I would be sure I had gone deaf. The absolute silence disturbs me, and my muscles strain, prepared to plunge into action. Flashes of light strobe between the boarded windows and the ground beneath me continues to quake.

Hold position, Nevermore says, his voice coating my nerves like an irritant in my mind. *Four radicals. One informant positively identified as Theus.* He must have received something from the team inside.

Vortex twitches near the door, poised to open a void should anyone attempt escape, but the way her silhouette tenses, it's evident to me that maintaining her position is turning into more of a challenge by the moment.

I can commiserate with her. I came here for vengeance, not to watch a light show.

The silence continues to deepen despite the light show inside and the shuddering earth. A few lights have switched on in houses around us, but as residents peer out their windows cautiously and identify the troopers and agents hunkered in the shadows, everyone swiftly dissolved back into the isolation of their homes.

My heartbeat stabilizes as my focus narrows on the target house. Breaths come easier. In. Out. In. Out. Steady as a beating drum. The cloth around my muscles stretches as I flex my Enhanced Strength.

Ivy is down, Nevermore reports. *Hound move in.*

Long seconds stretch past as the silent show proceeds.

I can't slip past Ivy's vines, Hound reports.

I'm moving in, Vortex says through the psychic channel.

She launches from her hiding place near the porch toward the door, but as she steps up to the stoop, a silhouette flashes in the light from within the house. Vortex flies back across the yard, slamming with a thunderous thud against the edge of the curb. Her head smacks the ground with a squelch that makes my gut churn. Blood pools on the ground beneath her skull and I know without needing to approach that it's already too late. The blood oozes out, and I cannot tear my gaze aside.

What just happened to her?

Will I be next?

Someone calls out in my mind, and to me it sounds like Vortex. But that's impossible.

I creep out of my hiding place and stumble toward her, freezing on the curb across the street. My feet have suddenly become too cumbersome to move.

Vortex's lifeless eyes gaze at the sky—an ultimate tribute to her Divinic Power, as if she is returning home.

Bile rises up my throat and I swallow it down.

Steele! Someone screams in my head, but in a stupor, I am only distantly aware.

A body sailing through the air toward me, skidding across the pavement at my feet. I blink, gawking down at the guy's wide-eyed shock.

Steele! Nevermore shrieks in my mind. *Snap out of it! They're escaping!*

The man scrambles to his feet—no; launches as if he has rockets in his shoes—and lands on the ground several feet away, running after a clump of non-DMA guys and girls. Two members of Unit 12 burst out of the house, panting and chasing down the escaping radicals.

They killed Vortex. With no effort. My blood thumps in my ears like drums of war.

Steele!

I snap out of the trance and join the chase. For Vortex. The pavement beneath us and the radicals seems to shrink—or more precisely, it stretches for them like they are running down a hallway in a nightmare, taking step after step and going nowhere as we continue unhindered.

Theus secured, Hound reports.

Rocket-boots man drops back, spinning to confront me. I charge toward him while his comrades continue their flight. His build is ordinary, not too big or small. He isn't Somatic despite his extraordinary leap into the air.

Another of the radicals, a girl roughly my age, soars through the air and strikes into a chain-link fence.

I toss a fleeting glance in her direction, then my focus zeros in on Rocket-boots.

He doesn't charge at me, but braces his feet against the concrete and clenches his hands into fists at his sides. *This should be entertaining.*

"Let's go!" a red-haired boy calls out.

The pavement beneath me shifts and a stone wall rises out of the concrete road. I crash into Rocket-boots with the complete force of my weight. We tumble across the flowing road, and he absorbs most of the impact of our collision, using it to boot me off him with considerably less effort than he should be capable of.

I roll backward and bound to my feet to discover him standing as he did before, feet planted and hands in fists. This close, excitement dances in his eyes and sweat cascading down his face. I wind back and deliver a jab into his gut that cracks a few ribs.

He grunts, stumbling back but not falling, clutching at his abdomen. *How did he not go down?*

Dimly, I am cognizant of others fighting in the street. Hound tangles with a man nearby, and as Hound lands a blow, the silence that had affected everything shatters as if some unseen boundary between us and sound has broken like a mirror.

The concrete wall continues to expand as my foe pulls back his fist and drives a left hook at my ribs.

I swing to block, but the jolt of the block slams against my arm as if I've just punched a steel wall. It only slows me briefly. I quickly throw another jab at his ribs.

He absorbs again.

What is his Power that he can absorb my blows without surrendering his footing? He isn't Somatic.

He draws back his fist again.

The ground beneath me shifts. I fall backward as his fist connects with my skull, whacking me to the pavement.

A gunshot rings out.

I blink, startled by the blow, trying to recover before these radicals can flee. Are we failing? The misery of failing Forrest presses down on my chest, and I get my hands under me to thrust myself up.

Another shot fires. Someone nearby grunts.

"Get him!" a male voice roars.

I peer up to see Rocket-boots dragged to his feet by a companion and the red-headed boy lugging a girl over his shoulder. Then the concrete wall seals off our view for good.

The world around me no longer looks the same. The house we targeted is still wrapped in Ivy's vines, but the foundation appears to have sunk into the ground in one corner. Ivy's vines might be the sole thing holding it up. The street ahead of me is blocked by a wall of concrete. Hound crouches beside Vortex, and the way his shoulders shake is distressing. Is he grieving? Stretch carries Ivy's limp body in his arms. Nevermore stands over a quivering Elpida Theus. I sit back on my heels, suck in breaths, and let the defeat sink in.

We failed.

General Sims wanted as many of them alive as possible. Instead, we lost all but the informant—including two of our own.

I rise.

We haven't failed yet.

"Steele, where are you going?" Nevermore calls.

I don't even realize I'm leaving until I arrive at the space between houses.

They slipped away, but they aren't gone yet.

"Steele!" Nevermore snaps.

I peer back at the others, but I've made my mind up. I enlisted in this war so I could finish these radicals. Now they have murdered my only friend and think they can flee.

I sprint between houses, but after a few steps my body is no longer in my command. My feet lift off the dead grass. My body draws back toward the street. The world rushes past as I float backward and land on my feet in front of Nevermore. Still, I struggle to run, but Hound crosses his arms, glowering at me.

"They took one of the guns," Hound says. "If you chase them now, they will shoot you with it."

"We can still capture them," I snap, infuriated that his Power has seized control of my body.

"I can't lose you, too," he says, inching toward me. "Please. Even if they don't get the shot off, they have a man with Naturalist Impact Absorption. Every punch you land will only fuel his Power."

That explained the man I fought. If he could absorb the power of my impacts, he probably collected more punch than ever before. Going toe-to-toe with him alone, I can handle. But he isn't alone.

I scan over at Vortex. Sure, chasing them down is a risk, but so is everything we do in this job.

We failed the DMA.

I failed Forrest.

Theus kneels beside Nevermore, golden hair framing her lovely face. She lifts her chin, angling her serene gaze on him. "It's okay. You will let me go." She suggests it as if it's a matter of fact.

Nevermore laughs, stooping in front of her a little too intimately. "That won't work on us, darling."

Her eyes grow into brilliant, entrancing circles. Suddenly her gaze slips past him to me. She chokes. "Bianca? I thought you were dead. Your parents will be so thankful."

My parents? She must be misinformed. My parents are the ones who died, not me.

"Don't resist," I say as pressure pushes at the barrier Nevermore placed on my mind. She is struggling to work her Power. "You are in the custody of the DMA. If you resist, we will be required to use force."

Theus's gorgeous face sags as sadness takes over, and her shoulders slump. "They got to you. Bianca, you can't—"

Nevermore backhands her before she can finish. "Enough of your lies. Remain silent."

Theus whimpers and collapses, but recovers quickly enough. Nevermore isn't that strong, after all.

"They betrayed you," Theus says through gasping breaths, tears pooling in her eyes.

Pressure builds against my skull as she attempts penetrating Nevermore's barrier. All I can think about is my parents. They can't possibly be alive. I remember the funeral. I remember signing up for this because of their deaths. If she slips past Nevermore's barrier, will she use me to kill them? My sudden fear is removed, entombed in the emotional void.

Hound grinds his teeth and punches Theus hard enough to knock her out. Everyone is staring at me, transfixed. Did I do something?

Hound rests a hand on my shoulder. He doesn't have to ask for me to know he is concerned about my mental state.

"I'm fine," I say.

"What the hell happened to you, Steele?" Nevermore snaps.

"Watch yourself, Nevermore," Hound says.

I don't need his defense.

"Screw off, Hound! They escaped because of her. If she had been ready and in position, we would have had all of them. Instead, she seized up like a clam." Nevermore sneers and I want to slug him directly in the teeth. He stalks closer as if daring me.

He might have a point. I locked up. Something about seeing Vortex dead on the ground kicked at my brain and rendered me wholly worthless.

"Maybe it's your fault," Hound hisses at Nevermore.

The others are hushed, averting their gazes.

I stare unblinking at a Nevermore. Whatever he has to say, I deserve it. I failed.

Nevermore doesn't seem to notice me staring. "My fault?" Nevermore snorts. "Of course you would take her side. You're still hoping she will climb into your bed."

Hound punches Nevermore in the nose.

Nevermore yelps and presses a hand to the blood now dripping from his nose.

"You aren't in charge anymore," Hound hisses. "And once I have a conversation with Forrest, you'll be lucky to remain in the Unit."

Was that punch really necessary? I frown at Hound but say nothing, bewildered by all of this.

"Please." Nevermore scowls at the blood on his hand. His nose has already stopped bleeding. "He needs me. Without me, his golden girl is a loose cannon."

Golden girl. Is he referring to me? Earlier today, I might have disputed being a loose cannon before, but tonight proved Nevermore right. I have to make up for this, but how? How can I make up such a profound failure when I realize how much everyone was depending on me?

"Enough," I say as anger blazes in my chest despite the emotional void. "Hound, let it go. He's right. I did seize up. Seeing Vortex like that … I screwed up. This failure is mine, and I will tell Forrest as much."

"Forrest will be the least of your problems," Nevermore says bitterly.

Who else could he be referring to?

"Let's get her back to the shuttle," Dyspnea says, nodding at Theus' unconscious form.

No one argues. I heave Theus off the ground and toss her over my shoulder. Hound gathers Vortex, slipping her eyelids closed and cradling her in his arms. The seven of us march toward the shuttle, with Hound and I in the center of the pack.

12

FORREST LOCKS THEUS IN A CAGE AT THE REAR OF THE shuttle after binding and gagging her so she cannot speak if she wakes during transport. He claims her Power comes from her words, and without speech, she is Powerless. Hound places Vortex near the rear as well so none of us have to see her body unless we turn in that direction. Silence settles over us as Forrest glares at the dead body. If only I could learn what he was thinking or feeling. Anger radiates off of him in waves.

"You assured me this would work," Forrest whispers, leaning close to Nevermore and dropping his voice.

A surge of fear and worry rushes through me from my link to Nevermore. I do my best not to look at the two of them so they don't notice I'm aware.

Whatever Nevermore did to defend our minds, I can feel it slip away like a discarded coat. Hound's sorrow is no longer lingering in a suppressed ball. Nevermore's revulsion is gone. Yet I still feel nothing. Numbness climbs through my limbs.

I stare at the floor, grasping the straps of my harness and avoiding meeting everybody else in the eye. Nothing about the mission makes sense. Why did she say I was dead? Shouldn't I remember something like that? And what about my parents? My toes bob on the metal floor of the shuttle as we fly back toward the DMA facility.

When we departed the facility, I hadn't noticed the black window behind the men sitting across from me. Now, I see a tinted Elpis skyline as the sun breaks over the horizon. Even distorted through this reinforced window, the city is beautiful as it comes to life. The gleaming towers of downtown are a stark contradiction to the conditions of the neighborhood we just left behind. I gaze out at the horizon as my mind continues churning through the encounter with Theus, and the failure of our mission.

I watch Elpis pass along the side of the shuttle as we glide over buildings, and the silence around me swallows me whole. All of this—the city, the people, our way of life—depends on the success of our missions, and I have failed. It can't happen again. The thought consumes me as I gaze at the Deadlands while the shuttle orbits around the DMA facility.

In the distance, something in the dwindling darkness catches my attention. A massive hole. It reminds me of Vortex's voids and I straighten as if I expect to discover her out there. It's impossible, of course. Her body is in the shuttle, tucked safely away from our eyes. Knowing this makes that void in the Deadlands ominous.

The DMA facility rests on a patch of arid ground near the northern edge of Elpis in a two-story building abandoned before the founding of the city. Or at least it appears abandoned. The building looks in disrepair on the outside, with structural defects that make it dilapidated. But inside, the facility is anything but derelict.

This must be why we have no actual windows to the outside world, either in our apartments or in the training facility ten floors down. Only the vehicle parking spaces are above ground. Everything else is deeper in the earth. They designed this facility to be overlooked.

The shuttle circles and drops to enter the docking bay. The doors slide closed silently behind us, and we touch down with a jolt. I unstrap my harness and store the vest and the new gun in the safety cage, just as the others do, before hopping out into the wide bay.

A dozen troopers open the back door to retrieve the prisoner and take her to whatever mysterious place they will question her in.

It's none of my concern. In fact, Elpida Theus's lies about my parents have left me even colder and emptier inside, as if the last reservoir of emotion has been drained away, leaving only unexpended energy.

Forrest accompanies Theus in one freight elevator, while our unit climbs into another. When we arrive at the apartment floor, they step out, but I linger behind.

Hound turns, planting a hand over the door so it doesn't close on him. "Steele?" he asks, brows stitched together in concern.

"I'm going down to train."

He glances at Nevermore, then steps into the elevator. "I'll join you."

"No." I place a hand against his chest and firmly nudge him out. "You can't keep up. I'll only be an hour or two."

Hound nods and releases the door. It slides shut with the rest of the agents watching me along the hallway.

My fingers linger over the buttons, prepared to punch in the training facility, but some strange voice in my head—a voice that isn't mine—urges me to find out where the prisoners were taken. Why? It doesn't matter where they go or what happens. My job was to place them in custody. The DMA officers can handle the rest.

But that voice won't leave me alone. With a grumble under my breath, I punch in the training floor, voice be damned. *Not my problem.*

The training floor is empty. The other agents haven't arrived to begin their day. I'm blissfully alone.

And I run.

I run like the past is creeping up on my heels.

I run as if I can reverse time and find my parents alive and well.

I run to escape that voice trailing along behind me, instructing me to delve deeper and find answers.

After seven miles, I switch to the weights, adding as much to the barbells as they can hold, then lock it in place. I practice Romanian Deadlifts at the bar's maximum weight, but after thirty reps my muscles still don't tire. A quick survey of the facility and I find two thick chains on the wall, looping them along the locks on the end of the barbell, then start the lifts again. At most, I've only added another hundred pounds and my muscles feel no real fatigue.

The routine shifts from deadlifts to squat press, but the chains get in the way and I have to shove them off, then I change on to clean and jerks, scarcely struggling more than a breath as I press the bar above my head. I can handle more than this.

Frustrated, I drop the barbell on the floor and move on to the rope obstacle course, running through it repeatedly, then on to the rock wall where I climb all the way to the top and jump down, landing nimbly on my feet.

Over and over, I repeat the routine of run, lift, course, climb, run, lift, course, climb until I obtain an audience as the two boys from Unit 14 watch; until my muscles final begin to ache; until hunger gnaws at my insides. Despite some irritation at not properly working my muscles, at least that nagging voice in the back of my head has ceased.

As I rack the weights, the lanky boy from Unit 14 stalks over. He says nothing. He just stands there behind me with his arms crossed as if waiting. Occasionally, he glances at the gangways above, but no one is up there.

I sigh and spin on my heel, "What?"

The other boy with crew-cut dark hair waits near him, fidgeting.

"It's your fault," the lanky boy says, and his voice is thick with anguish. He must have been close to Vortex.

I straighten my back and release my hands to my sides. I won't fight him. It is my fault.

"Sparky," the second boy hisses.

But Sparky isn't deterred. He takes a bold stride toward me, and his hands shift. Electric energy permeates the air around me.

"She's gone, and it's your fault," Sparky growls.

"I'm sorry."

"No you aren't." His lip curls up, baring yellowing teeth.

"Sparky, don't," the other boy jumps forward, grabbing Sparky's arm and drawing him backward. "Or you'll be next."

The energy in the air intensifies, causing the hair on my arms at stand at attention.

"Let go, Levi!" Sparky tries shrugging the other boy off, but Levi won't be stopped. He yanks on Sparky's arm. "You don't even remember her, do you?"

I frown at him, then glance askance at Levi, who just hangs his head and groans. Of course I remember Vortex. Why wouldn't I?

"Come on, or he will take you next," Levi snaps.

Sparky relents, stalking away from me toward the far side of the training facility. They argue in hushed tones as they depart, but I can't hear most of what they say. Something about murder, pets, Poly. It doesn't make sense to me.

Shaking off then encounter, I march to the elevator. I have no desire to remain around and await another encounter with them. I ride up and head toward my apartment.

Just outside Apartment 6, heated voices from within carry under the frame. I steady my breathing and hold my ear to the door. I don't naturally have Enhanced Hearing, but it does seem to be improved and the muffled voices become more distinct.

"All traces of Poly should be gone now," Forrest says.

Poly? Sparky and Levi mentioned Poly. Who is she?

"You need to make sure she doesn't remember. She seemed perilously close to a breakthrough today."

"Selective memory tracing can do that," Nevermore says. I can't feel his anger anymore, not like I could on the mission, but it's obvious enough in his tone. "At some point you will have to choose Forrest. It's all or nothing if you want to be positive your sister doesn't remember anything."

They're talking about me! Why would Forrest try to wipe my memory?

"I can tinker with a mind all I want, but someday the mind will fight back," Nevermore says.

"Bianca never was one to shy away from a fight either," Hound adds. His voice slams against me, battering the air from my lungs. He is part of this as well?

I lurch back from the door, and for the first time today my heart is racing. *If they find me here listening* ... What? What will they do to me? What have they already done?

Fear cripples my lungs in a way that the workout could not, and I dash to my own apartment and close the door, then race to my room and poke around for something, anything I can use to write on. No paper. No pencils or pens. Just the tablet, but I refuse to touch the device. I rush to the bathroom and dig around in the makeup drawer. Eyeliner.

What to write ... and where to write it?

A knock on the apartment door makes me jump.

I lift my tank top and quickly scribble a warning across my stomach, then toss the eyeliner back in the drawer and jerk the shirt down to cover it.

"Steele, you okay in there?" Hound calls from the entryway.

He let himself in.

I turn on the water for the shower and take a moment to collect myself. The girl staring back at me has hard copper eyes. Unforgiving. Is that really me? Who *am* I?

I open the bathroom door a crack. "I had a great workout. I'm about to shower."

He appears dubious and glances into the bathroom as if expecting the truth to loom over my shoulder. Does it? At least he can't read auras like my dad could. Or minds, like Nevermore.

"Is something wrong?" I ask, cramming my emotions into a void once more. It doesn't work too well.

"No. Just, we're holding a vigil for Vortex in the hallway soon." He steps backward.

"I'll be there."

Hound nods, and there's a sorrow in his eyes that almost forces me pity him. But I can't ignore what I heard. Without further comment, he leaves me blissfully alone.

I shower carefully and when I towel off, the message is only slightly smudged. I will leave it until morning and see what happens next.

By the time I tiptoe out my door, all the other agents are gathered in the hallway outside Apartment 3—including Sparky and Levi, who keep distance from me and never once make eye contact. I crave to ask them question, but the urgency Levi put on display earlier makes me falter.

The door to Vortex's apartment sits open, and someone has managed to obtain candles. Ivy has returned from medical, and her skin is a bit paler than normal, but she seems restored. She wanders around the small cluster of agents and places a leaf in our hands. One by one, she turns that leaf into a splendid bouquet of flowers. Each of them is unique, and after a half an hour of this, a wide assortment of colored roses, tulips, carnations, lilies, and more have been arranged by each of us around the narrow living space, enveloped by candles. No one speaks.

While, for the most part, the units don't interact with each other, we still have a feel of camaraderie and brother-sisterhood among each other. The loss of Vortex is met with profound sorrow. Everyone lends a little extra space to me, and even more to Hound, as we assemble around the cramped living room and hallway. Sparky and Levi continue to hold their distance, but every now and again I know Sparky is glowering at me.

Hound reminds me of an ancient statue: his hands are jammed in his pockets, back straight. The chiseled jaw line is even more distinctive as he gazes at a candle, unblinking. Since that moment beside Vortex in the street, I have not detected any emotional reaction from him. His face remains an unreadable mask. Every now and again, as others retire to their own apartments, they pass him and place a sympathetic hand on his arm or shoulder. His statuesque appearance only deviates slightly as he returns his gratitude with a trace of a smile on his lips, undoubtedly forced. Just how deep had the relationship between them been?

Nevermore leaves the two of us alone.

I linger near my own door, but Vortex's vigil is directly across from my apartment and it's impossible to turn aside. It happened so fast. One moment she was charging the door, just as I would have done—as I craved to do. The next, she was on the pavement with her back broken and head split open. That could have been me. It *should* have been me.

I peer at Hound, who remains fixed in place, staring at nothing. I can't just abandon him like this.

"Do you want to come in for a drink or something?" I ask.

"No."

I nod, opening my door. "Okay. Well if you change your mind …" I mean the invitation, though privately I pray he never takes up the offer.

Leaving him alone in the hallway, staring at nothing, doesn't sit right with me. But what else can I do?

"She died because of him," he says before I can close the door.

I halt, gripping the doorframe. "You can't blame Nevermore. We did our best." Well, everyone else did. I didn't.

"Not him."

I lean against the doorframe. "Who?"

"All of this is because of him," Hound says with vehemence, glaring at something I don't comprehend.

Does he blame Forrest? The General? The Directorate Chief?

"You know that feeling you experience around me sometimes? That anger?"

I grimace. "Yes."

"That's his fault, too. *Everything* in my life that has gone wrong is because of him." Hound turns, and I see an anger I've never witnessed in his eyes. It blazes with contempt and loathing, a pure blue flame of fury. "Your anger. My job. This program. Her death. It all ties back to that miserable runt. If I ever get my hands on him, I will make him suffer like he made me suffer."

"Wait. Who are you talking about and what does it have to do with my anger?" I step toward him, but Hound turns away to enter his apartment.

"Best not to tell anyone about this conversation. It won't end well for either of us."

Then he closes the door.

What was that all about? Levi said something similar in the training facility. What in the hell is happening?

The experience has my mind reeling as I shut my own door and remove a feast from the fridge. Very little about what he said made any sense to me, except Hound did confirm what I already believed. I am angry with him for a reason. Or at least I was at one time. Whatever that reason, it has something to do with this person he went on about tonight. Whoever this guy is. How do I find out who it is?

And why did I forget if it had such an emotional impact on me?

They are messing with my head somehow, but just what has happened to me? I need answers, but have no clue how to get them.

As I perch on the edge of the bed, my daily dose appears on the nightstand. If something is going on, I will need all the strength I can get to see me through. But as I hold the needle to my arm, something forces me hesitate. A warning not to dose. Why shouldn't I?

I sit in indecision, gripping the dose firmly in one hand, until something deep inside compels me to scramble to the bathroom. Before I understand what I'm doing, I depress the plunger and watch the blue fluid squirt into the sink. My hands shake as I turn on the water to wash away any trace. The water rolls remnants of the blue liquid into a mesmerizing swirl of color. The vivid color fades as it mixes and washes away.

Tonight, I will miss my dose.

Nevermore warned me never to miss a dose.

What will tomorrow bring without it?

13

"RUUUN!!!" I SCREAM.

Guns click. Shots fire. I kick out. Pain tears into my stomach.

A shadowy figure kneels beside me—mysterious and familiar at the same time. "It's okay," he says, as if trying to convince himself that it's true. His voice is filtered, muffled by the pain and slowing thump of my own heartbeat.

"Go!" The word barely escapes me. And then, nothing.

I bolt upright in bed, pressing a hand against my stomach and searching for a wound as if I actually expect to discover myself bleeding. That nightmare was so real. Sweat rolls down my temples and into my eyes. I rub fists against them to clear my vision and the room around me swims into view. My heartbeat steadies as the familiar canvas painting greets me. A pounding headache momentarily blinds me as I step out of bed. My stomach heaves in revolt, but the sensation quickly passes.

Such a bizarre nightmare. Why would I dream of my death? Is that what happened? And who was that figure beside me? Maybe it was spurred on by the mission yesterday. Maybe I was afraid of dying inside the void of emotion and it manifested in my sleep.

Shower. I need a nice cold shower.

What happened after the mission, anyway? I struggle to recall our return from the mission as the water runs and I prepare to step in. All I can remember is Vortex's death, Sparky and Levi's peculiar behavior, Hound's cryptic concession, and then I woke in my bed. I don't remember the exercise exhausting me, but it must have.

I strip off my tank top and am about to step into the shower when I see the smudged message on my stomach. It freezes me in my paths.

They wipe ur memry
Trust no1
Find Poly

My body tenses so thoroughly that my abs make the message more defined, as if an intense light is flashing the message in my face. That's my handwriting, but I don't remember this. Which would make sense if they are wiping my memory. But why? And when does it happen? And how can I remember so much about yesterday if they are wiping memories away?

Eager to eliminate the evidence, I jump into the shower and scrub. I scrub away the eyeliner and continue until my abs are raw and angry red.

I don't understand any of this. Who is doing this to me? Whoever it is, they can't see everything, or I could not have left myself that message. They would have washed away all evidence just like I did.

By the time I'm ready for the day, it's still early. I head down to the training facility alone and immerse myself in the lifting routine once more. Run, lift, course, climb. Run, lift, course, climb. Time has no place in my fitness routine. The action helps steady my racing mind, leaving my worries behind and soothing my jittery nerves. There is only me and the routine.

After my third round, a low whistle draws my attention. The rest of the team watches nearby, and Hound grins in that dangerously charming manner.

"Something on your mind this morning, Steele?" Nevermore asks.

The danger of my situation strikes me in that moment as his perceptive gaze peers right through me. Thankfully, the workout has settled my nerves and helped still my racing mind. I wipe a stray hair away from my face and shake my head.

"I just needed to work out before we start," I say. "It helps center me."

"And why would you need to be centered?" Nevermore asks, staring as if he knows, but he couldn't.

"Just thinking about my parents again." Not a lie, yet also not the entire truth. Hopefully he can't tell the difference. "And I need to find these radicals and arrest them."

Hound glances at Nevermore as if searching for some clue. Is he part of this as well? Hound, who I know from before the DMA. Either he is wondering why Nevermore is pressing me, or he can't be trusted either. But how to tell?

At last, Nevermore nods. "Well, that's good news, because we are being activated for nightly missions. Should be more than enough targets to keep us busy."

Before they allow our unit on regular missions, we spend the day undergoing special testing conducted by Forrest: briefings about rules and regulations, tests to ensure we absorbed and remember the information, and psychological questioning. It drains me more than any workout ever has before. How does anyone just think all day? How incredibly boring and tiresome!

As the day concludes, Forrest pulls me aside. *Can I trust him? Is he part of this, too?* The thought feels familiar, as if it isn't the first time I've had them.

"Nevermore mentioned you are still upset about Mom and Dad," he says, and Forrest's nature is all brotherly concern. "Is there anything I can do to help?"

What can he do? They are dead. Nothing he does will change that. I shake my head reluctantly.

"I just don't want to fail them, or you," I say, stunned at my honesty. I really don't want to fail Forrest.

"How has your sleep been?" he asks.

I glance at the other two as they hesitate near the elevator doors. Do they already know what I dream about?

I've seen things, Bianca, a male voice says, and for a moment my heart hammers against my ribs. It's him again. That mysterious male voice that dogs my steps. I've seen them and I can't unsee them.

My limbs shake, and Forrest grabs my arms to steady me. "Are you okay?"

I want to answer, feel compelled to tell him, but my breaths come in sharp gasps. I stiffen my clutch on Forrest's arms. Scattered fragments of a memory press against a barrier in my mind. A desert. Yearning. Desperation. Love. Agony. Nevermore. My gaze darts past Forrest to the rest of my unit, still lingering near the exit. Hound watches with intense curiosity.

But not Nevermore. A hint of a wicked smile plays at the corners of his mouth.

… he smiles at me, and there is a desperation in his dark eyes. For the first time, I see him—really see him—and my heart leaps into my throat. How did I not recognize what was always in front of me? Ugene …

The figure solidifies into Ugene, and the name feels so familiar and comforting, yet it also fills me with trepidation. Forrest's says something, but I don't hear him. He is distant to me as another memory slams against my mind and my knees buckle.

… "Bianca, stop!" Ugene is eight years old, like me, drenched from the puddles I splash in, driving the water up against him. He calls for me to stop, but he laughs, shielding his face …

"She missed her dose," Forrest snaps.

I'm on the floor now, with all three of them kneeling around me.

"It was empty," Nevermore says. "I confirmed it myself."

"Do something before she recovers," Forrest commands.

My memories. The warning. They are about to wipe my memories again. I try to resist, but before I can shift more than an inch, another memory slams against the cracks in the wall around my mind and I whimper his name, hoping that reciting it will help me remember even after they have wiped my mind again.

"Ugene …" I breathe it out like a cherished object, clinging to it. Hound growls.

Icy-cold hands clamp my skull.

I struggle to retreat, but the force of these memories has undermined my enhanced body, and the team pins me to the floor.

… grief tears at my heart. My own grief. Ugene's grief. The utter devastation on his face shatters any lingering doubts in my mind. I have never really loved anyone before. Now, all I want to do is help him, heal him. I open my mouth, but the words won't come out. His skin is warm against my hand, as are his tears. Unable to say the words, I close the narrow distance between us before I can chicken out and press my lips against his. And he pulls away …

"—all traces of him erased for good this time," Forrest snaps.

Ugene. "No," I whimper. Tears roll down my temples against Nevermore's hands.

… the compact room lights up when Ugene paces like that, waves of excitement at solving yet another puzzle rolling off him and crashing against me with such force. He spins on his heel, and a smile lights up his face in a way that makes my heart seize. He opens his mouth to declare his discovery …

The memory dissolves like sugar in water. Followed by the next, and the next. I battle against the barrier in my mind, locking these fragments of my life, my love, away, but the fight is futile. As if I have no control over my own mind.

Who was I even thinking about? I can no longer recall a name or face. Does it matter?

Forrest places a palm against my shoulder. I smile dumbly at him as tears slide out.

Why am I crying?

My heartbeat slows, steadies. I close my eyes, still beaming.

Forrest will be so proud of me …

14

"DO YOU KNOW WHERE YOU ARE?" A FAMILIAR MALE voice asks.

I squint as my vision slowly comes into focus. The room is plain with no door and only a wall of mirrors in front of me. Yes. I've been in this room before, when I first completed Phase One of the DMA Special Forces project. And that voice isn't just familiar. It's Forrest.

"The Department of Military Affairs Special Forces training facility," I answer. The chair beneath me is hard and cold. "What happened? Why am I here?"

"You missed your dose," Forrest says.

Missing a dose is dangerous. Why would I do such a thing? It must have been an accident.

"You aren't kicking me out of the program, are you?" I ask, dreading the answer.

"Not yet," Forrest says, and the reply has an ominous tone that settles into my bones and gives me chills. "First, we need to be sure missing the dose has not had adverse effects. Then we will return you to your unit. But if you miss a dose again, we may not allow you to continue the program."

I raise my chin, determined not to let Forrest down. He is counting on me to help avenge our parents and protect our very way of life. "I'm ready."

"I will show you images, and I need you to tell me your honest reaction. Do any of them feel familiar? Do you recognize anyone or any places in them? What do they make you feel inside?"

A sequence of images flash across one mirror, and I give Forrest my sincerest reactions: Paragon Tower, Paragon's lobby, a group of teens in gray scrubs, a desert, a boy my age with dark skin and curious eyes, houses, schools, burned buildings, the same boy again covered in grime with fury burning in his eyes. None of the people are familiar. A few of the locations are, but they don't illicit an emotional response.

This goes on for some time, then Forrest announces we are finished, and I will return home soon.

§

Forrest leads me to a shuttle, just the two of us, after retrieving me from my apartment. He promises a special surprise.

We now fly over Elpis. From this high up, the downtown flattens out into perfectly maintained and manicured streets, houses, businesses the further west we head. The sheer magnitude of Elpis is impressive.

The jarring motion of the shuttle touching down jars me out of my daze.

Forrest unfastens his harness and rises, gesturing for me to follow as he slides open the shuttle door.

I hurriedly unfasten my harness and dash out after him…

… and step out into a parking lot, nearly vacant so early in the morning. The shuttle occupies four stalls of the grocery store lot. The medians in the lot have topiaries, well-cared for and sculpted with expert hands. Across the street, a strip of smaller up-scale boutiques.

Forrest starts away from the shuttle, and after a few steps he pauses, holding a hand out to me. I accept and let him guild me along.

We round the corner toward a suburb of large, impressive homes surrounded by gardens and landscaping just as well sculpted as the parking lot—if not more so. As we approach a corner, past a string of two-story, wide houses, I peer up and locate the street sign, then freeze.

Dysart Lane.

Forrest gives my hand a reassuring tug.

The lane ends in a cul-de-sac, and everything about it is both alien and intimate. I recognize this place, yet I don't. Something about it makes my palms sweat and generates pressure in my chest.

Forrest's hand is also slick with perspiration. Is he apprehensive about this as well? It would make sense. He doesn't have to reveal to me which house belonged to our parents. I recognize the brown siding and white-trimmed windows, the familiar pillars over the front porch, and proud patches of pink staghorn sumac add a splash of color to the natural face of the home.

Forrest drops my hand as he perches on a bench beside the manicured garden sidewalk. I can't move my feet to join him.

Lights illuminate a few of the windows in the house across the street. Every minute, a shadowy form passes the curtained windows until, at last, a woman I don't recognize steps out and into the wide driveway, oblivious to our presence. She is in her middle years, with cropped black hair and pale white skin. Nothing about her resembles either of us. This woman is a stranger.

"The house sold quickly after they passed," Forrest says, his tone solemn. "You demanded to keep the house, but we just couldn't manage it. I wish you could remember it, B."

But I don't. I can't remember anything but their funeral and a few scattered images of Mom and Dad playing with me, hugging me. And there are broken images of me dancing in the rain as a child.

Except those memories weren't here. I spin and search the street for anything that resembles what I remember, but nothing stands out.

"What is it?" he asks. "Do you remember something?" Is that hope or trepidation in his voice?

"I remember playing in puddles as a kid, but not here." I didn't intend to say it, but the words tumble out.

"We moved here when you were about…" He pauses, and his brows scrunch up as he struggles to remember. "I think eleven."

I nod. That makes sense then. I was definitely younger than that when I remember the puddles.

"You did make Mom so mad when you came in dripping in water and mud though," Forrest says with a sad chuckle. "She used to say you might as well have rolled around in it like a pig."

Once more, my gaze is drawn to the house as the woman disappears down the road in her vehicle.

"We will stop them," Forrest says decisively, resentment and hate burning in his tone. It pairs with the ferocity I experienced myself, though I don't feel any of the emotion now.

"Why did you bring me here?" I ask, turning to face him, unable to look at the house a moment longer.

"To show you that Theus lied to you," Forrest says as he rises. "I need you to be confident you are on the proper side, and I can't afford for you to distrust me. I need *you* to do this."

"Why me?"

Forrest steps closer, settling his hands on my shoulders. For just a moment, he looks more like an older brother than a commanding liaison. "Because you have more Power than anyone else in Elpis. The enhancements far exceeded our expectations. Between your strength and my brains, we can finally root out these radicals and put an end to the threat against our city, against our very way of life."

I have more Power than anyone? Does that mean I have surpassed even Atmos—the Super who nearly ended the world? It's a chilling prospect to even contemplate.

15

I REPORT TO MY UNIT TO RESUME TRAINING, GREETED by Hound's grinning face and Nevermore's typical sneer. Hound's eagerness to return to work blows me away. Can he really just set his emotions regarding Vortex's death aside so easily? I almost resent it.

The hostility between the two boys remains palpable despite how carefree Hound acts. It's evident by the way the two of them interact with each other that they have not forgotten what transpired in the field despite going on with training. It's as if they reached some unspoken agreement that it would never be mentioned again.

"How are you feeling?" Hound asks.

"I should ask you that." I chew my lip and nod. "I'm ready to put an end to this." I have a lot to make up for.

On the other side of the facility, Ivy's unit is celebrating her recovery. They attempt keeping to themselves, but their happiness chaffs my nerves.

Nevermore's simulation is far more ruthless than before as he continues testing my mental stability. Vortex screams somewhere out of sight, but I can't find her. Radicals line agents along the sidewalk with guns to their heads. He forces me to watch as they squeeze the trigger. Over and over, Nevermore tests my ability to stare down death and function. The mental anguish creates a headache and acidic churning in my stomach. By the end of the day, I'm trembling.

But I won't fail again. Not when it could cost lives. Not when it means failing my brother.

Hound stalks over to Nevermore as I return the practice gun

to its case.

"… overdoing it," Hound whispers, glancing at me from the corner of his eyes.

I act as if I haven't noticed.

"I'm doing what I was ordered," Nevermore responds. "We can't afford to lose agents because she can't handle a little death."

I swallow the lump in my throat. Nevermore is right. I hate when he's right.

"If she has another mental break—"

"Better here than in the field," Nevermore snaps. "She will agree, if you ask."

I march to the lifting set. I *would* agree. I have no desire to suffer another mental lapse like I did in the field, and if Nevermore's simulations prevent that, all the better. Even if they hack out another chunk of my soul each time.

Hound strides toward me, but I shake my head. "Go rest," I advise him. "I'm going to lift a little before I go back up."

"I can spot you," he offers.

"That's sweet that you think I need a spotter," I tease. But that isn't why he offered, and we both realize it. Hound just prefers to remain near me.

He nods in dismay and leaves me alone to lift.

Nevermore has already vanished.

The weights do little for my muscles, but work wonders for my headache. After an hour of work, the dull throb in my head has faded, along with that churning in my gut.

I return to my room, shower, and thump down on my bed. Sleep is the farthest thing from my mind. The jolt my weight causes against the bed makes it shift on the hardwood floor. Something beneath the bed slaps against the floor and I roll over the lip to peer under. My black hair dangles against the floor and I have to press it back to see.

Beneath my bed, white envelope rests on the floor. Did that just drop from under my mattress? Curious, I roll off the bed and reach under, squirming part of the way under before my fingers work it toward me.

Pressing my back against the bed, I examine the white envelope. My name is scrawled in big, bold letters across the front. But not the name I go by here. This one reads: Bianca.

Just seeing the name in writing like this makes my heart thud against my chest. I flip the envelope over and over between my fingers. Who could this be from?

No point just thinking about it when I can find out, I tell myself, sliding a finger into the flap to rip the envelope open.

The handwriting on the note is not recognizable. It isn't mine.

> Bianca,
>
> If you are reading this, they got to me. My name is Polygraph, your roommate. By the time you read this, I'm sure you won't remember me at all. Or what I told you.
>
> The DMA is erasing your memories to control you. Your brother is working with them. All of this—the injections, the training, the people appointed to your team—it plays into their designs. I don't know exactly how, but I know for a fact that they are selectively wiping your memories. The dose reinforces the barrier. I know because my job, as your roommate, was to Detect when you were remembering and report to Nevermore.
>
> Don't trust anyone. They are all in on it.
> Poly

This can't be real.

Yet something about her warning seems familiar. Polygraph used Detect on me, which means she possibly was a Somatic, like me, but with smell or taste detection. She could also be Psionic, sensing through the mind when someone lies.

The terrible notion that what she says is true, or that she was real at all, makes my stomach twist and my brain hurt. I don't want to believe it, but the gaps in my memory make it tough to deny it as a lie. Why *do* I remember so little? I can't even remember why I'm mad at Hound, or why Nevermore makes me so uneasy, as if I have a sordid history with both of them. And I must. That way Nevermore sneers at me all the time can't be a coincidence … He remembers. He remembers, and he doesn't like me.

I press the note from this mysterious Poly against the hardwood floor as the anger grows in me.

This note from Poly cannot slip into other hands. I have to find a secure place to keep it in case they somehow wipe it from my memory.

I tuck the note back into the ripped envelope and slide it under a slat under the mattress loosely enough for it to fall again if I hit the bed hard enough. If they do wipe my memory and I discover this once more, I want to be sure I have already opened it. The envelope will present proof.

Levi and Sparky blamed me for "her" loss. I assumed they meant Vortex, but as they went away, they mentioned Poly. Maybe they have answers.

I bite my lip, brush my finger through my hair, and push off the floor. Someone owes me answers.

Levi and Sparky share an apartment three doors down the hall. I watched them retire to the apartment after Vortex's vigil. Licking my lips, I lift my fist and rap softly on the door. My heart hammers against my ribs. Will they answer? Will they tell me anything?

The door swings inward and Levi goes rigid when he sees me. "What?"

I wince. "I just … Who was Poly?"

Levi pales, glancing into the hallway suspiciously, then peering over his shoulder deeper into the apartment. "I don't know what you're talking about," he says sharply, then slams the door in my face.

I step back, gawking at the door. There's no way in hell he knew nothing. How will I ever learn the truth when no one will talk to me?

Our unit spends the evening in the city, hunting down several targets for the DMA, who collect the targets and gather intel to locate more targets for the next night. Nevermore, Hound, and I work with terrible efficiency.

Hound and Nevermore use their Powers to hunt down the target's location and zero in on them.

I pin the targets in and use my Strength and speed to arrest them.

When we return to our apartments, I pass Levi in the hallway. He scans me cautiously. What is that look for? I smile and wave, soliciting friendship, but he just rolls his eyes and rushes the opposite direction. Have I done something to him?

After showering off the filth of Pax, I spot something under my bed and frown, fetching an envelope that's previously been opened. Frowning, I perch on the floor and read the letter. Who is Poly? I remember her name from somewhere else. Didn't Levi mention her once? Maybe that is why he glares at me.

I knock on his door.

Levi opens groans. "Again?"

"What?"

"Leave us alone." He closes the door in my face.

Peculiar. Have I knocked on his door before? I suppose, if Poly is right and they are wiping my memory, it's altogether possible I sought answers from him.

The next night we only locate one target. She resists, and I get a thrill from chasing her down and overpowering her. Her Naturalist Power is nothing compared to my strength.

The unit returns to the facility and I spend some time on the training floor working off extra energy. On the way back to my apartment, I pick up an exchange between Forrest and Nevermore in his apartment.

"The doses seem to work now," Nevermore says. His voice is only slightly dampened by the door. They must be in the kitchen. "Bianca doesn't remember him at all anymore. I've tested her repeatedly. There seems to be some sort of echo from Poly. I can't pinpoint it, but I'm working on it. I should find it in a day or two."

My heart seizes. Who don't I remember? Who is Poly?

"Good," Forrest says. "The barrier was merely temporary, anyway. We both knew it. With Ugene erased completely, the doses will continue to tidy up traces of what we are doing. Once you can find Poly's echo, we shouldn't have any more unexpected complications."

Ugene. Who is Ugene? Who is Poly? What has my brother done to me?

I squeeze a hand against my mouth to stifle the cry of alarm rising in my throat. The hallway sways. Sweat beads on my forehead and my heart palpates. I gulp down breaths that provide no reprieve.

Forrest is my brother. What has he done to me? And why?

I hurry into my bedroom and slam the door, backing away as if a demon is about to break it down. I have to get out of here. I have to escape!

The dose appears on my nightstand as it does every night. I stumble away from it. My legs hit the bed and I sink down.

He is using that to clean my memories, I think, unable to tear my gaze away from the needle.

No. I won't take it. He can't force me.

Sick to my stomach and dizzy, I snatch up the dose and run to the bathroom to wash it down the sink.

The front door bursts open, and Nevermore, Forrest, and Hound dart in.

"Stop!" Forrest shouts.

I freeze in the bathroom doorway, gripping the needle with my thumb against the plunger. *I won't take this again. Never again!*

"She's going to waste it," Nevermore announces.

I squeeze my thumb against the plunger to spray the blue fluid onto the floor when Hound seizes me with his Power.

Forrest strides toward me and fetches the needle as it slips from my paralyzed fingers.

"Don't do this," I plead.

"I'm doing this *for* you," Forrest says.

I peer past him at Hound, appeal with my eyes. He averts his gaze.

"No!" I struggle against Hound's Power, shifting my arm as Forrest is about to stab the needle in.

"Dammit, hold her steady, Jimmy!" Forrest snaps.

"I'll do it," Nevermore grumbles.

The world drops away. I'm plunged into impenetrable darkness.

16

OUR BIGGEST SUCCESS ARRIVES ON THE FIFTH NIGHT of patrols, when we uncover one of the radical safehouses and arrest six men and women. One woman tries to flee, but Hound is positioned outside the back door and when she attempts fighting back, he seizes control of her body using her own blood against her. By the time I slip out the back door to help him, Hound is standing over her corpse. I have no idea what he did to her, but her body is shriveled and ashen, as if all the blood has gone from her. As Hound meets my gaze, I sense the shock in him. Whatever he did, even he did not know it was feasible before that moment. I never ask what happened. He never speaks of it. No one else cares.

No matter how hard we work or how many people we arrest, the stream of targets seems infinite. Are we even making a difference? Could there truly be hundreds, as General Sims implied? I had assumed the problem would be much simpler, that we would locate a hive of radicals and arrest them all, and that would be the end. But they seem more like insects. Regardless of how many we stamp out, more rise to the surface.

Forrest continues to assert that we are drawing closer, and the Directorate Chief is pleased with the results we have yielded, but the task is far from over. I pick up on the sense that he is hunting for someone more specific, and each time we arrest more than one radical, the disappointment on Forrest's face is crushing. He is searching for someone, but for whatever reason will not tell me about it.

The failure of that first mission persists in my mind, driving me to prove repeatedly that I can be successful. Maybe it's just me getting in my own way, but it feels like Forrest has not forgiven me for that failure, that a chasm is opening between us and I don't know how to fix it. Hound and Nevermore have accepted what happened on that mission, to some extent, after I have showed myself capable in the field since. But I don't seek their endorsement. I yearn for Forrest's approval. I desire it.

He said he needs me, that I'm stronger than anyone else in the city. With any luck, I will get a chance to convince him at last.

After another mission, I shower and change. My old leather jacket hangs over the back of the armchair. Mom and Dad gave me that jacket. I remember now. I begged and pleaded with them. On Unity Day—our celebration of the founding of Elpis—Mom proudly presented me with the box as Dad watched from the sofa.

I glide to the armchair and slip the jacket over my arms, hoping it will provide some comfort. I hug my arms around myself and close my eyes, wishing it was either of my parents holding me instead. Something in the jacket crinkles and I inspect the pockets. Nothing. I examine the lining and find an almost imperceptible hole in the fabric. I dig my fingers into it and produce an envelope with my name scrawled across it in big letters.

What is this?

I pull out the letter and unfold it. The paper is worn along the edges. How many times have I read this?

The message makes my pulse accelerate. The DMA is erasing my memories. My brother and Nevermore are part of the conspiracy. Trust no one.

But who is Poly? I battle for some recollection of the name, but nothing comes to mind.

This can't be real.

But the worn condition of the paper along the folds and edges gives away the truth. I have discovered this before. Many times.

I understand now why Nevermore doesn't like me. Maybe this is why I am uneasy around him. I return the note to the lining of my jacket, passing my fingers along the hole in the lining to make it hard to see.

Hound's glib comment after we arrested Theus surfaces. *Maybe it's your fault.* He spoke to Nevermore, but I must have missed something, some vital detail. Hound believed that what happened to me in the field was Nevermore's fault. I didn't think twice about it, assuming he meant Nevermore should have warned me. But now, after reading Poly's letter, I can't help but think Hound meant something very different; that maybe whatever they are doing to my memories and mind had an effect in the field, and that's why I froze up.

And Nevermore's snide comment when Hound threatened to report to Forrest: *He needs me. Without me, his golden girl is a loose cannon.* Just trying to puzzle all of this out makes my head split with a headache once more. If Nevermore is blocking me from losing control, or whatever the loose cannon comment related to, was Poly trying to warn me that Nevermore is responsible for the memory loss as well? He's a Telepath, but erasing memories is something else altogether.

This note from Poly has to remain safely tucked away in case they somehow wipe it from my memory again. Then my stomach sinks and I feel like I might throw up.

Again.

Hound warned me, *Best not to mention this conversation to anyone else. It won't end well for either of us.* I have no clue what Hound was referring to when he said that. Everything about that conversation was mysterious. But maybe he was trying to warn me. Maybe he is in on it but doesn't want to be. Someone is playing with our lives and if we voice anything we suspect is off, it could cause another memory wipe.

Or worse.

I bite my lip, brush my fingers through my hair, and head out the door. Hound won't inform me everything, but maybe I can drag something out of him.

In no time, I'm knocking on his door.

Nevermore opens and steps aside, waving me inside with an impatient swipe of his hand.

Have I done this before?

Nevermore narrows his bird-like eyes and I direct my thoughts to Testing Day, sitting on the sofa with Hound—Jimmy. Nevermore cannot know the truth.

A tense moment passes between us as he closes the door and enters the kitchen.

"Something wrong?" Nevermore asks, leaning on the counter.

The question throws me off and I flounder to identify a plausible answer.

"Steele?" Hound steps out of his room, rescuing me from this awkward moment.

I nudge past Nevermore and fold my arms around Hound, pressing my face against his neck. He doesn't question my reaction as his arms wrap around me and he rubs at my back.

A sense of ease flows through my limbs as his Power sooths me anxiety. Part of me wants to sever contact and refuse giving him this sort of influence over me. Another part of me is grateful for the respite.

Nevermore stomps away. "Just don't keep me up," he grumbles as he retreats into his bedroom and bangs the door.

For a moment after Nevermore leaves the living room, Hound continues to hold me and sooth my frazzled nerves. His hand slides up to my chin, and he tilts my face up. This close, his blue eyes are magnificent. For the first time since our argument in the hallway, I feel a tug of attraction toward him as my belly does flips.

"Please don't use your Power on me," I say, conscious that he is doing something to warm my blood.

Hound shakes his head. "I'm not doing anything. Just calming your nerves. What's wrong?"

I glance toward Nevermore's closed door.

He doesn't need me to add more. Hound slides a hand into mine and escorts me to his room.

I close the door. What comes next, Nevermore can never know.

The room is much like my own, but in deep hues of blue instead of bright splashes of color. His bed is a rumpled mess, with the navy comforter half hanging off on the floor. Dirty clothes pile in one corner and he kicks them into a tighter pile as if that will place them out of sight.

I proceed toward the bed, nudging the clump of blankets aside. Hound raises an eyebrow as I settle on the edge.

"What brings you here?" he asks. "I would hate to make false assumptions."

"I can't stop thinking about what you said in the hallway the other day…" My voice trails off. This has to be handled delicately. I can't just come out and ask him anything directly. What if he is part of this? He must be. I pick at my nails, averting eye contact to draw him in and lower his guard. "You were so angry, and I'm worried that your anger is directed at my brother."

Hound sighs dramatically as he sinks down on the edge of the bed beside me. "Forrest? No. He and I have always gotten along, though I'm pretty sure he assumes I'm a moron. I owe this new Power to him."

"Okay, well you were so angry, and somehow whoever you are angry with links back to the reason I feel angry around you. I guess I'm trying to understand. My mind wants to remember, it tries, but there's nothing." I free a trembling sigh and even invoke a few tears that well in my eyes. My ability to play the role of a damsel in distress is disturbing. "I don't want to be angry with you anymore. I need to know what happened."

With any luck, his hope that we might revive whatever might have been between will loosen his tongue.

"I'm not proud of myself," Hound says, and the melancholy in his voice is sincere. Unless he is as skilled at this game as me.

"Please, Jimmy," I plead, swinging my moist eyes to him.

Hound stares at his own hands until I utter his name, and it snaps his attention to me.

"I can't tell you," he says. Something about his tone tells me he prefers to, but is that fear in his eyes? "I would do just about anything to avoid you from being angry with me. If I break the rules and tell you the truth, I'm scared you will only get madder."

I slip my hand over his, granting it a light squeeze.

He stares at our joined hands while the conflicting desires play across his stiff face.

A tear slips out of my eye and rolls down my cheek.

Hound looks up, and his face falls. With his free hand, he reaches up and sweeps the tear away. "Bianca," he croaks my name, then his Adam's apple bobs. "If anyone finds out, we are both in danger."

I only reply by squeezing his hand.

Hound pulls in a heavy breath and lets it out, peering over my shoulder toward the door. He's afraid of Nevermore! *Maybe he* was *trying to warn me.*

"If he perceives anything—"

I shake my head. "He won't."

But Hound doesn't agree. "I've changed, Bianca. Please remember that. You were angry with me, and you had every right to be. But losing you woke me up. I'm not that guy anymore."

I actually believe him. Not because he is working his Power on me, but because of the shame and earnestness on his face. I must not have provided him a chance to explain himself before, so whatever he did, it can't be good.

Hound seems to await some signal that I accept his plea. I turn toward him, dragging a knee up onto the bed to face him.

"There was this kid in school who used to give us a hard time," Hound explains. "The two of us never got along, and he called me Jimmy the Idiot, told other people nasty stuff about me. Most of it was baseless allegations. I think he was just jealous that you were with me and not him. You wanted me to just ignore him, let it go. You insisted he wasn't worth the trouble."

That hardly sounds like me. Somewhere in my gut, I get the sense that I would stand up to any bully who intimidated people I care about. So far, I see no reason to be so angry with him.

"But I couldn't take it," Hound continues. "Soon after Career Day, I finally cracked. I tried to be the bigger man, but I knew I was stronger than him and I just couldn't take it anymore. He and I got into a fight. You showed up and tried to stop us, but I lost control. I went too far. I accidentally ... hit you with my Power during the fight. You were livid with me for it. You said I was no better than him, that I was a bully, and you broke up with me right there in front of him and everyone else."

That, I can believe. While something about his story doesn't feel quite right, it rings true enough to why I might be angry with him still. Especially if he used his Power and hurt me.

Hound's grasp on my hands tightens frantically. "He got what he wanted, to drive a wedge between us, and I've tried so hard since then to prove that I'm not that guy. I need you to believe me."

"If you're not that guy," I say deliberately, "then why did you say you would make him suffer when we were in the hallway?"

He hangs his head. "I let Vortex's death get the better of me. I didn't mean it."

But that hate in his eyes had been so real. I find it hard to accept he didn't mean what he said.

"So who was this guy?" I ask.

"A nobody, at the time."

An interesting remark. I cock my head.

Hound straightens, and the anguish in his eyes is real, but it only vaguely masks the anger. "A criminal, Bianca."

The response startles me. "What?"

"He is responsible for the bombing at Paragon Tower. He is known to be consorting with the radicals, maybe even as a leader. He is the one Forrest has been hunting for these past few weeks. Ugene Powers is the DMA's primary, number one target." He watches me, searching for a reaction, but the name doesn't ring any bells. All I feel is anger. "For a little while, before the attack, they had him at Paragon. He agreed to participate in their research, but now Forrest and General Sims believe he only agreed so he could get inside and attempt destroying the research and the building. Thankfully he failed at both, but he managed some significant damage to Paragon Tower. If I had known who he would become back then …"

Now that hate Hound revealed in the hallway makes much more sense. And this discovery makes me fear the next question.

"Was he responsible for what happened to my parents?" That would clarify why Forrest was also angry with the mysterious *him* he mentioned when I first came here.

"I don't know." Hound's words are dragged out, careful. "Forrest doesn't talk about it."

My grip on his hand tightens, and now the tears that roll down my cheeks are terribly real tears of rage.

Hound winces and tugs at his hand.

Realizing I am crushing it in my fist, I let go and mutter an apology. "And my memories? Why do I have so many gaps?"

Hound tenses, caressing the hand I crushed.

"I know something is going on," I say, praying that Hound really is here for me.

"I didn't want to do it," he says hastily. "But you told me to, because if I didn't help … I don't want you to forget me. Regardless of what you think of me, I still love you. I tried turning it off, but I can't. And if you forget me, if they make me disappear …"

Disappear. Is that what happened to Poly? What is he talking about?

"I don't want to forget you, either," I say. "Do whatever you must to protect us both. Nevermore can never know. But please, if you love me, don't let me forget either."

Hound's eyebrows knit together and his shoulders slump. "You said that last night, too. Keep the letter safe."

My heart thuds. I nod stiffly.

"Are you still angry with me?" he asks, shaking his hand out.

I swallow the anger and grief that tightens my throat, then shake my head. It's difficult to be angry with him for hurting someone who deserves far worse, or for doing what I requested. Hound is part of this vicious cycle, but I asked him to be.

"And as for Ugene," I say, "he's a criminal. A radical. He will be brought to justice just like all the others." A smoldering hatred born for a desire to recover this guy burns in my core.

And when I succeed, I will make him suffer worse than Hound ever could conceive.

17

THE SAME NIGHTMARE HAUNTS MY SLEEP. STRAPPED to a table. Screaming. Blood. Injections. I wake with a start, sweat casting a glaze over my face. Hound's steady, soft breathing reminds me I'm safe.

I hadn't meant to stay, but once we started chatting, it just carried on. It's easy to understand how the two of us were once so close. Conversation came naturally. He even told me a few stories from our time together that made me laugh. I don't remember laughing. It felt so wonderful and normal. When I asked him about his relationship with Vortex, he just grimaced and reassured me that nothing had truly happened. He never felt connected to her in any intimate ways, just as a really close friend.

Eventually I rested my head on his chest as we passed jokes about Nevermore's bird-like features or overall contempt for humanity until we fell asleep.

I slip my feet over the edge of the bed and search for my jacket. Despite the dreadful dream, this had been one of the best nights I can remember. Not that my memory is reliable these days.

As I slip out the door and close it softly, I try to keep my movements as silent as possible so I don't wake either of them. I turn once the door is firmly shut and yelp, pressing a hand to my chest.

Nevermore is perched on the arm of the sofa as if he knew I was coming. "Will this be a constant thing?"

My cheeks heat. Nothing happened. Hound and I just talked. But how this must look to anyone else! I want to tell him no, but the words fumble at my lips. Will it be the last time?

Nevermore just nods with that sneer on his face. "At least you kept the noise to a minimum."

"I gotta go. My dose …" I stab a thumb over my shoulder toward the front door.

"I wouldn't bother too much about that." He rises and stalks toward me. Something about how he moves makes my skin crawl.

"Um. Okay." Without meaning to, I step backward, away from him. "Can I ask you a private question?"

"No." Nevermore stops a foot away from me, and his beady eyes penetrate me in a manner that makes me feel violated.

"Why do we call you Nevermore?" I ask, hoping for a diversion from the utter discomfort. Why won't my feet move? "We all have call signs that make sense except you."

"Because my last name is Poe and I apparently remind people of a raven," Nevermore replies without flinching. He doesn't seem to look at me, but through me.

"I don't understand." Something presses against my mind, like a palm pushing down. What is he searching for?

"Of course you don't," he sneers, glaring at me as if I'm a complete moron. I want to punch the expression off his face. "Poe was a famous writer from the 19th century. Wrote a poem about a raven who drove a man into madness."

Madness. A sensation that is creeping up on me. What is it about him that makes me freeze up in dread when he peers at me like this? I only blink dumbly.

Nevermore sighs in revulsion, as if he considers me the dullest thing he has ever encountered. "The raven could only say nevermore," he explains flatly.

I swallow the lump lodged in my throat. "So can you drive people mad?"

The rim of his lip curls up in a way that makes my heart thump irregularly, and the bridge of his nose crinkles. "The mind is a delicate thing once you know where to prod."

My first day of training surfaces. The strange, arid plain. The lightning. The figure without a face. Was that his doing? Something else presses at my memory. Something I feel like I need to remember; something urgent. But I can't seem to pull it back.

At last, I regain command of my body and step away. "Okay. I was just curious. I'll, um, I'll see you later."

"Unless I see you first," he says as I try not to run for the door. The way he says the words suggests something much more sinister, despite the obviously fake jovial tone.

It takes all of my inner strength not to race back to the security of my apartment. I don't feel like I've really put distance between myself and Nevermore until I close the door to my bedroom.

There's no way I will sleep again now, so I change into workout clothes and go down to the training facility to run, lift, and climb. The exercise will help me feel like I'm in control of myself, even if it constantly feels like my body is not my own.

After hours of intense workout, I return to my apartment to shower and change. I had expected to see Nevermore and Hound in the training facility at some point, but they never came. Once I'm fresh and dressed, I knock on their door, curious about what has kept them. To my own astonishment, I'm also eager to see Hound and talk to him again. What if Hound got into trouble for talking to me last night? I only remember scattered fragments of our conversation.

No one answers the door.

Odd.

I knock again, and as I wait for one of them to answer, the elevator doors open at the end of the hallway.

"They aren't here," Forrest says, approaching with two plastic bags in hand.

"Where are they?"

"Patrols."

"Then why am I here? I should be out there with them? Did they search for me before leaving? I was only down training." The words spill out of me in a flood. The fact that they left me behind hurts. Are they still upset with me for freezing up on that mission? I thought we were past that.

Forrest holds up the takeout bags. "I figured you and I could dine and chat." Without waiting for my answer, he opens my apartment door and enters.

I cast a glance at Hound's door and my shoulders sag. Would they rather be out there without me?

I close the apartment door with a slap as Forrest sets up the sushi along the counter. We settle into the barstools.

"You're mad at me," I mumble, powerless to meet his gaze.

"For what?"

"Freezing in the field. Failing that first mission." I poke at the sushi roll.

"I'm not mad," he says around a mouthful of unagi. "Was I disappointed in your performance? Sure."

I wince.

"But I wasn't mad." Forrest shifts on the stool and leans an arm against the countertop. "Maybe I just expect too much from you."

The words are as efficient as a slap. I would almost rather have him mad at me. He sounds so much like Dad it makes my heart ache.

"But you didn't send me out into the field with my team," I say. My appetite is slipping despite the colorful rolls. "I feel like this chasm has opened between us."

Forrest rolls a piece in soy sauce. "You are all I have left, B. I will not cast you off because you failed to arrest someone. Everyone out there that night failed. Don't hold it all on yourself."

"Maybe, but I was the only one who froze up." I pop a piece of sushi into my mouth and chew slowly, deliberately.

"You've been through more than most of the others," Forrest points out, taking a drink of his root beer. The condensation collects on the glass bottle and fat drops roll away from his fingers. "But I want to make sure you are okay now."

I shrug, uncertain how to respond. Forrest lost parents, too. He must understand on some level.

"Nevermore said you spent the night with Hound," he says casually, as any big brother would when he discovers his sister is sleeping with someone. "Is this a thing again?"

"No. Maybe." I droop, dipping a yellowtail roll. "Nothing happened. We just talked."

For a split second, Forrest pauses. The moment passes so swiftly I'm uncertain if it was real or imagined. "Yeah? About what?" His tone is light and conversational, but something about the way his shoulders have strained up makes me feel like he is concerned.

"All sorts of stuff." I chew and swallow, my hunger returning gradually. "He told me stories about when we were together before, helped fill in some gaps. Forrest, we laughed. It felt so wonderful. I don't remember the last time I really laughed."

He absently brushes his thumb over the condensation on the bottle and starts picking at the label. "It's been a while."

"You know, you are always asking questions about me, but you never tell me about you," I say. "Are you seeing anyone? How are you getting along without Mom and Dad?"

Forrest puffs out his cheeks. "No, I'm not seeing anyone. Work has kept me so busy."

"Don't bury yourself in work to avoid grieving them," I say, lying a hand on his forearm. "I'm here, if you need to talk."

The smile on his face is sad as he meets my gaze. Deeply, profoundly sad in a manner that makes my heart clench up for him. How lonely he must be when he's alone!

The wailing of an abrasive alarm shatters the silence of the apartment. It blasts from my bedroom, making both of us start. A second later, an identical alarm screams from inside Forrest's pocket. He frowns and plucks out his phone, tapping at the clear surface. The alarm on his device ceases, but the one from my room continues to wail.

I rush to the bedroom to snatch my tablet and kill the noise, reading the message as I shuffled back out to join Forrest.

TARGET ACQUIRED
ALL UNITS ACTIVATED

Forrest is already on his feet, fingers gliding over the surface of his phone as I tap on the flashing red dot on my tablet screen. A map of Pax pops up off the surface, marking out one house. A red dot inside the house pulses.

"I have to go," Forrest says in a rush.

"Is this him?" I ask, slipping my tablet on the countertop.

"Who?" he asks, sliding on his jacket that he had draped over the back of the chair.

"Ugene Powers," I say in a near growl.

Forrest freezes, staring at me like I just grew extra limbs. I've just given Hound away, but I don't care.

"What do you know about him?" Forrest asks warily.

"That he's a terrorist. That's all I need to know."

Forrest shrugs his jacket on the rest of the way and nods as if satisfied with my answer. Providing no further information, he turns toward the door and moves in long, urgent strides.

"You are safer here," he says.

"The notice called for everyone!" I protest, following on his heels as I slip on my jacket.

"He is dangerous and I can't risk him getting his hands on you. No. You stay." He yanks open the door.

I slap a hand against it and slam the door shut hard enough to crack the frame and shake the entire wall. "Don't you dare! You are the one who told me I'm the strongest in the city, that you need me. I will not be left here like a helpless girl while you and my team are out there. Let me help you. I want to bring him in. Let me prove myself!"

"Bianca—"

"If I don't leave, you don't either, and I know how much you want to get your hands on him." I stand between him and the door. Let him try to move me. "I'm going."

Forrest emits a rare growl of frustration and rakes a hand over his neatly cut dark hair. He is usually so well composed, even under pressure. Am I wrong to insist on going? *No. I'm right. He needs me.*

"If he is so dangerous, I don't want you out there where he can harm you," I say, softening my tone. "Forrest, you are all I have left, too. If something happened to you and I was here, I would never forgive myself."

Forrest's lips thin in a tight line and he waves impatiently at the door. "Fine. But you stay with me."

"Obviously." I open the door and sprint toward the elevator

Excitement pumps through my limbs and my heart races as we ride up to the docking bay. Finally, a chance to hit the radicals hard and take down one of their leaders.

I won't fail Forrest a second time.

I won't fail my parents.

18

THE DOCKING BAY IS A FLURRY OF ACTIVITY. MEN AND women in uniforms slap on their troopers' helmets and climb into shuttles and armored trucks. Where did all these people come from? They shout orders through the air. Carts loaded with weapons are pushed at a full sprint toward vehicles. Others grab guns and refill cartridges off racks and out of cases along the walls. So many people for just one target. Is he really so dangerous?

Forrest moves with purpose and a stride that even I struggle to keep up with, as if a fire is burning at his heels. He doesn't look up as he crosses the massive docking bay, tapping on his phone, sending messages I don't see in rapid swipes. I have watched him at work, but this is different. His calm competence bolsters my confidence.

Despite the orderly chaos as everyone gathers materials and loads into shuttles, a path opens around Forrest and me as if he is Moses parting the Red Sea. The respect and authority these people automatically defer to him is a peculiar thing, and intriguing to witness.

General Sims waits at the open door of our shuttle, his arms crossed over his wide chest. "You better not screw this up, Pond. You and Cass have made a mess of things, and we expect you to tidy it up."

"Nevermore says he's cornered," Forrest says, finally looking up from his phone. "Even with help, he has nowhere to go this time. Hound has his scent."

Hound is out there hunting this guy down? My feet itch to run and help him.

"Seaduss will want him alive," Sims says, as if he needs to.

"We all do, sir," Forrest says. He nods me into the shuttle around Sims.

I offer Sims a salute as I pass him and clamber into the shuttle.

Forrest follows and closes the door, sealing us off from Sims. He then tucks his phone into his pocket and extracts bullet-proof vests from the armory cage. Forrest tosses one at me that I easily catch.

"Make no assumptions," he says. "Wear that at all times."

I'm about to order him to do the same, but he tosses his jacket aside and fastens a vest over his polo shirt.

Once vested, we sit beside each other and strap on the harnesses. The shuttle lurches into motion. I glance out the window, expecting sunlight, but am instead greeted by the deep darkness of night and the glow of city lights. In the distance, far from the edge of Elpis, a black hole pierces the earth, reminding me of one of Vortex's voids. I frown. *Talk about déjà vu.*

"Who told you about Ugene?" Forrest asks tersely.

"Hound." I turn away from the window and put a hand on his shoulder. "Don't get mad at him. I practically ripped it out of him." My hand falls to my lap. "He told me about the fight he had with Ugene, and how mad I got at him. Then he told me what the guy did. Forrest—" I have to work up the courage to ask the question Hound couldn't answer. "Was he responsible for what happened to Mom and Dad?"

Forrest grimaces and his phone buzzes. He pulls it out and taps out a quick message before answering. "I wish I could say yes. It would be simpler. You don't remember him from school at all?" His coppery eyes meet mine intently. What does he think I will say?

"No. I can't even remember what he looks like."

"What else do you know about him?"

"Nothing."

Forrest's eyes narrow as if he thinks I'm lying to him. Why would I lie about this? He must be satisfied with my answer, because he pulls out his phone and projects information above the surface to share with me.

"This is all you need to know about him," Forrest says.

I scan the details.

Ugene Powers: DMA Primary Target Number One.
Cass Scale Rank: 0.0001
Power: None
Wanted in connection with Paragon Tower bombing.
Paragon Diagnostics property.
Detain but do not kill.

He's Powerless?

"If he has no Power, why is he so dangerous?" I ask, tearing my gaze away from the bright blue letters.

"He is smart." The words almost seem to be dragged out of Forrest's throat, and he works his mouth as if trying to remove a foul taste. "Dangerously smart. People with regressing Powers are threatening the balance of our city, and he is leading the way. Bianca, I need you tell me you understand just how important it is that this doesn't happen."

I nod. "We need the balance to survive with our Powers. Regression will destroy us."

Forrest nods as if satisfied.

"So what does he look like?" I ask. "I have to know if I'm going to help you."

The request makes Forrest hesitate. His finger lingers over the phone as if nervous of showing me the picture. The seconds tick by before he finally swipes his finger over the surface, causing the image rises into the air in full color. Forrest's gaze remains locked on me, as if seeking some sign of recognition or hesitation from me.

I don't give him one.

The boy staring back at me is extraordinarily ordinary. Not built like a Somatic, but average—if a bit lanky. His dark skin is a warm walnut and his lips are full. The eyes pull me in: rich brown and shining with fierce curiosity. For reasons I can't explain, my stomach flips.

But I don't recognize him at all.

The image vanishes and Forrest tucks his phone back into his pocket.

"If he has no Power, I'm not worried," I proclaim confidently.

"I'm stronger than anyone else. You said so yourself. I can easily overtake him."

Forrest snorts. "A typical Somatic response. Bianca, he doesn't need a Power. He will outsmart you at every corner. If you have a chance to arrest him, make it quick. He won't need long to counteract anything you do."

I snort. "He can't be *that* smart."

"You need to remain absolutely focused," Forrest says. "There is no place for failure. If he escapes us again, we may never have another chance."

Again? What a curious statement. So Forrest had him once before.

Forrest produces a small blue pill from his jacket, offering it to me.

"What's this?" I take it between two fingers and study it.

"Nevermore is already in the field, so he can't reinforce the protection on your mind. This should help."

Such a small thing to provide so much safety. But Forrest needs me, and I need to focus. I won't get this wrong. I swallow the pill in one gulp.

"Location clear," someone says over the shuttle comm.

"Hem them in," Hound says. "They haven't gone far."

"Seal off a five-block radius," Nevermore says. "Then hold position and await further orders."

My fingers twitch. They are out there. I should be with them. I will be with them soon.

The shuttle touches down. Eager to join the fight, I unstrap the harness and a sense of calm washes over me.

Forrest grabs my arm. "I need you to remain out of sight," he says. "You may not remember him, but he will remember you and he will bolt. And please, don't judge me for what I will have to do. It's for our safety."

The shuttle door slides open as he releases my arm. I hop out and slip around the side of the vehicle before anyone can spot me from the house where the map showed his location. My breaths are steady, even, and my pulse is calm.

Dozens of troopers mill around the street and around corners. Shuttles hover over houses. An army has come out of the woodwork to arrest Ugene—a testament to how critical he is to the DMA, and possibly to the radicals. Being left out of such an important operation would have crushed my soul. I scan the masses for my team but come up blank.

"If he's here, we will flush him out," Forrest says to the surrounding troopers.

I peer around the vehicle to watch Forrest. He is motioning different squads of troopers around to various houses.

"Search every house," Forrest commands. "He can't have gone far with Hound and Nevermore tracking him. I want everyone brought outside for questioning. No exemptions."

The squads break off and charge up cracked porch steps all over the street. No one bothers to knock. They simply kick in the door and storm the houses.

I didn't come all this way for nothing. Ugene is here someplace and I intend to find him. Glancing at Forrest surrounded by his own squad of troopers, I break into a sprint to join one squad on the porch up the block as a woman is dragged into the street nearby. I kick in the door and the troopers flood in ahead of me.

"I didn't do anything! I pay my taxes!" the woman bellows as I slip into another house.

Flashlights bounce off walls in the dim living room. The stench of urine has penetrated into the floorboards and were it not for the peace that pill gave me, I would have gagged on it as some troopers do.

A few of them go to the back of the house.

I bound up the steps two or three at a time, with the thump of their boots following. We gather in the cramped hallway, scouring the rooms one at a time. The house appears abandoned, which would make it a perfect place to hide away from prying eyes.

Only one door remains closed, and Forrest's warning rings out in my mind. I wave the troopers aside and they separate for me as I charge the closed door and smash it off the hinges, then I tuck my body and roll in just in case they have firearms. Flashlights sweep the room as I couch and inspect the darkness.

A rotting bed and mattress, dirty and dusty. A dresser with broken drawers. A closet without a door. There is nowhere to hide here.

"Ugene!" Forrest's voice carries from the street, muted but distinct enough to hear. "We know you're still here. Come out and no one will get hurt."

Despite the calm, panic rises in my chest. What is he doing? Why did I leave him alone in the street? What if those troopers won't be prepared to protect him?

"I'll give you one minute to show your face," Forrest calls. "Citizens, harboring a fugitive will result in immediate expulsion from the city, but you will get one free pass. Right now."

One minute. I can close the gap in time.

As the troopers continue searching the house, I bound down the stairs, but when I hit the bottom, the floorboards snap and I plunge into the basement, banging my head against the concrete floor. Dust rolls up in waves around me. I shove myself upright and my head swims.

"Steele!" One trooper calls down to me.

"Toss me a flashlight," I say, then cough as dust fills my mouth and throat. I spit and grab the flashlight as it drops through the hold.

Every basement has an exit.

The space reeks of mold and mildew strong enough to even diminish the urine stench that saturates the rest of the house. I cross the floor, scanning the walls for the stairwell, and a rat scurries away from me.

At the back of the basement, a set of unstable concrete steps rises upward. I climb as far as I can until two doors close over the top of the space. Pressing my shoulder to one door, I push upward to heave the door. A chain rattles on the other side.

Forrest's voice carries from the distance, but this time I can't make out what he says.

Once more, panic penetrates my calm and I tense my muscles, feeling them strain against my skin, then thrust my shoulder against the door. The handles holding the chain snap and the door flies upward through the air, across the backyard.

Brushing the dust and debris off my body, I climb out of the basement and spit another wad of dust on the ground. Just as I'm about to break into a sprint to meet up with Forrest, a group of shadowy figures streak across another backyard up the block. *It must be him and his radicals!* I dive into action to chase them down.

By the time I reach the rusty chain-link fence between yards, another voice stops me in my tracks before I bound over the fence.

"Forrest! I'm right here."

Ugene.

I hesitate. Should I pursue the others and risk something happening to my brother, or do I allow the radicals to escape and defend my brother? The fear of losing Forrest is the sole emotion that can penetrate the inner calm. The radicals will have to wait for another day. Forrest is more important to me, and if Ugene is there with him, I have to help assure the boy is apprehended.

When I burst into the street again, squads of troopers have split off from where Forrest stands near the shuttle, charging the remaining houses. Two men hold the target in custody.

Once more, I feel the distant pang of failure. I wanted to bring him in, to redeem myself, to convince Forrest how efficient I can be. Seeing Ugene in custody already dashes that hope. I slow to a walk, in no rush now. Some part of me wonders if I should pursue those radicals, but that insistence that Ugene is smart and wily propels me toward Forrest.

Then Ugene lunges at Forrest and wraps his fingers around Forrest's throat.

Everything slows.

Troopers yank on Ugene's shirt to no effect.

I shoot into a sprint. The ground stretches before me, but it's just my imagination. *Forrest can't die. Not when I'm so close! Not now!*

But his face turns redder as he struggles for breath.

Nevermore steps out from a gap between two houses. A second later, Ugene is pressing his palms against his temples.

"Don't kill him!" Forrest rasps as he rubs at his throat. Blood trickles from a couple of scratches where Ugene's nails must have dug in.

I'm so close now, ready to strike, to knock him out before he can harm anyone else.

Ugene nearly doubles over from the pressure of whatever Nevermore is doing. He gasps for air and his body shifts ever so slightly. His muscles coil. I know precisely how a body reacts before an attack. A moment later he lunges at Forrest.

I bound to close the distance, seizing his wrists and pinning them behind his back before he harms Forrest further.

Forrest stumbles a step backward in surprise, rubbing at his throat. The marks on his throat are angry red. I stiffen my grasp on Ugene.

"Load him in the shuttle," Forrest says.

Without mercy, and without surrendering my grip in the slightest, I shove Ugene toward the open door of the shuttle. He tugs only a little at my grip, probably because he knows he cannot break free. *He's not so tough.*

The ground beneath my feet rumbles and jolts, driving my feet out from under me. I release my grasp on Ugene's arms to catch my balance. The concrete rolls in waves. I jump, but one wave smacks my heels and drives me headfirst into the steel reinforced door of the shuttle before tumbling backward. My visions tilts as my back smacks the road.

And I recognize my mistake instantly.

Sneakers pound against pavement.

I blink to clear my vision.

Ugene is running. The waves of concrete have not altered his balance at all. *He has help.* The radicals who dashed out of the back of the house. It must be them circling back to help him escape.

Cursing under my breath, I glance up the street and bound to my feet.

Ugene is sprinting full speed ahead.

I cast a questioning glance at Forrest. He didn't want me here in the first place and I'm concerned he won't let me chase, but Forrest waves me off with an exasperated expression pasted on his face. My heart sinks. I'm failing him again.

A wall of fog rolls down the street toward Ugene. Another use of Powers to help him escape, and now I'm convinced that those radicals I noticed before have circled back to provide protection. This was their plan all along, and a smart one to send Forrest off the scent. If I don't reach him before he reaches that fog, I will lose him.

I bolt after Ugene at full speed.

He tucks his arms tight to his side halfway up the block, and the speed he achieves impresses me. It's the speed of someone used to being chased, but it isn't quick enough to outrun me.

Several other DMA troopers have pulled their guns and are taking aim at Ugene.

"Don't shoot him!" Forrest howls from behind.

DMA troopers lower their weapons, and I tuck in and increase my speed. My feet are light and swift, despite the thudding sound they make against the ground. My body hurls along the road. It almost feels like flying. The distance is closing, but the fog continues to roll ever closer. The ground continues to rumble, but my feet hardly make contact long enough for it to influence my balance or pace.

I take calm, even breaths, not even cracking a sweat. Soon, I will be close enough to tackle him to the ground. Just a little closer now.

As if sensing me closing the divide, Ugene shifts course so abruptly I nearly run right past where he stood moments ago before circling just in time to see him disappear into a nearby apartment building. He knew I would catch him before the fog, and now he is hoping to escape through the building. I smirk, and adrenaline pumps through me.

As I snatch the rusty metal door before it can seal him inside, yanking hard enough on the handle that I nearly rip the door off the hinges, the fog wraps around me, obscuring me from those up the street. They won't know where I've gone.

I can't fail Forrest. This boy is a radical and the key to the continuity of Elpis. He's a terrorist. *I can't let him slip away,* I think, as if trying to convince myself that this is the truth.

19

THE LOBBY OF THE BUILDING IS DIM. ONLY A TRACE amount of light leaks in through the long thin windows near the door and even that is veiled and hazy because of the fog outside. The light isn't enough. I hold and listen. His sneakers thump against the stairs and I identify his form bounding up two at a time. I spring after him, reaching for his ankle. If I can get a grip of it, I can rip his feet out from under him. The steps groan beneath our weight.

My hand brushes against the hem of his pants. A stair snaps under me, plunging my leg into the hollow stairwell. I yelp as the shock of impact from the sudden split slams into my crotch. The pain passes swiftly, but extricating myself from the broken step and navigating toward the top of the stairs takes precious time I don't have to spare. Forrest warned me Ugene is smart. He chose these stairs for a reason. The density of my enhanced body is too heavy.

The building rumbles from another quake. I clutch the railing for stability, but it's old and brittle. The metal snaps under my enhanced grip and nearly sends me tumbling back down to the lobby. I drive my weight against the far wall, leaving behind a dent in the plaster. Dust rains down from the ceiling tiles. Can this building hold against the assault outside?

I finish picking my path to the top with caution. I can't afford any more of the steps to break on me. Before I arrive at the top, a thump echoes along the narrow, empty hallway. By the time I round the top step and penetrate the corridor, he has disappeared into the darkness. Instead of using my eyes to find Ugene, I close them and steer myself along with only the sounds of the building to guide me. The floor beneath me emits a groan that concerns me. It just might snap under my weight.

Ugene moves with remarkably light steps, but I detect a faint trace of subflooring creaking behind one door.

I halt, breathing carefully so dust doesn't reveal my position with an ill-placed cough.

A whisper of material against plaster emanates from within. I smirk, settle on the balls of my feet, and coil my muscles. He thinks he can hide from me. The element of surprise is my ally. I take one more measured breath, then discharge it as I launch into the door. The wood splinters and shatters inward. A fragment of light from the boarded window is just sufficient to locate him a few feet away. I charge him before he can counter.

Our bodies collide into the floor with the force of a car crash, but it hardly hinders my breathing. We plunge through tiles and sagging subflooring toward the first level. Instincts kick in. Forrest needs him alive and unharmed. If Ugene hits the ground beneath my weight, it could crush him. The decision takes a split second. I coil my limbs around him and twist our bodies mid-air so that my body receives most of the impact.

My head smashes against the tile floor on the first floor. The impact broke my grip.

Ugene presses off my shoulders as he coughs and scurries away.

I can't fail.

As he stumbles a step aside, clasping his ribs, I kick to my feet and seize his arm, jerking him toward me so he cannot flee again. *He won't escape me again.*

Ugene's entire body stiffens and I hear his breath catch. "Bianca..."

The intimate way he speaks my name, the utter confusion in his tone, induces momentary hesitation. His pulse is racing beneath my palm. *From the exertion. Yes, it must be.* But instead of tearing away as he should, Ugene steps closer, squinting at me as if to verify his hunch. Something tender and friendly crosses his face. I can see it plainly, even in the meager lighting. He does recognize me. *Of course he does,* I advise myself. *You went to school together. Stick to the mission.*

"Don't resist," I say, and my voice sounds empty, unfamiliar. "You are in DMA custody. If you resist—"

"Bianca, it's me."

"—I will be required to use force." Does he expect me to care? It certainly sounds like he does. I retain a solid grip. Forrest needs him. I can't fail my brother.

"Stop," Ugene says. But it isn't a command. It sounds almost desperate. "It's me. It's Ugene."

Ugene Powers. Terrorist. Wanted Criminal. I know exactly who he is. "Put your hands behind your back. Resisting is pointless."

Slowly, he turns his back to me, shifting his loose arm behind his back. He's just giving up without a fight?

I relinquish my control on his other arm just enough to allow him to move it into position without releasing fully. If I do, he will bolt again. I would rather finish this now. Eager to get moving, I nudge him toward the door.

Words flow out of his mouth like an open tap, so rushed that I have a tough time following. "Bianca, it's Ugene. We grew up together. I lived right across the street. We're friends."

I almost snort at that but manage to retain my professional composure, shoving my emotions into the void. He is working to get into my head, just as Forrest suspected, but there is no way we grew up as friends. I would remember that … right?

But I don't remember everything, a voice in the back of my head warns me.

"We played in the rain and built mud castles," he continues.

Rain and mud castles. I *do* remember those, but he was never there. How would he know how much I had loved the rain as a girl? Knowing me from school is one thing. Knowing these details—the few I actually remember—is something else altogether.

"Your brother, Forrest, broke your arm and blamed it on me."

The broken arm. That wasn't Forrest. It was an accident. But when

I try to recall the details, I can't summon them. It was an accident. That is all I can remember.

My steps slow, and he evidently accepts that as a signal that he is getting through to me. Slowly, he turns to face me, studying my face desperately, and there is something personal about how he measures me. Like he does know me. And not just from school. It's deeper, intimate.

He steps closer and my heart hammers against my ribs. It isn't an aggressive action, but one of desperation … or hope.

"At Paragon, you fought beside me, helped all of us escape," he says, dropping his voice as if someone will listen.

Paragon? Why would I be at Paragon, helping a terrorist, no less! I try to shake my head, reject his comments, but the shock of all of this has me suspended in place. *No, no! Don't freeze up again!*

"They shot you and I carried your body," he says, and the agony in his eyes is so genuine I almost believe him.

But I would remember being shot, right? *The nightmares … No. He's lying. He must be!*

"Just before you died, you told me to go and kissed me."

I squeeze my lips tighter at mention of dying, and a kiss. Every part of my body seems so much tighter than it should be, as if the slightest contact will cause the coils under my skin to snap and I will shatter apart.

My nightmares make sense. The blood. The anger. The echo of a gunshot. The mysterious figure. Are my nightmares stemming from lost memories? *No. It can't be. They were just dreams.* Forrest warned me about Ugene, that he knows just what to say to get under my skin. Regardless of how he knows what he knows, I cannot trust him.

He gasps for breath and nearly stumbles aside, reaching toward me. I snatch his wrist instinctively and wrench the arm away from me, unclear what I am afraid he will do. Stab me? With what? Overpower me? Not likely.

The abrupt motion emits a wail of pain from him.

I pack my confusion into the void with the rest of my emotions.

I have a duty.

"Don't touch me," I say coldly.

His face collapses. "What did they do to you?"

A thud against the outside wall near the back ally snaps me out of my trance. I twist Ugene around instinctively, depositing him between me and whoever is attempting to break through. More than likely, one of his comrades is coming for him and will attempt shooting first. Better if Ugene acts as a barrier to slow them down.

Once more, my breathing becomes even as my focus zeros in on the unnerving silence that follows. Thankfully, Ugene does not resist as I wait, listening for further signs of peril. He almost seems resigned to his fate.

Boots scuff the pavement outside, and for a moment, I'm sure I can see the shadow of a form move past a narrow window. Holding Ugene will slow me down, so I relax my grip. The moment I do, he shifts away as if understanding something is coming. Or maybe he already knows what it is. He remains close to me, though.

The glass shatters and a heartbeat later a Somatic barrels through the window into me. We tumble across the floor with his crushing weight settling on top of me. My fist connects with his kidneys as my knees come up with full force, launching him off. In seconds, we are both on our feet, engaged in savage hand-to-hand combat that rocks even my Enhanced Strength. My muscles instinctively kick in, flowing through the motions of my Muscle Memory training: a mix of judo, MMA, and boxing.

I crack his rib; he attempts returning the favor, but my body resists. He drags back his fist as I thrust my own into his ear with a satisfying crack! But he has already delivered an impressive uppercut that shoves me off my feet into the far wall, where I leave behind an imprint in the plaster. As he lurches back, I shrug off the blow and charge him. Pain is distant in the void. I wrap my arms around his body as my feet press against the floor, strong enough to snap the tiles. Then I launch us forward, driving our bodies into the wall like a wrestler propelling his opponent into a mat. We crash into the outer wall and burst through into the sunrise-filled alley.

Ugene will escape for sure if I can't break out of this fight quickly.

I roll on top of my assailant and spring to my feet, clutching the collar of his shirt in my fists and hoisting him up. The pure strength of my Power is intoxicating, potent. He's unusually light for one so broad.

I'm dimly conscious of others around, and the peril I am in surrounded by these radicals. This fight needs to resolve now, before Ugene's allies spirit him away. *Why is he not running already?*

With the Somatic dazed and securely in my grasp, I toss him like a doll at the brick wall strong enough to fix him in the stonework. The others in the alley aren't inactive, but I can't afford to take my eyes off the Somatic just yet. Eager to finish this, I leap toward him and hurl fists into his face, breaking bones with each punch.

Another body slams into me from the side, thrusting me off balance. I tuck and roll. All of Nevermore's vicious training has equipped me for this, and between my Enhanced Strength and Muscle Memory, even two attackers cannot easily overpower me. Where is the rest of my team? Nevermore and Hound must have some sense of where I am. They weren't far off when Ugene sprinted away. Help must be arriving soon. I can either win quickly or stall long enough for help to turn up.

Even as I hop back to my feet, the second Somatic—slightly smaller build but apparently strong—draws the massive man out of the way. I smirk, noticing how stunned the big guy is, stumbling and battling to keep from falling over. Big guy's right arm hangs limp at his side, and the blood trickling from his wounds exposes just how spent he is. One eye is swelling shut. The two of them function together to stabilize his balance. *Now is my chance!*

I clench my fists and concentrate on all my muscles, basking in the exhilarating pulse of each one bulging with strength.

Just past them, Ugene watches in awe. Why has he not run? A mousy girl grabs his arm and attempts pulling him toward the entrance of the alley. I can't fail again!

Before the two Somatics can recover, I sprint toward them and use an arm to take each down with all the power my arms can hold, aiming for their necks to clothesline them like those old wrestling videos Forrest made me examine. But the two of them surprise me, turning at the last second, catching my arms. Boots race across the pavement behind me.

Ugene holds a palm toward them helplessly. "Stop!"

Why is he trying to help me? I can break this grip.

"Get Ugene out of here!" A woman calls out from behind me. I try to twist and see who it is, to throw off the restraint of the two men. She lands on my back and weaves her limbs around me so completely I might as well be tangled in a web.

Two girls are pushing and pulling on Ugene to get him to leave, but for some reason he works against them. Is he hoping to aid his comrades? He shoves the girls away as the woman on my back clamps her hands against my temples in a vice-like grip.

I attempt breaking the men off my arms to snatch this woman and throw her off my back. But the strength slides out of my body. The world blurs and I fight against the exhaustion pouring through me.

Ugene dips into view, racing toward me instead of away.

And then darkness swirls around me.

20

DREAMS. NIGHTMARES, REALLY. I'M STANDING IN Paragon Tower as it collapses around me. I scream for Forrest to save me, but he steps back holding a syringe. Disembodied voices float in the nether around me.

"How is she here?" a girl whispers.

"She died, right?" a guy also whispers.

I can feel the prickling sensation in my limbs and try shifting to lessen the sensation. Cool hands chase away the voices and plunge me into the void again.

Repeatedly, as I surface the void, float through voices and dreams, the same cool touch plunges me into the void again, as if dunking me in freezing water over and over without a chance to come up for air.

My lungs burn and for a moment I can't breathe. The unsettling feeling startles me out of my dreams. My eyes snap open and Ugene's face fills my vision. I still have a chance to bring him to Forrest! I lunge toward him, but ropes around my wrists and ankles yank me back. The bed cracks as I rebound back to the mattress.

"Relax, Bianca," Ugene says, and his tone is soothing. "It's okay. I won't hurt you."

But he isn't alone. I take in the others around the small bedroom. Three other boys. Two girls. All close to my age. Neither of the Somatics I fought in the ally are present. All of them are tense, watching me with wary eyes. One girl lingers in the doorway, glaring at me with intense hatred. I will have to deal with her first. I coil my muscles. These ropes won't hold me. It might take a little extra effort, but I'm confident I can rip them free.

"They won't hurt you either," he says. "Bianca. Look at me, not them."

I flip my gaze back to him. The way Ugene watches me reveals he knows that the binding won't hold me. I remain tense, uncertain, but I nod. Maybe if he thinks I'm relaxing or trusting him, I can turn this to my advantage. He reaches for the ropes at my wrists and the girl in the doorway tenses. So do I.

"Ugene … don't!" The girl snaps, and the fear and hate bleed through her voice.

Yes. This girl will have to be the first I take out.

"It's okay, right?" He smiles at me so earnestly that it makes me almost feel bad for what will come next. The smile makes my stomach tumble. Ugene unties the ropes at my wrists, and for just a moment I am certain I catch a flash of uncertainty on his face. Not that it's unwarranted.

The second my hands are free, I snap one of them out to seize his arm and use him against the rest of the room. A shock hits my fist and a barrier between us hums against my hand.

"I told you," the girl in the doorway mutters.

But Ugene is unfazed by my reaction. He expected it. Our gazes lock, and his dark eyes pull me in as I rub at my wrists to relieve some of the lingering irritation from the ropes. Those eyes! They peer right into my very soul, and my body responds with pins and needles crawling across my skin.

Silence momentarily seizes us as we stare at each other, and I'm only dimly aware of the others in the room. Why is he so close to me?

As if reading my thoughts, he shifts back to give me a little more space to move on the bed. "I can't untie your legs," he says as I sit up and press my back into the wall. "I hope you understand."

I could break out of this room, take all of them down, but the barrier prevents me from moving off the bed. Are the ropes necessary if they can just put this barrier around me? There must be a weak point in it somewhere. Is it only in the free space? What about the walls or floor? I could try to break out that way.

"Do you know me?" Ugene asks.

No one else in the room seems to breathe as they watch and wait. The tension is stifling.

I narrow my eyes. Is this a trick? "I do."

He collapses ever so slightly at my tone. Is that sadness in his eyes? "I mean, do you know me as anything more than a person you're seeking to capture? Do you remember … us?"

He reaches for my hand.

I pull away. "Don't touch me."

Ugene eases back and his shoulders slump. "Sorry. I just … I need to know how badly they've hurt you."

Hurt me? What is he talking about? I wrap my arms around my knees, drawing them up to my chest to show them I don't intend to fight. It will only take a moment to uncoil and break through a wall if need be. The wall behind my back, most likely. Even if it tumbles a story or two outside, I can easily recover from the fall.

"Ugene Powers," I say matter-of-factly.

The corners of his mouth turn down ever so slightly. "No, to you I've always been just Ugene."

Hound told me about him. I knew Ugene before all of this, even if I don't remember him. But the way Ugene introduces himself is much more familiar, like he truly believes we were more than passing classmates. I cock my head to the side as I study him, wishing I could read minds or detect lies. Without meaning to, I chew my bottom lip.

Before this group kidnapped me, Ugene said I died. It isn't the first time I've heard it, and my nightmares don't help. It takes a moment to pull back what Elpida Theus said that night of our failed mission. The shock on her face; the statement that my parents would be happy to see me. Does Ugene know more about this? Forrest said Theus lied, but Ugene repeating that fact can't be a coincidence. *Unless they planned this!* Only one way to find out.

"I died. That's what you said back in that building. That at Paragon, I helped you escape, and they shot me. But you tried to carry me out of the building."

Ugene perks up. "Yes." He pulls his knee over the bed to face me more directly. "Do you remember any of it?"

You kissed me, he said earlier. But if what Hound said is true, why would I ever do that?

"Why would I kiss you?" I ask, hoping to make sense of this whole mess.

His breaths shorten and he appears nervous. "I … well … what?"

It must have been a lie, and now he doesn't even remember saying it. "You also said I kissed you," I repeat. "Why would I do that?"

The girl in the doorway is staring at me with so much intensity that if looks could kill, she would have struck me down a hundred times over. *She likes him and sees me as a threat.* If Ugene lied about the kiss, why would this girl hate me so much? I'm missing something here that should be obvious.

I grimace and press my back against the wall, testing the strength of it without alarming them. The barrier doesn't exist at my back.

The fact that Ugene can't answer my question only confuses me more. He seems to be lying, but the girl staring daggers at me doesn't think so. I switch course, hoping to buy a few moments of time. "Why would I help you?"

"We were friends before all of this," Ugene says.

Friends. Hound didn't seem to think so.

Ugene almost looks like he wants to reach for me again, but resists the urge. I wish he would. Then I could make contact and carry out my plan to use him against the others and escape.

"I realize that it's hard to believe," he says with complete, unveiled sincerity. "But, just for a second, would you at least be willing to consider there is more to us than what the Directorate has told you?"

The Directorate? He thinks they are the ones feeding me information? No. It's Forrest and my team. I haven't had contact with anyone else, except our targets.

"Like what?" I ask. Maybe he is lying to me. Maybe he isn't. But I need to know what he is thinking, and I need to buy a few more moments of time to escape.

The fact that I even ask almost makes him bounce with excitement. "Well, like we actually grew up in the same neighborhood, across the street in Salas, on Cante Road."

Cante Road? No, that's not right. *We moved when you were about eleven,* Forrest told me this when we visited the house on Dysart. When I told him I remembered the puddles, but not on that street. Did we live on Cante Road before?

"We rode the tram to school every day," he continues, "and more often than not I was late, and you had to pull me onboard."

No, that doesn't sound familiar at all.

"Your parents—Nick and Gloria Pond—favored your brother, and it drove you mad. And they used to have game night with my parents until Forrest broke your arm and blamed it on me, and they forbid you to be friends with me."

The broken arm. Forrest and I were at the creek, and he brought me home to Mom and Dad. But that wasn't Forrest's doing. And how does Ugene even know about that? He mentioned it before, as well. I pull in my bottom lip and chew again, cradling the arm I broke that day.

This reaction seems to lift Ugene's hopes, and he barrels on. "I can go on and on, Bianca. About your childhood. Your likes and dislikes. Our ... our kiss."

The girl in the doorway burns red hot with jealousy.

I shake my head slightly, stunned by all of this. He knows so much. It can't be true though. Forrest said Ugene was smart. Maybe he is using those brains against me now.

"Think about it, Bianca," he continues as if sensing my hesitation. "How is it possible I would know everything about you if we didn't know each other before?"

I need an answer and can only pull up one. "You ... probably have telepathy or something." But even as I stumble over the words, they don't feel right. Ugene is Powerless.

He chuckles, and the sound is warm, if a bit self-deprecating. "We both know that I have no Powers, even if you don't remember our childhood."

The redheaded guy looming near Ugene crosses his arms and shakes his head in amusement. Ugene isn't alone in this room. Any of them could feed him information.

"Fine. Then someone in your crew can read minds." I examine each for a clue. The redhead studies me curiously, but not in the way Nevermore does when he is reading my mind. The Asian boy cocks his head to the side curiously as the girl—his sister?—tries hiding behind him. I can't tell who it might be. "You stole my memories."

Ugene shakes his head. "The memories I have of us were not stolen," he says as he leans forward. "The memories I have were a gift, one that you gave to me over the years we spent together."

I simply glare at him, refusing to blink first. I want him to flinch. I want him to show some sign that this is a lie. I *need* him to be lying. He gives me nothing and I huff in frustration.

"All right then," I say tersely. "We knew one another. So what? Doesn't change the fact that you're a wanted criminal conspiring with criminals." My gaze once more sweeps the room.

His patience seems unending. "The only crime we have committed is saving people from the Directorate killing them," he says. And the way he speaks, I almost believe him. "Do you know what they have done to people with weaker Powers? Bianca, they send them into the Deadlands to die."

My stomach sinks, and that void I spotted in the darkness surfaces in my memory. No. That can't be true. What would the Directorate have to gain by sending people to their death? And if they do, why? Just because a Power is weak doesn't give anyone the right to kill anyone else. Forrest is working on a cure!

Ugene senses my hesitation as hope lights up his face.

Again, my stomach rolls.

Those weak Powers are the very thing bringing Elpis to its knees, though. I once again scan the room, looking for any tells, but I can feel my resolve dissolving.

"But people with regressing Powers are threatening the balance we need." My gaze settles on Ugene once more. "And you are leading the way. If we don't restore balance, regression will destroy us."

I can see the heartbreak on his face. He doesn't share the same belief. The way his face falls is a clear tell.

His next words are careful, measured, but full of passion. "The people I'm with here are regressing, yes, but they also save lives. They want equality for everyone, fairness. Is that really such a bad thing?" He shifts closer, the eagerness radiating off of him. It's almost intoxicating. "I want to help you, Bianca. More than anything. But these people want answers that I can't give them. Please." The way he meets my gaze isn't desperate, but it shines like a brilliant ray of hope. "What *do* you remember?"

Nothing. At least, none of what he is telling me. I let out a shaky breath, angry with myself for revealing just how unstable my certainty is. "My mission."

"And what's that?" he asks.

The redhead shifts slightly, drawing my attention and making me hesitate. What is his Power? My chest tightens. "To enforce Proposition 9, secure the city, find the dissenters, and bring you in to the DMA for questioning in connection with a bombing at Paragon."

The angry girl in the doorway blinks in shock. "Bombing?"

Her confusion echoes through the room on each and every one of them. If they were responsible for the bombing, why does the news create so much shock? I'm no longer certain of anything.

Hoping to push past the awkward moment, I recite the orders I saw on my tablet before leaving on this mission. "Ugene Powers: DMA Primary Target Number One. Paragon Diagnostics property. Detain but do not kill."

Ugene flinches. "Do you still feel that's necessary?"

I pull my hair over my shoulder and braid it as I chew my bottom lip. Do I? All of this has left my mind spinning in uncertainty. The lack of memories from my past make it hard to differentiate fact from fiction. "I'm not sure of anything," I say honestly.

Ugene nods as if he expected the answer. "Do you remember dying?"

Only in dreams, I think, but say, "No. But there are gaps in my memory."

Ugene motions toward the group, and the girl who tried hiding behind the boy inches close. The fear is clear on her face. Fear of me. Should she be? I don't know anymore.

"This is my friend, Lily," Ugene explains. "She won't hurt you. I promise. She can help fill in those gaps in your memory, but she needs to touch you to do it."

I examine the girl from head to toe. She isn't Somatic, and if she tries to hurt me, I can easily break her arm. I give a tight nod, a little surprised they are asking for permission to do this instead of just forcing it on me.

Ugene rises off the bed to give Lily space. As he steps back, he hesitates just a moment, like he would rather not give up his place. Lily sits beside me, trembling in fear. Good. She knows I'm stronger. Her quivering hand reaches toward my head.

Instinct takes over and I swat her away. Last time one of them touched my head, I woke up here. I stab a finger toward her. "Stay away from my head. You guys used that against me already. I won't fall for it again."

"This isn't the same thing," Ugene insists gently. "She just wants to use her Psychometry to read your history, if she can. No one here will knock you out again."

My history ... Can she truly do that? Should I trust that he will keep his word? Somehow, I'm compelled to believe him. Does someone in the room have that Power? Frustrated with myself and my uncertainty, eager for some sort of answer, I huff and thrust my hand toward Lily. The girl edges closer and places her cold, clammy hand in mine gingerly. Then her eyes glaze over.

... cold tungsten bites into my wrists, binding me to the metal table. A shriek echoes off the stark white walls of the room and rings in my ears, and I wonder, What moron is making that racket? It only takes a moment lover for my sore throat to make me realize it's me.

I tug at the metal straps as they cut into my wrists, but they bend against my strength. A team of doctors in white coats and surgical masks crowd around me, trying to hold me steady.

"Calm down, Bianca," Forrest says, holding a needle to my skin. It bends but doesn't puncture.

"Let me out!" I shriek.

The straps break free.

Forrest finds a weak spot, plunging the blue fluid into my arm. I throw a fist into his chest and rush the tungsten door with all my might. It buckles, but doesn't break ...

"That's enough," someone in the room says. "Stop her now."

Ugene bites his bottom lip as his shoulders tense.

... I punch the door again and again. With each impact, it bends but never breaks off the hinges.

"Ugene!" I scream his name as if he will magically appear to help me. But he doesn't. My fists bloody as I continue hammering at the door.

"We have to start again," Forrest says from somewhere behind me.

I spin on my heel, pure fury burning in my veins. Forrest takes aim ...

My heart hammers against my ribs. I said his name. I said it as if I expected him to rescue me. And Forrest aimed a gun at me. *It can't be real. It can't be!* I hardly have time to meet Ugene's anxious, curious gaze before I'm plunged into another memory.

... Injection after injection. Everything comes in flashes. I cry. I scream. I fight. I don't fight. The terror seizes my chest over and over and over until I can't breathe ...

... Someone looms over me. Dark hair, penetrating eyes, but I can't make out his face. He is familiar, yet he isn't. His icy hands pinch my head in a vice-like grip, and I can feel pieces of myself falling away, like he is erasing the data from my mind ...

"Ugene, enough!" The Asian boy stomps closer.

Ugene places a hand on Lily's shoulder and she breaks away, releasing my hand and falling backward into Ugene's arms as she gasps for breath like a fish out of water. The redhead sweeps in to help Ugene ease Lily into the chair beside the door. Her boyfriend—or at least I assume it's her boyfriend—kneels beside her and touches her face so tenderly.

My heart is hammering so hard I'm certain it will explode. Those memories were so vivid, so real, yet as the seconds melts away, so does my recollection of what I saw.

The others tend to Lily, arguing amongst each other. The dark-haired girl in the doorway watches me with suspicion all over her face.

I'm too stunned to do more than stare at them all blankly.

Until Lily speaks. "Paragon. They experimented on her. They pumped her with epinephrine over and over after healing her wounds. There were so many different injections I couldn't distinguish what they all did. And …" Pain and sorrow create lines on her face as she buries her face in her hands. Her boyfriend rubs her back.

Ugene doesn't relent. "And what, Lily?"

I try to close out her voice, not wanting to hear what she says next. But I can't. The words slam against my chest.

"They killed her."

Forrest killed me, I think, and numbness spreads through my body. Forrest is my brother. Why would he do that to me? I no longer can feel anything. Not the rhythmic beating of my heart or the mattress clenched in my fists. No emotion. I dump everything into a void in a desperate attempt to maintain control.

"… selectively wipe her memories and insert new ones," Lily says. Her voice is distant, miles away.

My vision narrows, and only Ugene remains in view. The look on his face can only be described as grief and disappointment. That hurts more than anything else. He stares at me as if I'm still dead, lost to him forever. He sinks down on the edge of the bed beside me and I almost shrink away, not needing any further rejection.

"Do you remember your family, Bianca?" Ugene asks, and the

sadness in his voice reflects the grief on his face.

I lick suddenly dry lips. "Forrest is the Paragon liaison in the DMA."

"And your parents?"

I blink slowly, as if waking from a dream … or a nightmare. "The radicals killed my parents, so I joined the DMA to help them fight back."

Ugene's jaw drops ever so slightly, and he tries to cover it by scrubbing his hands over his face. As they fall away into his lap, I swear I can see a light flip on in his eyes. An eagerness as if he is about to close in on all doubt and shatter it completely.

And then he does.

"Your parents are alive."

The words rock me to my core. *No. No, it can't be true. Everything I've done, everything they led me to believe, was all founded on that one purpose.*

Ugene's reaches a hand halfway toward me, as if he expects me to close the distance. I stare at the dark skin, smooth and soft. Not the hands of a fighter.

My words fall out of my mouth as if spoken by someone else. "I've been to their house on Dysart Lane. A different family lives there now."

That gets his attention. "Did you say Dysart Lane?"

I nod numbly.

"No." That single word is like a breath of relief from his lips, as if he is about to seize victory. "They have always lived on Cante Road, right across from my parents. I can prove it if you let me."

I'm not aware of just how much I'm chewing my lip until the metallic tang of blood touches my tongue. I stop and press my tongue to the wound inside my mouth. My hand inches closer to his, almost as if I have no control over it. Then my fingers wrap around his. Warm. Familiar. I tighten my grip, afraid he will pull away and I will lose this intimacy.

"I want to see them," I say, and I can hear the heat of anger singeing the edges of my voice. If he can prove my parents are alive,

Forrest will have a lot of reckoning to deal with.

"We will." He sounds so confident that I want to believe him. "Soon. Tonight. But first I need to tie you back up, or Willow will be suspicious."

I tense. He wants to tie me back up? I thought we were just coming to an agreement here! Ugene gives the redheaded boy a warning look, as if challenging him to say something.

But the redhead is stunned, staring at me with wide eyes.

If they tie me back up, I will break free. I won't be held prisoner if they want me to trust them. But the way Ugene gazes at me is so sincere that I believe he means well. Why do I so willingly believe him?

"I also need you to promise me you won't leave this room or start a fight with anyone," he adds, as if sensing my hesitation. Was that just a lucky guess? "I'll come for you."

The resolution, the firmness in those four words draws a nod out of me. Because I do believe him.

The jealous girl in the doorway makes a noise of disgust and storms off. I won't do anything, but something tells me she will.

21

UGENE BINDS THE ROPES AROUND MY WRISTS AGAIN, just as they were before but not nearly as tight. I could slip my hands out of these without breaking or ripping anything. The tenderness Ugene has when he completes the task contradicts what I expected of him, and I struggle to figure out of something to say. His attention shifts quickly away once he's finished. As if I'm no longer there. Why does that sting?

Only three of them linger in the bedroom with me now. Ugene, a blonde boy Ugene calls Miller, and the redhead whose name turns out to be Jayme. They are absorbed in some discussion that makes their words and gestures passionate, but I continue speculating about my parents. Ugene says they are alive. If he takes me to them, what does that mean? What do I do? It doesn't negate what he has done or who he is, but maybe everything I was told about this group isn't altogether accurate. He believes I helped them escape Paragon Tower. Should I accept that as well? All of this is overwhelming and I can't think straight. A headache is setting in.

"… get your Powers back," Ugene says, pacing the room. An excited energy radiates off of him. I don't follow what is progressing as he hands a sheet of paper to Miller.

But I can't concentrate on them. I continue thinking about my parents. Do they assume I'm dead, like I thought they were? And Forrest was so convincing. That sadness he displayed, the vulnerability couldn't have been an act. Forrest isn't that cunning … is he?

Ugene mentions the Protectorate, capturing my attention as he explains to Miller how his Power was unplugged and just needs to be jumpstarted.

Jayme looms at Miller's shoulder, narrowed eyes on Ugene. He doesn't trust Ugene. He flings up his hands at mention of a knife, and now I can't glance away. Are they plotting to use that knife against me?

I'm captivated, observing as Ugene gives Miller a switchblade, and Miller doesn't hesitate slicing open his arm. He doesn't even flinch! I can't see what he is digging for though, and I stretch my neck to get a better line of sight.

Jayme grabs Miller's wrist to draw away the knife when Miller produces something small and covered in blood between his fingers.

"How long has that been there?" Jayme asks, bewildered by the entire ordeal.

Miller's answer is so calm I almost envy it. "Since we left Paragon."

Ugene reaches toward the bed and I intuitively understand what he reaches for. I snatch the pillow and hand it to him, observing as he tears the case and uses the cloth to wipe the object off, exposing a homemade data drive. My stomach drops. They stole that information from Paragon. From Forrest, probably. Is that why Sims was angry with Forrest when we left to arrest Ugene? Should I take it from him? I could. I could steal it from his hand and break out of this house before they could intercept me.

But I don't. Instead, I stare at Ugene as he slips out of the room, leaving me alone with Miller and Jayme.

"Don't look at me like that, Murph," Miller says. "You don't tell me everything either."

Jayme flinches. "What does that mean? Alex, you've been hauling that thing around, doubtless with information we needed. You promised you wouldn't keep anything from me anymore. But you keep hiding things from me. Things about *him*."

Miller's face darkens in a manner that reminds me of Nevermore in one of his ugly attitudes. "When will you accept that he is a friend? My best friend!"

Jayme steps back and shakes his head, misery written all over his face. "I thought I was your best friend."

Miller closes the gap, placing his hands against Jayme's face in a tight grasp. "No, Murph. He is my best friend, but you are so much more than that."

Jayme's shoulders tense, but he slides his arms around Miller. "You still can't say it, can you?"

"Do I really need to?"

I avert my gaze, thinking like I'm intruding on an intimate moment.

Ugene rushes back into the bedroom, his face alight with restless excitement, a defibrillator in his hands.

The two guys pull apart instantly.

"Are you ready to jumpstart your Power?" Ugene asks Miller.

Miller agrees, but the way his full body tenses makes it obvious he isn't on board with whatever is happening. Nor is Jayme. As they argue, I struggle to understand what's going on. Forrest said Ugene is smart, but it seems even his friends question just how smart he is. Maybe Forest overestimates him. But the pure certainty on Ugene's face makes me suspect he means what he says. Somehow, Miller lost his Powers, and Ugene is positive this will restore him. How can they doubt him? I don't even know if I trust him, yet I don't doubt the sheer confidence in his assessment.

"You told me you were broken," Ugene says, and the kindness of his tone makes me wonder if we are mistaken and he does have a Power. "I'm telling you that you're right, but this can fix it. The defibrillator's electric current will give your Power the surge it needs to restart. You can't really expect to fight the Directorate in your condition. You need to be ready."

Fight the Directorate? I sit up straighter, hoping I don't seem too hungry for intelligence.

"Ready for what?" Jayme asks as he crosses his arms and places himself between the two boys.

I tense, feeling the delightful intoxication of my muscles swelling for a battle. I can't describe why I feel the need to protect Ugene—*because Forrest wants him alive and unharmed*—but the way Jayme is acting makes me worry he is about to strike out.

But Ugene almost looks bored by Jayme's antics as he says, "The Directorate is ready to launch its Purification Project. If we don't want to stand by while they Directorate forces thousands into the DMA's arms—and potentially to their deaths—we have to stop them now. The time for falling back to regroup has passed. We need to act."

Suddenly, the air slips out of the room. I drag in precise, shallow breaths. They assume the Directorate is going to execute thousands? What is the Purification Project? And more notably, what does Ugene mean by act?

Miller paces the floor like a caged beast. And the way he scowls at Ugene makes me wonder if *he* won't start the fight instead of Jayme. "Do you have any idea how much it hurt losing my Powers? What do you think it'll be like having them jumpstarted like this? No." Miller shakes his head.

Ugene deflates. He genuinely believed he could do this, and Miller's rejection has dashed his hope.

Jayme shifts and I lean forward, bracing to slip my bonds and defend Ugene against them, but Jayme steps in front of Miller.

The exchange between Jayme and Miller is so heartfelt, so rich of love that it makes my heart twinge. I will never experience love like that. I don't even know who to trust anymore. How could I ever love someone when I don't know what they demand from me—or what they've done to me?

"You told me to trust him," Jayme says. "Do you trust him?"

Miller's shoulder droop. "Yes."

Jayme nods as if that settles it and smirks. "And anyway, if he kills you, there'll be nothing stopping me from ripping him apart, limb by limb."

Like hell there won't, I think. Whether I elect to trust Ugene or take him to Forrest, I need him unharmed. If Jayme tries anything, I will toss him out through the wall before he can get his hands on Ugene.

Everyone moves into position and Ugene counts down, then holds his finger to a button on the device. In the blink of an eye,

Miller's body turns rigid, and he roars as the convulsions take over. Jayme watches with pain creasing his face as if he can feel agony with Miller. After a few moments, Jayme steps forward and I move to my knees. If he plants a finger on Ugene, I'm ready.

"Don't," I call to him. It's a distinct warning. "It won't work if you stop it now."

I don't know this for sure, but I do know that I will say just about anything to stop him from interrupting Ugene. Thankfully, Jayme freezes, and his hands shake in horror. He clenches and unclenches them. I don't dare lift my eyes off him as Miller's back arches off the ground.

"You're killing him!" Jayme's voice is scored with anguish.

Ugene doesn't acknowledge Jayme. All of his focus is centered on the task.

All of my focus is on Jayme … until two others rush into the room with a collection of faces behind them. Recognizing the Somatic I attacked in the apartment building and alley, I push back against the wall once more.

In a heartbeat, a blonde woman and Jayme are closing in on Ugene. My gaze darts to him, and the tears rolling down his cheeks as the blonde woman catches his shoulder. If that Somatic wasn't lingering at her shoulder, I would stop her. But I can't take them all. Not with him in the room. I delayed too long.

Ugene releases the button as the woman yanks him backward.

As the woman tends to Miller, Jayme shoves Ugene into a wall.

I cringe. I can't save him now, but if he tries to kill Ugene, I will accept the risk. Thankfully, I don't have to find out.

As Jayme pins Ugene against a wall, three others catch a grip on him to jerk him backward. I recognize one of them from earlier.

Jayme has gone feral in his misery, grappling like a trapped animal against those holding him as if he is starving and Ugene is his last meal.

And Ugene doesn't fight back. He accepts the abuse in shock.

A mousy girl I remember from the alley knees beside Miller and as she probes for his pulse, her face drains of color.

Jayme completely falls into hysterics.

The blonde woman questions Ugene, but his gaze is distantly locked on Miller's body. He won't respond, and what will they do if he doesn't?

I have to support him somehow. "He tried giving him his Power back," I say sharply, observing the others for backlash.

The blonde woman rounds on me. "And who gave him the idea it was possible?"

I don't cower from her gaze. I'm not frightened of her. "All his idea."

The Somatic moves between Jayme and Ugene. At least they are protecting him, even if I couldn't.

"Get Jayme out of here," the blonde woman snaps. "This is exactly why I can't trust your decisions, Ugene!"

So he isn't in charge then. I attempt taking stock of everybody in the room, memorizing as much as I can about who each of them is.

And then Miller is breathing again and the entire room freezes, examining the rise and fall of Miller's chest.

Ugene is first to split the silence with delirious glee. He thought he killed Miller. He doubted himself.

Jayme rushes to Miller's side, touching Miller's face with so much affection as Miller's body trembles violently.

I toss a blanket toward them to help ward off the chill. If it is a chill.

Ugene crawls across the floor. No one stops him, but the glare Jayme throws at him is adequate to make Ugene pause.

"Go away, you—"

"It's fine." Miller's voice is a croak as Jayme helps prop him against a wall.

Something passes between Miller and Ugene. I don't know what, but Miller points at Ugene and a second later, Ugene's back stiffens, and he grates his teeth, glowering at Miller.

Please don't make me start a fight now.

But they laugh.

"You got it back," Ugene says as if he just ran a mile. "How much?"

I can't concentrate on what's transpiring anymore. Ugene isn't just smart. He's brilliant. How did he give Powers back to someone who lost their Power? I gawk at him with a newfound sense of awe and respect. What he just did should be impossible! No wonder Forrest seemed jealous of Ugene's intelligence. Forrest dedicates his life to correcting regression. Ugene just fixed a Powerless.

The others extend Ugene congratulations before gathering around Miller, but that seems drastically inadequate for what he just did. Ugene meets my gaze, and all the excitement I feel drains away at the melancholy in his dark eyes.

Then he leaves me alone in the room with everyone else. And it aches more than I can understand.

22

THE EXCITEMENT DIES DOWN AND EVERYONE FILTERS out of the room. The blonde woman dismisses Jayme and Miller so they can rest. As soon as the two disappear into the hallway, she spins to me, hands folded behind her back with the Somatic—now healed—lingering at her shoulder like a guard dog. Her gaze is hard, calculating as she studies me.

Don't start a fight, I remind myself. Ugene asked for my word. I don't know if I will keep it or not, but I'm positive I need him on my side to contact my parents.

This woman is in charge here. That much is undeniable by the way everyone else deferred to her. *Everyone but Ugene*, I think. He doesn't trust her either, does he? Should I?

"He tried to set her loose," the woman says to her guard dog.

The Somatic scratches the woolly hair on his skull.

"Make sure she's secure," the woman commands.

But the Somatic hesitates. He doesn't inch toward me until she lifts her eyebrows at him.

A grin curls one corner of my mouth. Clearly I left behind an imprint on him the first time. I seek weak spots, places where maybe a rib is still cracked or his vision isn't quite normal. Any indications that my smack down on him earlier left an impression—but there's nothing. *They have a healer!*

Of course they would. It's wise to bring a healer into battle with you. Whoever it is, he or she is good at it.

The big guy tightens the ropes Ugene had relaxed, maintaining a vigilant view on me. I can't help the surge of pleasure at his worry. His touch has none of the tenderness of Ugene's as he yanks on the ropes, stretching the ones tethered around my ankles tight so I can no longer sit up. I examine how he secures it around the footboard. There will be no undoing that, but I can break the bed in a pinch. After testing the rope around my ankles, he checks my wrists, grimacing when he realizes my wrists are loose.

"His soft spot for this girl will cost us everything," the woman grumbles as she sits in the wooden armchair and crosses her legs.

Are they talking about Ugene? *You kissed me.* His statement repeats in my head. Was there something between us? My heart plummets. Is that why Hound hates him so much? How could I not recall something like that? The questions are piling up unanswered.

The Somatic simply grunts in reply as he finishes tightening my wrists and cinching them so tight I'm force to settle on my back to avoid stretching my muscles too far.

"Just send him back now, before he does anything else stupid," the Somatic says, his voice hard and deep.

"I have to wait until we are certain the Directorate isn't on us." The woman casually rests her arms on the arms of the chair and surveys me. "I have a few questions you will answer," she says to me.

"What makes you so sure?" I ask, amused by her confidence.

Something pushes at a wall in my mind, attempting to smash through. The blonde's eyes are commanding and I almost feel compelled to obey her, but the moment passes as something else in my mind resists. *She's trying to Influence me,* I realize, recognizing the sensation from when Theus did the same. But it doesn't work.

"How did you find Ugene so fast?" she asks.

I clamp my jaw shut and glower at her in rebellion. The pressure rises in my mind but still doesn't penetrate the wall.

Once she understands I won't explain, she exhales.

"Why did you help Ugene escape Paragon only to try to capture him again?" she asks.

I give her nothing.

"Okay. Tell us about what the Directorate is planning." The pressure she forces on my mind becomes unpleasant. I grit my teeth and clench my fists, which her guard dog notices. He steps backward.

Ugene seemed to know what was going on in the Directorate and DMA. If he works with this woman, why doesn't she know what he does?

The pain becomes blinding, but I don't yield to her Power.

"Chase, persuade her to answer me."

He grins and cracks his knuckles as he stalks toward me, drawing back a fist. The muscles in his arm twitch and rope for the windup. I tense my own muscles to absorb as much of the impact as possible.

Don't fight back. I close my eyes as Ugene's voice reminds me to comply.

Chase's fist hammers against my abs and one of my ribs cracks, but I don't cry out. My eyes shoot open and I glower at him. He drags back for another jab and it takes everything in me not to break the footboard and slam my feet into his chest. Another rib cracks.

The woman rises and stalks closer, but I notice how she is certain to hold her goon between us. "If you think someone is coming for you, you're wrong," she says. "We deactivated your tracker. Whether you submit won't matter Bianca Pond. We will still use you against your brother. We will still get what we need from you—one way or another."

I lift my chin in spite. "How do you know this wasn't part of his plan?" I ask, unsure where the thought came from.

She falters, but it hardly lasts a moment. "I know Forrest *very* well. And while he would be willing to sacrifice his little sister for the greater good as he sees it, he would not endanger you by tossing you into the lion's den. I would guess he didn't even want you in that street yesterday. Forrest wouldn't save your life if it meant failing, but that doesn't mean he would place you in harm's way."

The way she talks of my brother makes my chest tighten. "How do you know what he would or wouldn't do?"

She cocks her head to the side. "Because he did the same to me."

All the predatory tension in her melts away as she sinks down onto the mattress beside me. Something about her feels familiar, and instead of producing off an impression of menace, she becomes warm. "Forrest and I were close, once. I trusted him unconditionally when we were in school together. He was such a sweet boy, but I guess I saw even then how driven he was. I blame your dad for the shift in him. All he ever craved was to prove himself, and it never satisfied your dad."

My heart hammers against my ribs. How does she know all of this?

"Forrest loved me once," she says, and her spine bends. "Or at least he said he did. Right until the Directorate took me into custody on bogus charges and tossed me into Paragon. Right until he launched his experiments on me."

No. She's seeking to muddle with my head through words since she can't apply her Power on me. These are lies.

"Your brother nearly murdered me for the sake of his own ambition." She stiffens her spine and lifts her chin, matching my gaze. "I won't let him do it to anyone else. Now, you can help us by telling me what the Directorate is up to and how Paragon plays into the plans, or I can give Chase the room."

Poison. Her words are poison in my heart. Forrest isn't hurting anyone. He is struggling to preserve this city from extinction.

Is he, though?

She waits patiently, peering at me.

Ever since leaving the facility, nothing has made sense. Will Hound find me with his Power? Surely he can track my blood trail to wherever we are. *Unless we aren't in Elpis,* I think, remembering mention of a place called The Shield outside the city. How far can Hound's Power reach?

The blond woman heaves a sigh and rises. "See if you can't loosen her tongue," she tells Chase, then strides out of the room.

Chase eyes me as if waiting for me to break loose. But I can't. I need Ugene to locate my parents and sort this out. Everything that woman said only reinforces Ugene's story. His soft spot for me. The escape from Paragon. Forrest.

My throat constricts as Chase punches me in the kidney, but I don't weep or scream. Instead, I close my eyes against the agony and bear it as his blows hammer against my torso over again and again.

And later I let that woman believe she is Influencing me by only providing what will not harm my own desire for answers.

23

FORREST CALLS FOR SOMEONE. TERRY. HE AIMS A GUN *at me and the expression in his eyes is cold, but not without remorse. A bullet rips into my chest.*

I jump awake, but the ropes binding me keep my body against the mattress. None of the pain from Chase's assault remains. No broken bones or fractures. No collapsed lung or stabbing pain from my kidneys. Someone healed me. My body can't do all of this without aid. Not so expeditiously. Yet pain persists in my chest, a stabbing ache in my heart as the grisly memory haunts me even awake. Forrest had such a cold look in his eye, so calculating. *It's my mind playing tricks on me*, I think, but it convinces no one.

How long was I out? They boarded the window in the room, and not even a trace of light from the outside world could peek through the cracks.

The ropes loosen on my wrists as I test them. Chase secured them tight before. But now they nearly fall off my arms as I pull. Someone else did that. I bite my lip. Is this a trap? Maybe they need me to think I can slip my bonds so they can catch me trying to escape and abuse me some more. Or maybe they are hoping to poison Ugene against me. Everyone seems so sure he is on my side. Should I trust him? What if this was his work, easing the ropes? Maybe he needs me to be ready to escape with him when the time arrives.

I hold my breath and listen for sounds of movement in the hallway. Nothing. Voices come from elsewhere in the building.

I can slip these bonds without leaving the house. As long as I don't flee without him, I should be safe, right?

As I slide my hands out of the ropes and work on untying the ones around my ankles, I chew my lip. *I'm not running. I'm not.*

Moving through the bedroom is troublesome when the floor insists on creaking with each step. I tiptoe across the floor and hold my back to the wall beside the door, listening. No one is watching me. Maybe they didn't expect me to wake for a while.

I peep out into the hallway, monitoring in both directions. One door at the end of the hall is closed: a closet, maybe? One door across the hall is sealed tight, but the other stands open. I creep out, placing my back to the wall as I slink along, snooping into the open door before traveling on. The bathroom door is open at the top of the steps, and humid air rolls out.

To my right, a narrow stairwell descends to the first floor. This is a house. Literally a house and not some storehouse somewhere. How many safe houses does this group have? My team tracked down so many already!

The voices are all coming from downstairs, and as they speak, I remember some from earlier.

"… threw me out when the experiment failed," Jayme says from the room below. "Like garbage. Thought I was dead until Chase found me in the Deadlands in a pit with …" Grief and fear make his voice tight as he attempts pushing on. "… With other bodies."

A pit in the Deadlands. The void I saw in the dark as the shuttle returned to the facility. Could it be the pit of bodies Jayme mentioned?

Jayme goes on, confessing his fear of losing someone—Miller?— and jealousy toward whoever he is speaking to. I shuffle delicately and secretly, trying to keep my weight equally distributed on the step before gently easing down to the next.

"But you brought him back to me," Jayme says. "Three times."

Silence settles below, and I freeze, nervous the slightest squeak of the stairs will give me away.

Then I hear Ugene say, "I have an idea."

The plan hinges on me and my family. My dad, more precisely. The conviction he has as he explains only convinces me that my parents just might be alive still, and that Forrest lied to me. Yet as I freeze on the staircase listening to the discussion in the room below, a peculiar sense of my heart shrinking presses down on my heart as my lips compress. Ugene is using me.

But my parents are alive.

"Her dad runs the network," Ugene says. "If he can't broadcast the news for me, maybe he can connect me to Elpida Theus."

My heart thumps and I grow dizzy. *No.* I close my eyes and draw a quiet, even breath.

"Ugene, she's been missing for at least two weeks," Jayme says.

"Missing? Why?" Ugene's tone is a blend of confusion and devastation.

Something tells me I know precisely what happened to Theus. Will Ugene forgive me if he discovers the truth? That I was responsible for her arrest?

Jayme explains what he knows, and that the Directorate blamed her disappearance on the Protectorate. I have a tough time focusing as a lump grows in my throat. I lean my head against the wall of the stairwell. Blood hammers in my ears, obscure their voices.

"Willow and Doc ..." Jayme's voice is scattered as my panic overtakes my body. "... Directorate silenced her."

Did Theus end up in that pit Jayme mentioned earlier? I squeeze a hand to my mouth, stunned as wet tears brush against my fingers.

"Then I will have to convince Mr. Pond," Ugene says with confidence. "If I can share the truth with the city, the Directorate's grip on the city will evaporate. But to get him on our side, I need to take Bianca to him and Willow will never go for it."

I concentrate. Now is not a moment for frailty. Willow must be the blonde woman who interrogated me. Willow. Chase. Doc. Jayme. Miller. Lily. I collect their names, even though I'm not positive what I will do with this information. Feeding it back to Forrest or anyone else on my team no longer sounds like the ideal action.

What even is the right thing anymore?

"I need to go alone," Ugene says, drawing my awareness back to the discussion below.

No one else agrees. Their voices rise in protest all at once. A moment later, all is silent.

I peer up the stairwell as movement above catches my attention. I stop listening to the conversation below to be sure no one will discover me missing upstairs. What if it's Willow checking in on me? I can't be missing if she checks.

"Even if you do make it to his house, Pond is in the Directorate's pocket," Jayme says. "He won't turn against them. It could ruin him and his family."

What family? I think bitterly. A few hours ago, I thought my parents were dead and Forrest was all I had left.

"Mr. Pond is a decent man," Ugene says. "He might be in their pocket, but if the truth strikes close to home, he might reconsider. Especially once he finds out what they did to his daughter."

What *did* they do to me? Ugene said I was dead. Lily said they killed me again. How am I standing here? Why can't I remember anything? Frustration makes my body shudder. My jaw aches as my teeth grate together. I'm not a whole person, just a shadow of myself. An illusion.

"You're asking him to choose between his two children," Jayme says.

Who would Dad choose? Would he support Forrest as he has always done? Would he choose my side and stand against Forrest? Not likely. It's not something he has ever done before. Forrest was his favorite; his special, gifted child. Whatever I am now is because of Forrest. Dad will know that and still praise Forrest for his brilliance while condemning my shortcomings.

"Bianca will be with me," Ugene says, attracting my attention back.

Something slaps and I jump, ready to flee. But no one appears.

"She could be a spy," a girl says. "We have no idea if we can trust her or not."

Am I? Would I even know if I was?

"I realize the risk," Ugene says, and once more his unshakable confidence is admirable, "but we don't have a choice."

"Don't go alone with her!" the girl demands. The short girl with dark hair whose eyes blazed through me upstairs. No one here trusts me, and maybe they are right not to.

Silence falls over the room below and I glance upstairs again to reassure myself no one is near. Ugene breaks the silence in such a gentle, reassuring voice that I have to lean against the railing to hear him. "You told me that I saved those people from Paragon. Willow and Doc keep telling me that I'm looking at the small fish instead of a much bigger one in the pond. It's time for me to do for this city what I did for the test subjects."

I can't define what it is about his tone, his courage, his faith that inspires me. Does he have the Power of Influence as well? Nothing else explains why I would be so swayed by him, so eager to trust and follow him. Yet Willow tried the same thing on me and it didn't work.

"I started this fight," Ugene says, and I can practically feel the sadness coming from him. "Now it's time to finish it."

I feel like a fish out of water, floundering for air, trying to make sense of this strange new world. Nothing makes any sense to me anymore. Never has my heart beat so rapidly before. Everything I thought I understood has become a tangled mess in less than a day, and the more I fight to unravel the mystery, the worse that knot becomes, trapping my very existence within.

"Enid found schematics of Paragon with strange marks on them," Ugene says. His voice centers me. I gulp a few more breaths to calm myself and hear movement upstairs for real this time.

I carefully edge back up the stairs and slither into the bathroom, closing the door as I spot Willow emerging from one of the rooms. The last thing I see is the pure rage on her face and the papers clutched in her fists.

I push my back to the closed door and slip down as my knees give out. My body trembles. Weight like a mountain presses against my chest and my shoulders slump as I wrap my arms around my aching gut. Something in my jacket crinkles and I reach a quivering hand into the pockets, only to come up empty. But inside the lining, a hole in the fabric reveals a precisely folded envelope with a piece of paper tucked inside. My fingers fumble to draw it out, nearly ripping the worn paper.

The letter is not in my own hand, yet it seems familiar to me. I've read it before. If the familiarity doesn't prove that much, the worn condition of the paper does. I skim the page and choke. A note from someone named Poly, warning me that the DMA and my brother are working together to erase my memory and control me. A strangle sob slides out and I slap my hand over my mouth to smother it. How many times have I read this letter? Who is Poly?

Steele.

I jump as Nevermore's voice thunders in my head. "No," I mutter, knowing that the others are in danger. Why do I care? Everyone is using me!

Take cover, he says.

There's no chance to do more than jump into the bathtub as the house erupts around me. It's too late. The DMA is here.

24

THE TUB PROTECTS ME FROM FRAGMENTS OF PLASTER
and splinters of wood. I cough as the dust coats my mouth and clings
to my tongue, then assess the weight of the debris on my back.

Forrest.

This is his doing. He stripped away my life, my memories, my soul.
I will return to him, kowtow at his feet like a perfect little sister ...
then destroy everything he has worked so hard to achieve.

I thrust the debris off and clamber out of the cracked claw-foot
tub. The house is little more than a heap of rubble with one broken
wall remaining vertical. A DMA trooper picks his path through the
debris, hunting.

I crouch for a time, studying his movements. I can turn myself in
and hope that it leads me straight back to Forrest, but that risks him
erasing my memories again. No, I have to take Forrest by surprise. I have
to go now, before anybody sees me. Do they already know I'm here?

"Enid?" Ugene's terror-soaked voice attracts the trooper's
attention directly to him.

Thank you for the diversion, Ugene, I think, rising to a crouch and
reviewing my surroundings for fresh signs of concern. More than one
trooper patrols the wreckage.

"Enid!" Ugene calls out.

I spin, prepared to leave as soon as the second trooper at my six
turns his back to my hiding place.

But Ugene will doubtless end up in a pit—or worse—if I don't
do something. *What if I need him?* If he is going to use me, I'm going

to return the favor. I can't risk his capture when I might have need of him later. He can show me to my parents' house. I can't recall where Cante Road is.

I leap out of my crouch to take the trooper closing in on Ugene by surprise. Tiles crack and damaged plaster splinters beneath my boots. He doesn't notice as he drops into a gap between two joists. Ugene attempts pushing to his knees, but I reach his side and force down on his shoulder with one hand. I snatch the trooper's vest in a fist. Ending this fight as quickly as possible is in all of our best interest. Thankfully, Ugene doesn't push back against my shove.

I thrust a punch at the trooper's ribs. They register a satisfactory crack. He gasps and lifts a hand to defend with his Power. I surrender my grip on his vest and use both hands to jerk his neck, astonished with the cold efficiency of my own actions. Thankfully, his visor keeps me from seeing his eyes as he dies. I toss his body elsewhere. It smashes through the solitary wall and his body rolls with flailing limbs to a halt in the grass.

Ugene is on his hands and knees now, and I grasp his jacket to hoist him to his feet. His gaze is latched on the dead trooper in horror. Seeing that expression on his face is more painful than anything I can remember.

As he stumbles on his feet, clutching my arm for assistance, I avert my gaze.

"You said my parents are alive," I say. "Prove it. We need to go now."

The crunch of boots moving through the wreckage of the house draws my attention toward the street. Nevermore is near. Were it not for the time we spent together in the shadow of night these past weeks, I might not have noticed him. Without a doubt, he is conscious of me. At the end of the block, a DMA shuttle waits with the door open.

And I have a split second to decide: turn Ugene in as Forrest wants, or allow him to escort me back to my parents and, with any luck, answers.

Or I can trick them into thinking I'm turning him in.

I jerk Ugene closer, tightening my control on his jacket. "Play along," I murmur in his ear.

I need answers. I deserve them! Ugene is my key.

Whether Ugene plays along by resisting, tugging futilely at my grip as he whimpers Enid's name, or he genuinely is doubting me now, I can't say. But his struggle seems to satisfy Nevermore as I drag Ugene along beside me into the street.

"I have the suspect," I say, soliciting the most lukewarm, robotic tone I can manage. "Thanks for coming to get me."

Nevermore sneers, his tone tinged with revulsion as he says, "We didn't come for *you*. You allowed them to capture you."

Ugene freezes the moment Nevermore speaks, as if he knows Nevermore. I shove Ugene mercilessly to his knees on the pavement. He grunts.

"Allowed?" I sneer right back at him, allowing the bloating of my muscles to disclose to Nevermore just what I think of his assessment. "They used some sort of Power on my mind and knocked me out."

A squirrelly girl rubs her palms together anxiously nearby, scanning the destruction with wide, terror-filled eyes.

I glance toward the remnants of the house as wood clunks and rolls. Other survivors are attempting to climb out of the rubble. I'm nearly out of time. Once the radicals surface, a fight will break out.

Ugene's gaze is latched on the squirrelly girl, and the hurt is evident in the way his mouth turns downward. The girl's face turns brilliant crimson and her hair falls around her face as she bows her head.

Nevermore grunts in irritation, then stalks toward the girl, glaring at her down his beak-like nose.

"I did what you asked," the girl whimpers. Her entire body is shaking. "I reactivated her tracking, and you said you would let me go."

My tracking? *Play the part!* I instruct myself. I snort and roll my eyes, pretending that I know precisely what that promise is worth. I guess it doesn't actually require pretending. I *do* know. Nevermore never would have upheld his side of whatever trade they struck.

As if to verify this, Nevermore bares his teeth. "Did you really think the Directorate would forgive you for siding with radicals?"

The girl snarls, screeches, and vaults at Nevermore, clawing at his face like a feral cat. I almost laugh as Nevermore stumbles back, but she sinks into desperation, echoing the same thing over and over. "You promised."

I peek at Ugene, trying to puzzle out how to get us out of this. His gaze slides past me.

I spin around as Hound holds his hand in the air and the girl's whimpers choke off. Her eyes pop. Her feet rise off the ground. I've felt the intensity of Hound's Power like this before, though he never choked me with it. His shoulders rise as he scowls at the girl. The Power is appalling.

From the corner of my eyes, I spot Ugene pushing to his feet and I hold a steady hand on his shoulder. What does he think he can do?

Apparently bored with the proceedings, Nevermore turns his scrutiny to the rubble. He stalks toward it.

We are wasting time. There must be a way out of this. I just can't think.

Ugene shudders violently under my palm and I follow his gaze back toward the girl as blood oozes from her pores and churns around her in a red hazy mist. The body shrivels up and the girl's already pale skin turns ashen white. I want to look away, but can't divert my gaze. My stomach roils and I clench my jaw firmly closed to avoid throwing up. Hound tosses the girl's body aside carelessly and her blood rains down, painting the pavement.

My grasp on Ugene's shoulder falters, and he topples forward, vomiting in the road. I avert my gaze so I don't join him.

Intense burning sears my throat. I've seen this before, or at least, the aftermath of it. At the time, Hound had seemed so astonished by it. Why would he do this again? How many times has he done it before? That Power is a terrible thing of nightmares.

Hound is a monster, I think, horrified by his performance. How could I ever have considered him a victim? Hound has never been a victim.

As Hound marches toward Ugene and me, I lock my stunned gaze on him. Quick breaths make my chest heave and my body goes rigid. I can beat him in any of our sparring bouts, but he never exhibited such crude, emotionless Power before. Will he apply that Power to Ugene? Could I stop him if he tried?

Ugene shakes out of his stupor long before me and charges at Hound. I want to snag him, stop him, but I'm fixed in place. Frozen. *Not again.*

Hound sneers at Ugene, just like Nevermore always does to me. I know that look. Hate. Disgust.

Ugene stumbles, collapsing to his side as if someone shoved him down.

"You've really become full of yourself in the past few months," Hound sneers.

I watch everything play out like a horror film, powerless to interact with the characters. My body declines to heed my orders to move. Is Hound doing this to me? *Move, dammit!*

Ugene pushes himself to his knees, struggling for breath.

I will make him suffer as he made me suffer. Hound's declaration in the hallway hammers against me.

"Time to face the facts," Hound says, looming over Ugene who struggles to rise. "You're too pathetic and weak to survive. You were never meant for this world."

If I had known back then who he would become, Hound had said. I hadn't thought twice about it that night. Now, I doubt everything he ever said to me, with one exception.

He *will* kill Ugene instead of bringing him in. This absolute certainty finally frees me from my spell, and I press my way between them.

"That's enough, Jimmy." I apply his name, hoping that the familiarity will stop him just as it influenced him that night. "They want him alive."

Hound's back stiffens as he straightens, lifting his chin and squaring off against me. Would he harm me to get to Ugene? "They didn't say unharmed."

Yes. Yes, he did!

Everything happens so rapidly. Ugene falls back on the road, gasping for air. Then Hound raises his palm skyward and Ugene's body lifts off. Hound's arms quiver with Power and his eyes redden as the blood vessels swell and engulf the whites of his eyes. Blood trickles from Ugene's nose.

"I do owe you one debt of gratitude, though," Hound says, tilting his hand.

I strain my muscles, feeling them cable and grow. He doesn't notice. His focus remains locked on Ugene. "Thanks to you, I'm more powerful than just about everyone in this city. Who knew you could make me stronger?"

More powerful than just about everyone, I think. *But not me.* Forrest told me I was stronger than everyone else. Stronger than Hound.

Ugene glares at Hound in clear defiance I can't help but envy. Blood coats his lips as it slips from his nose.

I shove Hound back. "Jimmy, that's enough!"

He stumbles, but his focus doesn't break, as if he's in a trance.

"I said *enough!*"

Animal fury takes over and I heave a punch into his jaw strong enough to break bones and make his eyes water.

Ugene's body strikes the pavement.

I crash into Hound with a growl of pure rage. Nothing else exists except Hound and me. We hit the pavement hard enough to crack the concrete.

"You always were soft on him," Hound says as he clutches my jacket and twists it to secure me in place.

Idiot. Holding a Super Somatic over you isn't the wisest choice.

I drive a punch into his ribs and he chokes in pain, then laughs. The sound sends chills down my spine, like a madman accepting his lunacy. "I should have known you would turn," he says, exposing blood on his teeth.

Adrenaline pumps through my veins, suddenly the world tips and my vision spins. My blood heats and my chest compresses. He is using his Hematology Power to thicken my blood. It slows my blows as I kneel over him, making my fists feels as if they are traveling through water.

Somewhere around us, a gunshot splits the air.

I grab Hound's waistband as I lurch to my feet, staggering, and toss him aside like a bag of trash. *He* is *trash*.

Ugene's shout follows, calling out to Willow.

Hound catches himself, applying his Power, and rises off the ground a few inches, hovering in the air with his arms up. It's magnificent and terrible to behold.

A scream lodges in my throat as I charge toward Hound, but he catches me with his Power as plainly as an athlete catching a ball in the air. I sail backward, air rushing past my ears as all command of my body is surrendered. A wall cracks against my back, leaving me momentarily disoriented. But his Power releases its grasp and I wobble to my feet.

Hound rushes toward Ugene as if nothing in the world can stop him, and at his back, another open DMA shuttle. If he gets a hold of Ugene, I will never get the help I need. Nearly a hundred feet separate me from the action—from Ugene, who is between Hound and me. I thrust away from the wall of the shuttle at my back, using it to enhance the launch velocity and vault me across the distance. The shuttle rolls across the road when I shove off, propelled away.

Someone shouts. Another gunshot fires, striking Hound in the shoulder. He barely even blinks. He directs his palm out toward Willow. She crumbles to the ground as if something crushed her downward. The gun drops from her hands and clatters on the pavement.

Why does it feel like I'm moving so slowly?

Hound wraps Ugene's collar in his fist and tugs him to his feet, then tosses Ugene into the open shuttle.

That's it. If that door closes, this is over.

Blinding light streaks down from the sky and angles straight at Hound's chest. He slumps over with a thump—right on top of Ugene.

Hope lifts in my heart for the first time.

Then the shuttle door slides shut, sealing Ugene inside.

25

YOU BETRAYED US, STEELE, NEVERMORE'S VOICE shouts in my head, making me stumble to the side and press my hands to my ears. As I right myself, I spot Nevermore attempting to fight off Chase. The shuttle lurches into the air. Chase falls to his knees. All around me is chaos, but I don't care about anyone except Ugene and Nevermore.

Nevermore is distracted momentarily by Chase, and I throw a punch as hard as I can into Nevermore's temple. Nevermore collapses to the ground as a ball of lightning streaks across the sky and slams into the shuttle. I watch, heart in my throat and helpless as it tumbles toward the ground. This fight is over.

The shuttle slams into an apartment building, breaking a hole in the brick wall, and then rolls to a stop on one side. The shuttle door faces the sky, and I launch myself at it, leaping up and grabbing hold of the handle. My muscles strain, tug, pull, ache as I yank at the locked steel door. It makes horrible shrieking noises as metal scratches against metal before finally giving away. With a roar, I grasp it in both hands and send the door soaring through the air, dimly aware of the troopers who are crushed and killed by it.

I jump down into the shuttle and the metal vibrates with a thump. No one else occupies the space except Ugene and the body of Hound with a gaping hole through his chest. The harness has Ugene pinned in place and he is fumbling with it, his hands shaking violently. I grab a hold and snap it off the seat easily. Ugene tumbles to the shuttle floor and I hold a hand out to help him up.

"Are you okay?"

His trembling hand slides into my own. "I think so."

Miller calls for Ugene from the street outside.

"He's okay," I call back. "Let's get out of here before more reinforcements show up."

Ugene nods numbly as he follows me to the door. I crouch, then launch myself up and land on the edge of the doorway. Ugene grabs my wrist as I reach in for him and haul him easily out through the opening. In seconds, we are on the street again, and Ugene leans back against the shuttle, sucking in deep breaths.

The dark-haired girl—Enid?—limps over, jerking away from the mousy girl and rushing at Ugene. He eagerly throws his arms around her. Watching the two of them together makes my heart ache, though I don't have any good reason to feel that way. *Do I?* I can't stand around and watch, so I stalk away, giving them a moment alone.

Everything happened so fast, and more reinforcements will arrive soon enough. I have to make sure we don't linger too long.

Hoping for a distraction, I help Chase move rubble from the house in search of anyone who might be missing. Most of the people I remember seeing while in the house are already accounted for, but I continue to search, giving Ugene a minute to collect himself. *Then we leave.*

Fire climbs up the walls of the building the shuttle hit, and residents are filling the street. I glance over my shoulder and watch as Enid attempts funneling the fire out of the building and away with her obviously Naturalist wind Power.

"Please," Ugene calls, drawing my attention. He stands on the shuttle. "For your safety, move away from the building."

The residents comply.

I hoist a beam Chase couldn't move and flip it aside as the crowd gathers around where Ugene stands. I listen as he addresses the crowd.

"The Directorate sent super soldiers into Pax to attack while we slept," he says.

I avert my gaze at the mention of super soldiers. Just what side am I on here, anyway?

"They blew up our house, killed at least one of our friends, and injured several more just to protect themselves from the truth we now know." He captivates the crowd, and I turn to watch as he continues. "That we are stronger united than divided. Most of these people want nothing more than the same freedom the Directorate affords itself. Most of us have little to no Power to speak if, but together, we are a real danger to them because we want equality for everyone."

Equality. But at what cost?

"Take this night and tell everyone you know," he says. "The Protectorate is here and united we will make the necessary change."

What is he doing! Is he trying to spark revolution?

I run to the edge of the shuttle and motion urgently for him to jump down. More shuttles approach from the distance. *We need to run ... now!*

Ugene hears the sound, watching the sky, then turns his attention to the crowd, more concerned for their safety than his own.

"Go, before the DMA comes back. And tell your friends that the Protectorate is here."

He hops down as the crowd disperse, and Willow marches over, her expression as dangerous as a perfect storm.

"What are you doing?" she growls.

For a moment, I'm certain she is about to strike out against him.

Ugene doesn't back down. He raises his chin defiantly at her. "Sparking the flame," he says, as if that makes perfect sense, then simply walks away.

And judging by the way Willow's face heats, she understands.

I effortlessly match his stride. "We need to move," I say, watching Willow to be sure she won't do anything stupid.

"We need to kill that tracking device the Directorate put in you for good," he says.

I flinch. Tracking. Of course they would track me.

"Bri somehow reactivated it while you were asleep," he says, and I can only assume the girl Hound killed was Bri. "She claimed it was impossible to remove, but I'm not sure I trust her judgment anymore."

As we approach the house, a boy Ugene calls Sho approaches, holding out a messy stack of papers. Without hesitation, Ugene takes them and folds them into his jacket, then zips it. The hum of an engine draws my attention as a shuttle rounds a corner up the block.

"Cover them!" Ugene commands, pointing at the shuttle.

Enid doesn't move from his side, flicking glares at me when he doesn't look her way. Ugene nudges her toward the street, but she resists, clinging to his arm.

"It's too soon," she says, and the tremble in her voice gives away just how scared she is.

Ugene touches her face so tenderly that I look away. "I need you to help them. Keep Willow from losing control. And don't trust anything she tells you. She's using everyone. I don't know what she will do once she finds out what I'm up to. Please." He kisses her hand. "It's time. Meet me at Harvey's place."

I want to leave them alone, but there is no privacy here, and I don't dare leave his side. Instead, I distract myself by watching the others line up to defend their position. Enid joins them, casting a last look at Ugene that reveals she doesn't believe they will see each other again. The fight begins again, but now the radicals are holding the DMA troopers at bay. Only six special forces agents remain, not including myself. The DMA will send them after me and Ugene.

Miller supports Jayme as they limp toward us and says, "I can kill the tracker."

Kill the tracker. Where is it? What is it?

Ugene nods and turns his attention to the mousey girl. "Rosie, Bianca will need immediate healing."

Healing? Why will I need healing? What exactly do they think I will allow them to do to me? Miller stretches his hands toward my head and I dodge away, pushing him down. Jayme limps forward, but he's hardly menacing injured as he is.

Ugene puts himself between me and the others, holding out a hand as if the sheer force of his will could stop me.

And it does.

"Bianca, let him do this, we don't have time!" Ugene says firmly.

No. They haven't even explained just what they will do.

"Please," he says, his dark eyes pleading with me. "It will hurt like hell, but the DMA will find you, find *us*, no matter where we go."

The emphasis on "no matter where" isn't lost on me. My parents. With the tracker active, I will put my parents at risk. I nod, but my muscles remain tight. It's obvious Miller doesn't want to do this either, judging by the way he glares at me as his hands settle against the back of my head.

A shock hits my brain, and I jump. Miller's Power punches me in the back of the head. The shock spreads like a net over my head, striking every nerve. My muscles lock up. It doesn't burn, but feels like someone has sucked the air from my lungs as some unseen force constantly pokes my nerves with needles. My head buzzes with electric power.

Then the pain kicks in. The thousand-needle nerve touch becomes a burning, searing, stabling pain all over my skull. The sensation makes my eyes ache and water. Air rushes into my lungs as I suck in a breath and scream. No. Not scream. Shriek, like I do in my nightmares. Like I haven't done for as long as I can remember. Of their own accord, my muscles tense and flex against the pain. The tang of blood touches my tongue.

I'm doing this for my parents. For my family. I just have to get through it.

But the agony is overwhelming, and even my enhanced muscles can't support me any longer. My legs buckle as heat courses over my skull, rolling like a burning hot electrical fire. For a moment, I black out, unable to take the pain a second longer.   When   my vision returns, a girl, Rosie, kneels beside Ugene at my side. The pain has subsided, but isn't gone. I can still feel it buzzing in my brain like a bad migraine.

Regardless of what Ugene wants from me, I know exactly what I want from him. I snatch the collar of his shirt in a viper-like strike, making Rosie leap back in alarm.

"Now," I growl, then release with a small shove.

Ugene stumbles, hurt by my reaction, but he says nothing as he dusts himself off and stands.

Another house explodes nearby. Jayme nudges Ugene in the opposite direction.

"Go!" Jayme calls. "You're right. That information needs to get out. Willow won't agree, but we can't get out of Pax now. I'll deal with Willow. But you won't have long, Ugene."

Ugene nods. "Try to protect these houses and the people inside."

They wave us off as the others rush to join the front line of defense. I don't have to be told twice and run into a gap between houses. Ugene hesitates, though, and I grab his arm to yank him along. "Ugene!"

There's no more time to delay. We already waited too long.

Now, it's time to get to my parents.

And then the truth.

26

UGENE'S PACE IS IRRITATINGLY SLOW FOR SOMEONE who ran from me like death was on his heels. He falls back repeatedly, forcing me to stop and press my back to houses, watching for signs of trouble as he recovers his gasping breaths. Good lord, a deaf man could hear him breathing like this! And then he has the nerve to question where I'm going.

"I can't keep running like this," he says. "I'm not Super Somatic like you."

Clearly.

But our direction doesn't matter as much at the moment as just putting distance between us and the DMA. Hound won't be tracking us now. The image of his dead body lying in the shuttle, a hole burned straight through his chest, makes my stomach churn. Maybe the DMA has done some questionable stuff, but this Protectorate has killed without remorse, too. *As have I.*

"I'm just trying to put distance between us and them," I say. "We can worry about direction later."

Ugene scowls, gulping down a big breath. "Unless we're going the wrong way."

Compressing my irritation presses at my last nerve. How ungrateful can he possibly be? I've saved him from the DMA.

The scowl slides off his face, and he rubs his neck in exhaustion. "Just give me a second."

How many seconds does this guy need? Every instinct in me says we need to move. Now. But if Ugene collapses from exhaustion, I will have to carry him, and I have no intention to haul his unspectacular backside across town. Instead of arguing, I watch the street, scanning windows, shadows, doorways, and even the sky as Ugene regains his breath.

Few people would dare to be up and about at this time of night, but I swear I spot movement in some shadows. "People are watching us. We need to keep moving."

Headlights flash from the intersection, and my heart leaps into my throat. Who would be out here driving in Pax at this time of night? *No one good,* I think.

Enough resting. We have to go now. I seize Ugene's arm and yank him along toward the mouth of an alley across the street. Ugene stumbles behind me and we slip into the shadows of the alley as a DMA shuttle glides past.

Ugene's gaze follows the shuttle as well, and he expresses concern for his comrades. Does he not understand we are in danger here?

"They can hold their own," I say curtly. "But we need to hurry before the streets are crawling with DMA shuttles."

By some miracle, Ugene only nods in agreement and we continue on. I try to moderate my pace so he can keep up, starting slow at first, and pushing our steps with a little more haste once I'm sure he can manage the speed. Even so, after another mile Ugene lags, and his breaths are ragged as he sucks them in, making enough noise to wake the neighborhood. He makes a reasonable argument for us walking from this point—not wanting to draw unnecessary attention to ourselves. My DMA-issues clothing doesn't exactly help make us inconspicuous. We have made it far enough now from where we started, maybe a couple of miles, so I agree to walk from here.

Elpis is quieter at night, but it isn't really so late that, as we get closer to downtown, no one is out and about. Vehicles appear and disappear sporadically. The streets get wider and more people are walking home from work or a night out with their friends. At one point, Ugene stumbles over his own feet. *Seriously, we're walking. What is his problem?* I grab his arm to help balance him and say nothing.

The lights grow brighter as we reach the southern edge of downtown, right on the edge of the Clement borough. More and more people walk in small knots. My mouth goes dry as I wonder who among them might recognize us.

At an intersection, Ugene grabs me and pulls me back into an alley. I peer out and spot the DMA shuttle parked near the intersection. The shuttle door is closed. There could be agents inside, but odds are that here, so close to downtown, this is just a regular trooper patrol of two uniformed officers.

"There are only two," I whisper to Ugene, watching the troopers lean against the shuttle and talk to each other. "I can take them." It wouldn't even be a challenge.

"If we attack, even if you get to them before they alert others, the DMA will figure out where we are when those guys don't check in. We can't leave a trace."

I hate that his logic makes sense. Why had I not considered that? "Then what do we do? If we cross the street, they'll spot us."

Ugene just stares at the sky. The silence irritates me. We can't just stand here. Just when I'm about to give up on waiting for him, Ugene nudges me in another direction. He's going the wrong way! But Ugene doesn't wait for me to make my case. He's already moving away, leaving me to choose between following him or going my own way. I clench my jaw and follow on his heels.

This strange zig-zag pattern continues for miles. Every time he tries changing direction, I attempt arguing against it. But he doesn't listen. Ugene is so confident in his sense of direction.

And somehow, we avoid any confrontation. Does he know where the DMA is? Maybe Forrest is wrong. Maybe Ugene has some sort of Echolocation. He seems to know exactly which way to go and when. No one's instincts would just naturally be this good without a Power.

At last, as we round a corner, I spot the entrance to the metro and grin, slapping Ugene on the shoulder in congratulations. He winces, stumbling a step.

Eager to get off the streets, I bound down the metro steps two at a time, then stop when Ugene's sneakers don't hit the stairs behind me. I turn, motioning for him to follow.

But he's frozen in place.

Ugene refuses to enter the metro, insisting that something is off. Why does he keep looking at the sky? I follow his gaze, irritated. We are so close! There's nothing in the sky but stars. Maybe it isn't Echolocation, but a Divinic Power, like Astrological Tracking or something, similar to what Vortex could do without the Power enhancer.

Without warning, Ugene turns away from the station at a sprint.

"What is wrong with you?" I snap as I rush to catch up.

"The lights went out."

"What?" I have no idea what that means.

Ugene doesn't bother to explain, but the second we disappear around the corner, I can hear the heavy thump of dozens of boots coming from where we just stood. From the station. My gut sinks. How did he know?

I pick up the pace, forcing Ugene to run faster. This time he doesn't protest. We run, and the blocks breeze past. Our haste only catches a few eyes, but at the sight of my DMA clothing, people avert their gazes as if they don't see us at all.

After several blocks and a few turns, Ugene collapses onto a tram-stop bench. I ease down beside him, wincing with each of his shuddering breaths. I'm not winded at all.

"Do you care to explain how you knew they were coming?" I ask.

Ugene is leaning forward, wiping sweat from his forehead. He turns his gaze to me, resting his elbows on his legs, and I spot the slight tremor in his hands. He just stares at me, calculating, sad, curious. It takes everything in me not to deflect my gaze.

"I just ... had a feeling," he says at last.

"A feeling." My jaw twitches. For someone who wants me to trust him, he holds a lot close to the chest. There's definitely something he isn't telling me.

"It's gotten me this far," he says.

I grimace as a self-driving tram approaches from the east. I can't trust him. I can't trust anyone. Can I even trust myself?

Ugene grins at the tram map and announces we will ride. Is there even a point to argue how vulnerable we will be?

The tram ride is terribly silent. Ugene sits beside me with his hood up and his head down. He fidgets like he has a condition, and the toes of his shoes bounce on the metal tram floor. I want to put my hands on his knees to stop the endless motion. His anxiety bleeds through to me.

My parents are alive. I would have continued to question it had I not overheard them talking about Dad when they didn't know I was listening. Why would Forrest lie to me? Our childhood was always a bit strained. Forrest and I were never really friends growing up, but he cared about me. At least, I remember him caring about me. Is that a lie, too? All I wanted since waking up in the DMA program was to make Forrest proud, but that desire has evaporated. Who can I trust if I can't even trust my own memories?

The note from Poly remains in my jacket. I close my eyes and try to picture her, remember anything at all about her, but the harder I struggle to remember, the more my mind resists. I can't even remember her hair color or how tall she was. Attempting to resurrect her is like trying to create a complete stranger from memory. I have nothing to work with except a name and a Power. Not enough.

I watch as Elpis passes the tram windows. The buildings make way to residential streets and wider lawns surrounding bigger houses the further west we ride. This is familiar to me. Salas. The borough I grew up in. Home.

Do my parents know I'm alive? Did they know what happened to me at all? Ugene seems to think they believe me dead. *Because according to him and his friends, I was dead,* I think.

Wouldn't that be something I should remember? Death seems like a pretty traumatic event. How could I not remember? Unless it was so traumatic my brain walled it off. The nightmares may contain some morsel of truth.

The tram slows, and I recognize the stop. I've been here so many times before. I catch Ugene's attention and we step off into the street.

Everything here is so pristine; a stark contrast to what life in Pax is like. The houses are mansions by comparison, and the yards are all well-maintained. As we walk toward Cante Road, my feet carry me as if they know this path by heart. The scent of fresh flowers fills the air like a perfume, too many to identify.

A few residents are outside unloading groceries from their vehicles or playing games in the dark yards. Some talk to each other about tomorrow's weather and how it might affect the plants, or how they heard rumors about another neighbor. The entire atmosphere is very cookie-cutter perfect and peaceful. No one speaks to us as we pass, but a few people watch curiously—watch me curiously. Is it my DMA clothes, or do they know me? If they know me, do they think I've died, too?

"We need to take the alleys," Ugene says under his breath. He keeps his head down and face masked by his hood. The Directorate has been hunting him down for weeks, if not longer. Surely these people would recognize his face.

I nod and lead the way into the shadows of the alleyway.

At this point, I could run. I could leave him to his fate and find my own way home. But for some reason I'm tethered to his side, afraid to pull away, afraid to return to my house alone in case my parents aren't there. And in case they are.

"I need you to make me a promise," he says, keeping his voice to a soft whisper. I glance at him expectantly. "No more killing. Not the DMA recruits, at least. Some of them had no other choice but to join. They don't deserve death."

No choice? How could someone not have a choice? I *didn't*, I remind myself, which makes me grimace. If Forrest lied to me and used me at the Directorate's bidding, I want to burn the whole system down. Those DMA troopers will get in my way. I need answers. I need revenge. If my parents are alive, and I stand in front of them tonight, I intend to make the Directorate pay for what they did to me.

I intend to make Forrest pay.

"Please?" Ugene gazes at me with so much compassion and desperation that I can't deny him what he wants.

I sigh. "I will ... try."

"Promise?" he asks as if he doesn't believe me.

Can I take down the Directorate without killing troopers? Probably not. Yet I'm compelled to appease Ugene. "I promise. Unless I'm left with no other choice."

There. That should leave me enough wiggle room to remove anyone who gets in my way. If they leave me no choice, I will do what is necessary. Whatever that ends up being.

Ugene falls into silence, hands stuffed into his pockets as he slinks along beside me.

A backyard comes into view a few feet ahead, and a sense of familiarity slams against me. And fear. What if my parents know what happened to me and they were okay with it? What if they don't want me back? I'm not sure I could handle the rejection. My steps slow and my palms sweat. I wipe them on my pants as we climb the back steps, then reach a trembling hand toward the doorknob.

Ugene watches with concern and sympathy. *I don't need his sympathy!*

"We could knock," he says.

No. If this is my home, if my parents are inside right now, knocking doesn't seem right.

And if Ugene is lying to me, using this as a ploy to get me where he needs me, I will snap his neck like a twig.

"You had better be right, Powers."

He flinches, and I'm satisfied that he understands the danger he is in.

Steeling myself against rejection, I turn the knob and step through.

27

THE AROMA OF CHOCOLATE CHIP COOKIES PERMEATES
the kitchen as we step in. The odor makes my chest tighten and reminds
me of home. I want to weep. The kitchen is wonderfully clean. Not a
single dish or crumb in sight. A bowl of fruit on the island countertop
adds a splash of yellow, red, and orange. I glide my fingers along
the granite countertop as I head toward the living room—where I
can hear the holotv broadcasting. The counter is remarkably cool to
touch, and it causes my fingers to tingle. I remember pressing my
arms against this very countertop when I was burning up with a fever
years ago. The countertop offered respite. Mom had to nudge me
awake when I fell asleep on a stool.

My gaze wanders to the light emanating from the living room.
Mom and Dad are in there. Only feet away now, though absolute
terror threatens to bar me from continuing. Ugene trails along behind
me without judgment. Somehow, just having him at my back in this
moment offers me the courage I require to tiptoe into the living room
doorway.

And I freeze, beaming at them with wide eyes.

Mom and Dad sit on the sofa as if this were an ordinary night.
There is no doubt. I remember the crow's feet around Mom's eyes
and the streak of gray in her dark hair. I remember the lines of white
along Dad's temples, peppering his black hair, and the way his reading
glasses perched on the point of his nose. These are, without a doubt,
my parents. Alive.

Forrest lied to me. Until this point, I clung to the hope that Ugene was mistaken, scared that the only person left in my family had duped me, used me. My knees threaten to give out.

Dad is absorbed in work, fumbling with his phone, but Mom senses movement and matches my gaze. A bird-like squawk escapes her lips and she clings to Dad's arm. The commotion draws his gaze from the phone and his eyes grow two times their typical size. Copper eyes. Just like mine.

My breaths come in swift succession.

"Bianca?" Dad eases away from Mom and rises.

I gulp, striving to recover my voice. "Dad?" Sorrow, relief, anger, joy all develop into a maelstrom in my head, making me dizzy. I lose command of my limbs and my arms drop at my sides. "Mom?"

No one moves. The seconds seem to stretch on forever as they only gawk at me as if I'm a ghost. Why aren't they welcoming me home? Dear lord, the rejection is coming. Suddenly, I can't breathe.

Dad crosses the living room so hurriedly I jump back, but he sweeps me into his arms, hugging me fiercely. And I almost cry, pressing my face against his shoulder. I feel protected here as Mom joins us, like nobody could ever touch me as long as my parents are around.

Forrest lied to me ... and Ugene didn't.

Mom kisses my forehead, tears rolling down her cheeks as pure joy accentuates her crow's feet. Her fingers are cool as she grasps my face, taking me in as if I've been away for years. Perhaps to them it seemed like years.

"My girl ..."

Dad's arm slips around my shoulders and I shudder with relief and delight. "How? Forrest told us you died. He ..."

Forrest. Anger burns in my heart. "He told me the same about you."

Dad's gaze is calculating as he attempts putting the fragments together. "But why?"

Mom's gaze slides past me and she steps back, joy slipping from her face as she sees Ugene. "What is he doing here?"

"Gloria, get my phone," Dad says.

I catch her arm. "Please, Mom. Don't. I wouldn't be here if it wasn't for Ugene."

Dad seems to have forgotten I'm in the room at all as he studies Ugene, as if waiting for him to remove a gun or threaten any of us. "What do you want?"

Ugene licks his lips and strides forward. "Please, sir, we need your help."

Dad puffs out his chest as if preparing to blow Ugene over. "Why would we help a radical terrorist?"

Ugene frowns at this, taken aback. "Wait, why do you think I'm a radical terrorist?"

"Because of the crimes you've committed," Dad snarls. This exchange is rapidly shifting to perilous ground. "They say you are responsible for what happened at Paragon, and you are now leading a group of radicals against Elpis and may be behind this attack tonight. Anyone who helps you will be sent out of the city."

If Dad calls Ugene in, the DMA will capture me and erase my memory again. "Dad, I'm not sure that's true."

Dad flinches as if I slapped him. His job is to run the network, to regulate the news. Telling him that his own station has lied to him is doubtless as good as a physical slap in the face. Unless he already knows all of this.

"He risked everything to bring me here and prove the DMA lied to me," I say. My jaw twitches as I reflect on all I've been through these past few weeks. "That *Forrest* lied to me."

Dad's face contorts, twisting up in fury as his neck turns crimson. "Forrest knew?"

I can't match his gaze. What am I ashamed of? It wasn't the one who lied to the family.

Ugene sees his opportunity and seizes it. He tells my dad all about what the Directorate has been doing to families, how he saw it all for himself, how people have gone missing. Then he inquires about Elpida Theus.

I try not to give away my guilt, gazing at the floor, and my shoulders pull down as if the guilt is very literally swallowing me into the earth. I don't miss the knowing glance that passes between my parents. What would they think of me if they found out the truth? That I was to blame for Theus's disappearance.

Ugene doesn't imply he notices my sudden tension and guilt. He barrels on as if the DMA will smash down the door any second. The words fly out as he strives to persuade Dad.

"You have the power to bring the truth to light," Ugene says.

Mom clings to Dad, beseeching him with her eyes to at least consider this.

Dad stares back at her, then swings his head. "Even if I wanted to, we can't help you." He gestures to the holotv. "If we don't report you, the Directorate will order our arrests."

Ugene is remarkably calm and sympathetic as he acknowledges Dad's apprehension, spouting off about people being sheep and knowledge being our salvation. Dad can't meet his gaze, and even I can see how responsible he feels over his part in all of this. *He won't agree,* I realize.

Ugene has to present him whatever that kid handed him at the safehouse. It's still tucked into his jacket. That's the reason Ugene wanted to come here, after all.

I take Dad's hand. It's warm against my cold, clammy palm. "Daddy, Ugene helped. Now we need to help him." I nod at Ugene. "Show him, Ugene."

But he falters, and I see his Adam's apple bob. He wanted to come here, to share this with my dad, but now it's as if he doesn't trust Dad. Finally, Ugene's fingers move with distinct apprehension toward his jacket.

Dad tenses.

"Ugene," I hiss.

He grimaces and wrenches the papers from his jacket lining, thrusting them at Dad. "This is why they are after me."

The seconds tick by painfully slow as Dad weighs whether he

should trust Ugene. He takes Ugene in with critical eyes before studying the papers. I have no clue what is in those papers, but I know it's valuable. Important enough that Sho dug through the wreckage of that house to recover as much of it as he could. The anger melts off Dad's face, supplanted by utter shock. What did he just read? I try to peer at the papers, but Dad shields them very subtly from both me and Mom.

"Where did you get this?" Dad asks, breathless—and fearful.

"Dad left it for me."

Mom tenses at mention of Ugene's dad. Why?

"And what am I supposed to do with this?" Dad waves the stack of papers.

Ugene proposes his idea to share the knowledge across the network with everyone, but Dad is convinced it will kill us all. He shoves the papers against Ugene's chest, forcing him to stumble back.

"No. I won't risk my family," Dad says with newfound conviction.

I don't quite get what is going on. All I wanted was to see my parents, to verify they are alive. And they are. But something far more lethal is taking place here. The two launch into a heated debate and Ugene produces a copy drive from his jacket as well.

"This is from Paragon," Ugene says, holding it out insistently toward Dad, who shies away from it like it's a viper. "It shows the experiments they are performing on test subjects. Deadly experiments. Formulas, project notes, test readings. It's all there. Most of the data is encrypted, so I can't unlock it."

The injection doesn't work for everyone, and those who fail are eliminated from the program. Nevermore said this on my first day. Was I one of the experiments?

Dad accepts the drive. "Just like that, huh? You're just handing it over."

"Yes." The conviction once again bolster's Ugene's manner.

"Why?"

Ugene glances at me, and as he speaks he doesn't balk, doesn't blink. His words feel like pure, genuine sincerity. "Because I trust

Bianca, and she trusts you."

I almost laugh as my heart races. He *does* trust me. We must have more of a past than Hound would prefer me to know about. Why else would he trust me so thoroughly? Why else would I feel so tethered to him? How much of Hound's story about Ugene was a fact, and how much is a lie? After seeing what Hound did to that girl, Bri, it's difficult to believe Hound had anything but scorn and vengeance in his soul. Maybe I was just a weapon for him to strike back. He certainly seemed to hate Ugene in the street tonight.

"It's Forrest," Ugene says, drawing me back to the present.

It takes a second for me to grasp what Ugene just said. The researcher who experimented on those test subjects is my brother? The nightmare of being strapped to the table, of the forced injection rushes back, making me dizzy. Did Forrest put that in me?

… Forrest calls for someone. Terry. He aims a gun at me and the look in his eyes is cold. The bullet rips into my chest…

All the air sucks out of the room.

All along, it was my brother. I try packing all my emotions into a void, but it proves more of a challenge than I anticipated. If Ugene has evidence of what my brother has done, I want it out there. I want to know. I want everyone to know.

"I trust Ugene, Dad." And I do. How thoroughly, I can't be sure. But I know with certainty that every instinct in me has told me right from the moment he spoke my name that I should believe him.

Dad's lips thin. "Of course you do."

I flinch. What does that mean?

Dad paces the room, as if standing still will allow the truth to catch up to him. "You've always trusted him. Even when he led you into trouble, you trusted him. But this … Bianca, this will tear our family apart and put all of us in grave danger."

Everyone keeps telling me I know him, but I have no memory of Ugene at all. Nothing I can trust is my own.

I shake my head. "I don't know him."

Dad stops pacing, whirling on his heel to face me. Mom cocks her head. Neither of them understands.

I press on. "He says I do, that we grew up together, but I only met him a day ago. Still, he is the only person who has been honest with me, and who trusted me when—by all rights—he shouldn't have. I owe him the same." How I wish I could recall just a fragment of what others seem to believe I had with Ugene.

Ugene steps forward. "They did something to her, sir. Experiments. I'm not sure the extent of it, but Paragon somehow selectively erased some of her memories—her time in PSECT at Paragon, me—and implanted some false memories, like your deaths."

My parents cling to each other.

I have no reply. By now, all of this is so far over my head, so far from my grasp, that I can't even begin to fathom how to feel or what to say. It just leaves me cold.

"Experiments?" Dad's gaze shifts to me and his forehead creases, shoulders tense.

"I died," I reply coldly, avoiding mention of Forrest shooting me. That is for me to avenge, and no one else. "And Paragon did something to bring me back. They also somehow enhanced my Power to make me their super soldier."

Ugene displays his capacity to recognize the precise time to press his own motives by seizing the hesitation in my parents. He offers them hope that Forrest was corrupted, like me, and works their empathy against them as he correlates the people the Directorate is abusing to brainwashing ... to me. I want to be angry with him for the comparison, but how could I possibly dispute his logic? After all, they have actually washed my brain and twisted me into what they required. A weapon. Just another monster. The terrible notion that the DMA and Directorate are forcing people to into these dangerous experiments, then using them as fodder for their own means only reaffirms my burning desire to tear down the entire system.

Forrest. The Directorate. The Department of Military Affairs. Paragon.

You have more Power than anyone else in Elpis, Forrest told me that day he showed me the false house.

They created me. They gave me these Powers. They developed the very weapon that will tear them down. My hands clench into fists and the intoxicating allure of my Super Strength rushes through my arms.

Dad strides into the kitchen, and Ugene spares me a glance before stuffing his hands deep into his pockets and following.

"Are you okay, Bianca?" Mom asks, placing a hand on my shoulder. I jump.

"Oh my poor girl. What has he done to you?" She pats my cheek, then places her palm on my back. "Come. You need rest. Your room is exactly as you left it."

I don't need rest.

I need vengeance.

But Mom coaxes me toward the stairs. I peer over my shoulder into the kitchen as I let her guide me along. Dad's form is threatening as he leans against the countertop. Ugene stands across the island, his straight back to me. He nods stiffly.

Forrest lied to me. Ugene didn't.

Mom can escort me to my room, but when Ugene leaves, I'm leaving with him. I'm going to impose my own brand of justice, and to help him rip this entire corrupt system to the ground.

Brick by brick.

Part Three

"SOMETIMES, IT'S NECESSARY TO PUSH TO THE limits of what we, as people, are capable of to achieve the greater good. No one can stand in the way of that."

~ Dr. Forrest Pond
Moments Before the Bombing of Paragon Tower

28

THE ROOM SMELLS OF LILACS. THE BED IS NEATLY made, covered in a sage down comforter with pale gray accent pillows and walls that match them, much like my room at the facility. Did Forrest do that on purpose? All the clothes have been washed and put away. After my "death," Mom must have come in here and cleaned. Now, she lingers in the doorway as I enter, watching with her hand bracing the frame.

My desk stands in front of the window. The surface is clean as well. All the pens are in a cup, while papers or notebooks have been tucked away in drawers. Above the desk beside the window, my magnetic whiteboard holds remnants from a life I don't remember anymore: ticket stubs from a Crossfit Tournaments, movie passes, pictures of people I don't recognize—girls and boys all my age, smiling at the camera oblivious to my current ignorance. Including me.

"I didn't have the heart to remove anything," Mom explains as I brush my fingers over a ceramic pot that looks like a child created it. "I wasn't ready to accept what happened."

I sink into the gray desk chair and swivel to face her. "What did happen?"

Mom frowns as if bewildered by the question, then enters the room like she's crossing a sacred threshold. She perches carefully on the edge of my bed, running hands over the comforter. "Forrest said you were in Paragon Tower the night of the accident, that you sacrificed your life to save people trapped in the building."

"You mean the night of the bombing?"

Mom twitches. "Bombing? The report said it was an unexpected explosion resulting from a controlled experiment."

Just another one of Forrest's lies. How deep do they go? I wonder. And just who did he lie to? Mom or me?

After a moment of silence, Mom rises and kisses the top of my head. "I'm so happy to have you back, Bianca. I'll give you a moment."

"Thanks, Mom," I say as she heads out the door.

The silence becomes unbearably deep once her steps recede downstairs. My stomach grumbles, but I ignore its persistence and explore my room. The bottom of the clay pot on my desk has Ugene's name and the year which would have been when we were eleven. The desk drawers only contain ordinary objects: a couple of school notebooks, envelopes, earbuds, an open pack of gum, a makeup pouch, paperclips. I flip through the pages of the notebooks, but they're just notes from classes and doodles. As I drop the notebooks back into the desk drawer, producing a hollow thump noise. I tip my head to the side and notice the drawer is deeper on the outside than the inside.

A hollow drawer? I yank the drawer out of the desk completely and spill it on the desk, then search for a switch or something indicating a hiding place. Nothing. But the back of the drawer isn't attached that firmly. I pop it off, and it gives easily, as if I've done this a hundred times before. I tilt the drawer up so the contents slide out.

A journal thumps against the desktop, along with a Paragon I.D. that has my name and picture, and security clearance of three. *So I did work there.* I flip open the journal, skimming the pages for something helpful. The first half of the journal tells of utterly mundane crap that I can't believe I bothered putting to the page: fights with friends and how they resolved, a downhill progression of my relationship with Jimmy, and more. Ugene's name crops up again and again and often causing tension between me and Jimmy. At first I write about my regrets, how badly I screwed up our friendship and the shame I felt over it. But one passage stands out.

> Something was wrong with Ugene tonight. In all the years I've known him, I've never known him to go walking alone at night. But tonight he had his bag with him. The way he tensed around me, and the way he dismissed what he was really up to makes me wonder what he is doing. He was hiding something.

The next passage is dated the following day, on the last day of school. It tells about my official offer from Paragon to join the security team—a job I was certain Forrest used his influence to get for me—and about Ugene's absence from school the next day. The one day no one would wish to miss. After school, I went to his house to ask his parent's if he was okay. His mom was near tears but wouldn't tell me what happened.

> I don't understand what has happened to him. Marion's reaction was standoffish, and Gavin avoided me altogether, hiding in his office. I hope Ugene is okay.

Clearly, Ugene told me the truth earlier. We were friends, and tight for a time. Why else would I be so concerned about him, or so filled with regret about how I treated him after Testing Day?

Hoping to locate answers about what happened to him, and to me, I flip through the journal. Everyone has lied to me, but these are my own words, in my own hand. The answers in this journal are the only answers I can trust.

Some of what I recorded is boring. However, I do find answers about what happened between Jimmy and me. He bullied Ugene—which is not what Hound had told me at all—but I finally had enough. Then, as I worried about what happened to Ugene, Jimmy became controlling, demanding I leave it alone and forbidding me to search for "that Powerless runt." The duration of time I dealt with Jimmy's crap makes me angry with myself. At least I finally had the good sense to dump him.

In the months leading up to the bombing at Paragon Tower, my journal becomes much darker:

Ugene is a test subject.

Something isn't right about what is going on.

Forrest is at the center of it all, watching Ugene obsessing over his work and how Ugene fits into the puzzle.

Ugene doesn't trust me, and it hurts. If only I could tell him how I really feel.

Somehow, I have to make up for what I've done to him.

Forrest is conducting covert experiments on test subjects. I will help Ugene and the other test subjects escape.

I think someone is following me.

Dr. Cass knows. I don't understand how. She knows about the escape, about Ugene and his friends accessing Forrest's tablet for information. I tried to deceive to her, to tell her I was only working to protect Ugene from himself, but she didn't believe me. She threatened to employ some sort of injection on everyone to get them to tell her the truth. She thinks I'm too close to the subjects. I've been granted leave and discharged from PSECT. How will I help Ugene now?

Something much worse is approaching. Forrest has sealed me out, but the strain in him around my parents these last couple days has been palpable. He snaps at the littlest thing, dodges even casual questions about work. I may have been removed from PSECT, but I still have access to Paragon. If I can't help Ugene directly, I will do it indirectly. Ugene wanted to visit floor 189. I'm going to discover out why.

And if I don't come back, I hope I can at least

help free the others and stop my brother and Dr. Cass before it's too late.

I flip through the journal. But this was the last entry. A photo flutters out from the back of the notebook. Ugene and I, sitting together at a school picnic maybe three or four years ago. His arm is around my shoulders. We look so happy. The pure joy on our faces makes my heart twinge. This girl doesn't exist anymore. I don't even know who I am now.

But I know one thing: Ugene didn't lie to me like everyone else. This journal proves it.

Anger boils in my gut. Forrest stripped away my life and left behind only what he required to achieve his ambitions. Do I hunt him down or help Ugene? Either course could end the same—with Paragon and the DMA failing; with Forrest failing. But only if Ugene succeeds. I can help make sure that happens.

My stomach grumbles. Before I leave the room, I tuck the journal back where I found it and pocket my Paragon I.D., then return the drawer back where it belongs before skipping down the stairs. It might come in handy when I hunt down Forrest.

"Ugene?" I call as I reach the bottom.

No answer.

The living room is unoccupied. The kitchen as well. I tiptoe to Dad's office, but it's empty. I cling to the doorway, digging my nails so hard the woodwork splinters.

My heart plummets. Regardless of what Ugene and I might have been in the past, he just used me like everyone else to get what he wanted. Then he abandoned me.

I don't need him to get my answers. I'll go to Paragon and find them myself.

I return to the kitchen and fetch some protein bars from the pantry to help keep my energy up. It won't be enough—this enhanced Power creates voracious hunger—but it will hopefully get me where I need to go. First, the facility. Then Paragon and Forrest.

As I tear open the back door, Mom's trembling voice jerks me to a standstill.

"You can't go, Bianca. It isn't safe."

She doesn't understand. I want to remain here, in the comfort of my parents' home where I will be safe. But I *need* answers, justice, vengeance. I can't find any of that hiding away in my bedroom.

"Did you hear me?" she asks, stepping deeper into the kitchen and bumps into one of the barstools, incapable of keeping her gaze in one place.

"I did."

"But you will not listen to me."

Nothing I say will reassure her.

The complete devastation makes the crow's feet around her eyes sharper. "Please don't do this. I just got you back."

"I don't know what was done to me," I say. "But Forrest said I am stronger than anyone else in the city. They created me for a purpose."

Mom rushes toward me, taking my arms in her clammy hands.

I draw away.

Mom flinches.

"I love you, Mom. I don't expect you to understand, but this is something I have to do." I rush out the door before she can stop me.

Ugene didn't want my help.

I will handle with Forrest then.

29

LAST TIME I VISITED THE SALAS BOROUGH OF ELPIS, Forrest took me to the house on Dysart. That turned out to be a lie. How well he played the part of the grief-stricken son. All that bitterness and anger toward Forrest mutates into adrenaline I use to sprint across the city, devouring several protein bars to replenish my Strength.

Few people are out so late. It must be near ten or eleven at night. City lights streak past in a blur as I race at top speed through Salas, across the corner of upper Downtown, and into the Concordia borough in the northern part of Elpis. Here, the houses are smaller than Salas. Concordia plays home to the upper middle class. While not as spacious or pristine as the upper class section of town, it is clear that none of these families struggle to get by. Yards are cared for, as are houses. Some have cars in the driveway. The shops here are not as up-scale as one might find downtown or in Salas, but they cater to the residents.

I run past all of this without much of a second glance. Only a few people take notice of me—or at least, I think no more do. It doesn't matter much to me. My target is obvious. I need to find that dark void I spotted from the shuttle. To do that, I have to leave the safety of Elpis behind.

The edge of Elpis comes abruptly. Green lawns stop so suddenly I can literally see the line where the grass dies off into arid, cracked earth. My feet skid on the pavement that comes to a sudden stop. The darkness beyond the city limits is deep, and the moon offers extraordinarily little light. I reach back to braid my hair, but it's already up in a ponytail. My gut churns as if acid eats away at it. Another step, and I'll be outside of Elpis.

No one steps outside of Elpis.

In the distance, shadows loom tall, jagged, imposing. One of those is the facility. The void was about a mile northwest, if I remember correctly.

Yet I can't make my feet move. I'm rooted in place.

Forrest created me for a purpose, I think, attempting to convince myself that this is necessary. "Get a grip, Bianca."

I close my eyes, take a deep breath, and let it out slowly to center myself. Before I can change my mind, I dash across the Deadlands, away from Elpis. Away from the facility.

Sprinting at full speed in the darkness of night is dangerous. More than once, I have to launch myself over a sudden obstacle in my path. Broken statues. Fallen streetlamps. Rusting abandoned vehicles. The longer I run, the more uncertain I am that I'm headed the right direction. Without a light to guide me, I will never find what I'm looking for.

After a couple of miles, I stop and scan the horizon for any clue where I should go.

A star streaks across the sky, beautiful beyond the lights of the city. So many stars!

Another star streaks across the sky, along the same path. My back stiffens. *What?*

Then another.

And another.

All of them follow the exact same path. Is that normal?

Curiosity compels me onward, headed in the direction of the repeating falling stars. I jog, afraid of stumbling over something in my path as I follow the direction.

Suddenly, the stars stop falling. I glance down at the ground, only to find my feet on the edge of a massive ditch. It stretches as far as I can see east and west and is much deeper than I expected. The downward slope is steep, but nothing I can't scale.

Leaning back, I crab-crawl down the slope, then immediately gag at the sickly sweet stench of rot, urine, and feces. My boot brushes something stiff and I yelp, slapping a hand over my mouth as I climb to my feet.

Hundreds of bodies.

Maybe even thousands.

No one would ever discover this ditch, this pit of death, so far from Elpis. Faint moonlight peeks out from behind a cloud and casts an eerie glow on the bloated face of Elpida Theus. I tremble and whimper as my nostrils flare. I wish they wouldn't! It only enhances the stench of death around me. Tears burn my eyes. My legs grow weak and I fear I might collapse on the stack of dead bodies.

The DMA killed her. When I turned her over with my team, Theus was alive and relatively unharmed. My heart hammers against my ribs.

I stumble a few steps along the ditch, then freeze as I spot a familiar face.

Vortex.

They just dumped her body here! Did she not have family or friends? Does no one care what happened to her? *I have to get out of here.*

Before turning to climb back up the wall of the ditch, I scan the bodies. So many! And all in various stages of decomposition. The ditch is long and wide as well—a good twenty feet across. One girl catches my eye. She can't be much older than me, if she is at all. Her brilliant red hair covers part of her face, blown around by the wind. She's been here for weeks. Something about her feels familiar and makes my stomach retch. I gag in a lame attempt at swallowing down the vomit.

Turning away, I squeeze my eyes shut, but the girls' dead eyes still stare at me. A girl's voice surfaces from my memories: *My name is Polygraph. They are lying to you.*

The note remains safely tucked away in my jacket.

I scramble back up the edge of the ditch and gaze at the distant lights of Elpis shining in the night. Who would do such a thing? And why? This can't all be Forrest's work.

Somewhere to my east is the facility. If I squint, I think I can make it out even in the dark. My muscles tense and strain against the fabric of my jacket, making the leather creak. I flex my hands into fists at my sides, then glare toward the city. The Directorate did this. Paragon did this. The DMA did this … Forrest did this.

They will all pay.

Intoxicating power pumps through my veins as I race toward the facility.

The DMA facility rests on a patch of arid ground near the northern edge of Elpis. The building is a two-story complex that appears completely abandoned on the outside. But I know better. The boarded-up windows and dilapidated state of the garage doors don't fool me.

First, I circle the building, seeking a good entry point. Going straight in through the docking bay could be catastrophic alone. Who knows how many troopers are inside?

Near the northeast corner of the building, a rusted steel door remains firmly closed. I can't tell what's on the other side, but it's far enough from the docking bay that hopefully I won't be walking into a mess of DMA officers. I test the door, and it doesn't budge from the frame. The door isn't stuck by age and disuse. A scanner beside the door is almost invisible in the dark, but clearly meant for a keycard of some sort. I fumble out my keycard and try it, but the lock remains firmly shut.

Fine. I'll force it open.

There's no quiet way to go about breaking in. All I can hope is that no one will be around at this time of night.

Mustering all my Enhanced Strength, I throw my weight against the door. The frame breaks inward easily enough.

The inside of the facility is lit only with dim security lights. The overhead lights are off, confirming my suspicion that no one is around right now. Ahead of me, a long hallway of offices stretches toward a double door at the far end of the hall. I've been here before. The briefing room is near the end of the hall. I don't bother closing the broken door behind me and shuffle as quietly as possible along the windowed offices, peering into each to confirm they are empty before continuing.

I don't even know what I'm looking for here. Proof of what they did to me, or what they did to all those bodies in the ditch. Someone to punish for these crimes. Evidence that might redeem my brother, if that's even possible. It's hard to accept that he would do all of this without something dangling over his head. Forrest can't be that bad, can he?

He broke my arm, I think bitterly.

As I reach the office at the end of the hall, I spot his name on a door. Dr. Forrest Pond. I turn the knob. The lock breaks, unable to resist my strength.

The office is very orderly. No files remain in the open. The shelves are all free of dust, and the binders and books along the shelf are all organized precisely. I resist the petulant urge to rip everything off the shelves and throw it on the floor.

A holodisk shimmers with hibernating light on a side table next to the lounge chair.

A single potted plant rests in the corner of the office. I don't know enough about plants to identify it—except that it isn't a tree or flower. A fern maybe? I edge closer to it and discover a message inscribed on the edge of the pot. *Fern-ever growing toward a brighter future – Willow*

I blink. It can't be the same Willow. Can it? She said she knew Forrest before all of this.

The desk is empty, except for a computer. I ease into his desk chair and turn the computer on. It immediately prompts me for a password. What would he use as a password?

I type in Dysart1254—the house number he took me to. Nope.

Cante4893. Negative. One more try, and the system will lock me out if I get it wrong, which will probably alert Forrest to the problem.

The holodisk activates and I nearly jump out of my skin as Ugene's voice shatters the silence of the office. "For anyone who doesn't know, my name is Ugene Powers."

I press a hand against my racing heart and take a few breaths, turning to the device as Ugene continues.

"The Directorate has said a lot about the Protectorate radicals, and about me. That I am a tyrant, a liar, an extremist determined to destroy this city. But I'm here to tell you the truth. The Directorate has lied to you."

I snort and roll my eyes. *Get in line.*

He leans forward on the desk, pressing his forearms against it. Ugene seems uneasy, but as he continues to speak, his confidence gains stride. He explains who he is, what happened to him and his friends at Paragon, how he watched them kill. A chill runs down my spine. I was part of the problem. I brought in Theus and so many others whose bodies are probably in that ditch. I didn't have the heart to check for all the citizens I arrested.

Ugene carries on, telling the world about the Protectorate, how the DMA has ripped apart families and shot people in the street. *Did my work fuel this action? God help me, what have I been a part of? Can I ever make up for it?* I have to believe it's possible. I can't really be a monster created for the Directorate's own means. I have to be something more.

Beside Ugene's image, a video plays of the DMA attacking citizens in Pax, in broad daylight, of children getting ripped away from their parents. I brush away my tears and firm my jaw.

"But we are not weak," Ugene continues. "I call on all of you to take a stand with us, to show the Directorate and Paragon that our Powers can be combined into a source of strength. This is how we survive. United."

I clench my fists.

"This battle will not be won with a few of the strong holding against the tide of tyranny, but with fists raised in unity to build an indestructible wall against the tide, forcing it away from our shores. Let's stand together and show the Directorate that all lives matter. That we will not back down. We will not hide."

No, I think. *I'm done hiding.*

Maybe Ugene used me to get this chance to spread his message, but I can no longer be angry with him about it. The people needed the truth. They deserved it.

"I'm not asking you to believe my words as truth," he says. "I'm asking you to believe your eyes and see what's right in front of you. No matter what you choose to do, I will continue forward with confidence that my path will lead to liberation for everyone. Tomorrow, we fight for that right outside the Administration Building. I vow never to stop until Elpis achieves freedom. I fight for equality. I fight for balance. And I hope I survive to see it become a reality. But if I don't see another sunset in exchange for that freedom, I welcome my fate. For you."

Ugene vanishes. In his place, the holodisk reveals a message:

Share your story on social media. Tag photos & videos #DirectorateLies.

Below the message, a box appears with each of the social feeds. In just a few seconds, the first picture pops up. A girl on the curb, pressing a blood-soaked cloth to her head as DMA troopers linger in the smoky street background.

I glance back at the fern again, then try one last password: Fernever23

The box closes and the screen changes to a normal desktop background.

So Forrest did care about something, I think as I click on the files and search for my name. Nothing comes up under Bianca, but when I type in Steel, I get well over 100 results. It takes a while for the first video to load, and as I wait, I glance at the holodisk again. #DirectorateLies is trending, with images and videos rolling past. Men, women, and children at all ages beaten, abducted in broad daylight. Troopers destroying homes.

And in one video, my team capturing a target we were told was another radical. Nevermore places his hand on the woman's head and she shrieks, then collapses the ground in a heap. I didn't think twice about this before, but watching it now, my stomach churns.

What did we do?

What was I part of?

"Bianca Pond," Forrest's voice draws my attention to the computer screen as the video begins.

I'm lying on a metal table in a room that looks like a morgue. My lifeless eyes are turned toward the ceiling, and blood soaks my clothing.

His voice is thick with grief as he continues. "Attempt number one." He steps toward my body and places hands against my stomach. Sweat rolls down his forehead. His arms shake. After a minute of this, he collapses to the floor.

What is he doing to me?

The video cuts to another attempt, and another, and another. Forrest works on my dead body with fevered despair. At last, after dozens of attempts using his own Power, the video shows someone else in the room. A guy with sunken eyes in gray scrubs. He places his hands on me and I can't tell what he is doing, but I can guess it's healing. He sags, his shoulders slump, and he appears ready to give up when Forrest puts his hand on the guy's head, pumping his own Power through the guy to give him the strength to continue.

I fast forward nearly five minutes, stopping when the guy collapses to the floor, just as Forrest did repeatedly. I hold my breath, watching for some sign of movement, but there's nothing. The guy just lays there.

Forrest nudges him with the toe of his dress shoes and frowns. "Subject spent," he says almost sadly. Forrest then inspects my stomach, using a wet cloth to wipe over the bloody skin.

But the wound that caused the bleeding is gone.

I fast forward again, watching as Forrest and his small team of assistants work on me, injecting my body with drugs I can't identify. Tears shimmer in my eyes, blurring my vision as I watch Forrest's growing frustration—and fear. He thinks he is saving me!

After yet another injection, my dead body gasps in a deep breath and everyone in the room stumbles back, pressing against walls and bumping into equipment.

I press my hand over my mouth. He did it. Forrest resurrected me from the dead.

"Ugene!" I scream the name in the video.

Before I can move, though, Forrest is sticking another needle in my arm. My head lolls to the side and my eyes close. He just knocked me out.

Forrest sets down the syringe and smiles at the camera like a man who just conquered death.

Because he did.

My stomach churns. I want to run away from here, but I am compelled to continue working through the videos.

Forrest injects me with the blue serum.

My former self tires breaking out of the room, screams for Ugene as if he can save me, then starts breaking bones and crushing skulls as orderlies attempt restraining me.

Forrest aims a gun at my back, presses his finger to the trigger, and sags, turning his head away as one of his assistants shoots me. They haul my dead body onto the table and start over again. Injections. Healing. Sedatives.

In another video, Nevermore enters and places his hands against my temples as I lay unconscious.

In another, the tests I remember after first waking in that doorless cell.

The more I watch, the deeper my contempt becomes. I can't watch any more. There must be some way to get my memories back. There must be some way to become the girl I was before.

But do I want to?

The Bianca I have learned about in the last few hours was weak despite her Strength. All of her strength came from others, and she allowed people to abuse her for so long. People like Forrest. Like Jimmy.

I can't be that weak-willed girl anymore.

Angry, I click through the social feeds and begin uploading some of the videos.

30

THE WHISPER OF SHUFFLING FEET ALONG THE hallway draws my attention. I turn off the computer and rush to the door, pressing my back to the wall. Whoever is coming, they are in for a surprise.

"Let's just get what we came for and get out of here," Levi says as he passes the office windows.

Sparky follows close behind Levi. Both of them are agents from Unit 14. Did they come for me? Does Forrest know I'm here? They pause outside Forrest's office listening and my breath catches. Can they sense me nearby? I struggle to recall what their Powers are. Why am I so terrible at remembering things?

"We are clearing the block right now," Levi says to no one.

Communication devices. Or Telepathy. I can't be sure, but I am certain Levi speaks to someone somewhere else.

All they have to do is turn and look through the open door to see me pressed against the wall. My hiding place is far from perfect. If they spot me first, I lose the element of surprise. What will they do if they see me? I have no doubt Forrest probably wants me back, maybe to control me again. I can't let that happen. I won't be controlled or influenced by anyone else ever again.

"Copy," Levi says, then motions to Sparky forward.

Their boots shift in my direction. There's no time to think. I burst out of the office, throwing my fist into Sparky's face before slamming my shoulder into Levi's ribs. Sparky slumps to the floor in a heap as my weight carries me and Levi through the wall of the office across the hall. Tempered glass from the windows along the wall shatters into a million pieces. I land in a couch on top of Levi and throw my fist with controlled strength at his head. I mean to knock him out, not crush his skull.

But my fist slams against some invisible force, stopping so suddenly the shock of it ripples up into my shoulder and causes searing pain. No matter how hard I push, I can't move more than a fraction at a time. Sweat rolls down Levi's temples and into his dark hair.

My body lifts off the ground, off of Levi, and floats helplessly in the air. He rolls to his feet and spits blood on the floor, then scowls at me.

"What the hell, Steele? Forrest is looking everywhere for you."

Sparky stumbles into the room, and I can see the dazed glaze over his eyes. My punch stunned him, perhaps even left him with a concussion.

"Good. Tell me where he is and I'll go right to him," I snap, tugging fruitlessly at whatever invisible force is holding me.

"Levi, we should call her in," Sparky says, his words slightly slurred.

Somehow, I have to break out of Levi's Psionic Levitation.

If you depend on your fists in the field, you won't last long, Nevermore told me this on my first day. If I want these two to work with me and let me down, I have to make them believe I mean no harm. How do I do that after I just tried punching them both out?

"I'm was here looking for Dr. Pond," I say. Struggling against Levi's hold will do me little good to convince them. "Why do you think I was in his office?"

Sparky glances across the hall as if to confirm.

"Tell me where he is and I'll go right to him," I say again.

Both of them hesitate.

"We know what he did to Poly," Levi says, glancing past me at his partner.

Sparky tenses and sparks fire from a nearby outlet.

"Calm down, Sparky," Levi says. "Don't start another electrical fire."

Poly. They knew Poly.

"She tried to warn me," I say, praying my hunch is right and these two are bitter about what happened to her. "If you let me down, I can prove it."

"Let me burn her," Sparky says, glaring at me as his fists clench and unclench at his sides. The sparks from the outlet coalesce around him. He's gathering his Power.

He really means to burn me alive! "Wait!"

Levi edges toward Sparky, keeping his gaze fixed firmly on me. If he breaks visual contact, does that break his concentration?

"I don't know why you are here, in the Special Forces, but my guess is it's a lie and you suspect it, but you don't remember why," I say, praying I'm right. Vortex admitted that not everyone retains their memories. "I can show you. Forrest recorded all of it. It's on his computer in the office." I nudge my head across the hall.

"No one knows his password," Levi says. Did they already try that?

"I do."

Levi wets his lips as he considered my offer. He taps his fingers against his leg. "What if we trust you and you fight back again?"

"Levi, no!" Sparky's Power grows in brightness, like a hundred fireflies zipping around him. His fingers twitch.

"Then Sparky can burn me, just like he wants," I say. "Please. Just a chance to prove it to you."

I'm playing a dangerous game here. I can run fast, but a powerful Psionic will still easily catch me, and I have no idea if I'm fast enough to outrun whatever Sparky is doing.

"Fine." Levi waves a hand.

My boots thump hard enough against the floor to crack the tiles. Sparky doesn't release his Electromancy Power as he trails along behind me, leaving Levi at the back as we make our way into Forrest's office. Sparky continues lingering close by, and the static charge of his Electromancy worries me.

"Can you step back so you don't fry the computer?" I say sharply.

"I have control."

"Sparky." Levi stands at my shoulder, arms crossed and stance wide. Just by the way he stands I can see he is a skilled fighter even if he isn't Somatic, not that he would be able to hold up against me in a fist fight.

Sparky grumbles and shuffles back.

I type in the password again and search for Poly. Nothing.

"Try Polygraph," Sparky says.

I type it in, and a file with several videos pops up. Just as I'm about to click the first one, Sparky stops me.

"Show me that one." He points at one of the files.

Levi frowns and leans closer. "That's the day she died."

I click the video.

An apartment fills the computer screen. Not just any apartment. That's my apartment! Forrest was watching me all along? How much did he see?

A girl with brilliant red hair in smooth layers enters the room, and she's terrified of something. The door opens and Forrest enters with a handful of troopers. Poly runs to her room, but some Power stops her in her tracks. The troopers surround her, pinning her in place.

Forrest stalks toward her, tapping on his tablet. "You put our entire operation in jeopardy, Poly. Did you think we wouldn't find out?"

Poly whimpers and sags. Troopers seize her arms.

"I fought for you," Forrest continues, speaking as if this is a casual conversation and not a threat. "But General Sims, Dr. Cass, and the Directorate insisted I give you this before your mission."

Then she raises her chin in defiance and spits at Forrest.

"That's my girl," Sparky mutters behind me.

"She deserves to know what you're doing to her," Poly says, a tremble in her voice.

Forrest remains composed as he removes a syringe from his pocket. Poly struggles against the men holding her.

Forrest jabs the needle into her arm and depresses the plunger. She slumps.

Sparky growls behind me as the video ends.

Why would Forrest keep a video that's so damning?

Levi reaches past me and clicks on the final video.

Poly is in a plain room, lying on a metal table and held in place by straps. Tungsten straps. My gut churns. Oh god, what is about to happen to her?

Her head lolls to the side, and it takes a moment to recognize she is watching someone off the camera.

"I'm beginning to think you've failed tonight on purpose, Polygraph," Forrest says from behind the camera. "I am tempted to call in Nevermore, but something tells me you have left yourself a trail of breadcrumbs to follow should we try wiping your memory."

Poly's voice weak and distant. "What you are doing to your sister isn't right."

"I am saving her from herself!" Forrest snaps.

Sparky shifts behind me. "That son of a—"

"Get a hold of yourself, Sparky," Levi warns.

I glance back and see the fury of his emotions making his Electromancy brighter.

"Turn it off," Levi says.

"No!" Sparky places a searing hot hand on my shoulder. The hair on my arms rises.

"Your time in our program has, unfortunately, come to an end," Forrest says.

An assistant in white surgical papper suit enters the frame, holding a syringe. She injects the needle and depresses the plunger into Poly's arm.

"You have breached your contract. Dr. Cass and the Directorate cannot permit you to put the rest of the program at risk," Forrest says. "Paragon and the Directorate thank you for your service."

My blood runs cold as Poly's angry, defiant eyes dull. I close the video before Sparky can see the light leave her eyes.

"He killed her because she stood up to him," Sparky says, fury burning in his voice. "Because she tried to help you!"

I jump up and edge around the desk before he touches me. "Hang on. I had no idea what was going on. Poly left me a note, but I don't even remember her."

Tears well in Sparky's eyes. "I do."

"Then help me."

Levi has taken my place in the chair and is watching something on the screen. His gaze flicks up to me after a minute. What did he just watch?

Sparky rounds the desk, stalking toward me. "Dr. Pond doesn't have much of a heart, but there is one thing he cares about. And I will rip it away from him."

I don't have to ask. He means me.

"It won't matter. He will just bring me back."

"Not if there's nothing to bring back."

"Stop!" Levi stands, seizing Sparky with his Levitation and hoisting him away from me. "Sparky, we need her."

"Like hell! Let me go."

"Think about it," Levi says, closing the computer and rounding the desk. "He has manipulated her, too. But she is his weakness. We can use that to get to him directly."

Just another person who wants to use me. I'm getting sick of it, but I need them on my side, so I nod. "Forrest's door will always open for me. What he has done is monstrous, but he has created a monster to assure his own destruction. Help me find him, and I will help you reach him."

The sparks around Sparky swirl and merge into one brilliant ball of electric Power. "Fine." He throws the ball at the computer and it explodes in a shower of sparks and flames that quickly spread. "Let's go."

Levi releases his hold on Sparky and the three of us leave the office and head toward the door I used to enter the building. Along the way, Sparky holds his hands toward the floor, fingers splayed out. Sparks fly and catch from electrical wires in the walls as we pass. By the time we reach the door at the end of the hallway, everything is on fire.

We slip out into the darkness. I don't trust these two, but I understand their thirst for revenge.

Another hour has passed since I entered the building. It's well past midnight as we make our way toward Elpis on foot. I could run, but these two could never keep up.

Once we reach a safe distance from the facility, the two of them stop and turn back. My heart jumps into my throat. Are they going to go back after all of this?

Levi kneels on the packed dirt ground, and his arms shake violently as he sluggishly raises them. The ground rumbles, cracks, breaks apart. Then the facility rises out of the ground. Sweat pours in buckets down Levi's face, but he doesn't move to wipe it away. All of his attention is on the facility as he raises the top levels several feet in the air. It's amazing to witness such Power.

Sparky's energy buzzes, and in the distance, the facility floats several feet in the air like a massive ball of electric fire. It explodes, shattering windows and breaking down walls. Levi releases his hold and falls to his hands and knees, sucking in deep breaths.

The facility hammers against the ground. The force of impact and fire within creates an explosion that produces a mushroom cloud high into the night sky.

"Way to send up a warning flare," I mutter.

Like no one will notice.

Though I can understand why they would do this. Taking out that facility removes a significant portion of the threat the DMA and Directorate pose. All they have left are the troopers already in the city.

And with any luck, no more agents.

31

SPARKY FALLS INTO SULLEN SILENCE AS THE THREE OF us make our way toward Paragon Tower. It's apparent that he cared deeply for Poly. Levi doesn't have to bother explaining, though he tries, keeping his voice down as Sparky leads the way. Levi tells me about how Poly was placed with me for some reason she wouldn't share with anyone else because she was afraid of what would happen if she said something. They know that Nevermore was part of it. A few times, Sparky would twist into fits of jealousy, thinking that Poly and Nevermore had something going on, though Levi never believed it.

On their last mission as a full team, they went after a target, Elpida Theus. She turned Poly and Touche against each other. Touche used his Enhanced Touch on Poly; he could read anything though Touch and expose the truth—sometimes to devastating psychological effect. It crippled Poly mentally. With Theus Influencing them, when Touche realized Poly had turned against the DMA to help me, the two of them broke into a fight. By the time Levi and Sparky arrived and intervened, she was already gravely injured and unconscious. Sparky lost it and torched Touche on the spot. Meanwhile, Theus escaped. Levi had to lie and cover for Sparky to avoid losing his entire team in one day.

"We thought Poly would just be healed and everything would be fine, but she never came back, and they told us her injuries killed her before she could be healed," Levi says, watching Sparky's slumped form with deep sadness. Neither of them believed what they were told.

All of this only affirms what I already sense deep in my bones. Dr. Cass and Forrest are at the root of this, and I will rip them from the ground, stem and root.

"Change is coming," I say with unexpected confidence, hoping my determination to end this will bolster him.

"You mean the radical, Ugene Powers?" Levi shakes his head.

I blink. That isn't what I meant.

Levi continues, unaware of my surprise. "We got a report just before finding you in the office. The Directorate has him. There's no changing this, but if we can get our hands on Dr. Pond …"

My mouth goes dry. "Where is Ugene?"

Levi shrugs. "They won't tell us, but they said that something is happening at Paragon Tower. They've called all units to the tower and the Administration Building."

Ugene must be in one of them.

"Then we find him at one of them and get him out," I say with certainty.

"Why do you care what happens to him?" Levi asks.

"I don't." That isn't entirely true. I do care, but I can't fully admit it to the world. My silence has no logical explanation. "But my brother is obsessed with Ugene. Wherever Ugene is, my brother won't be far."

Forrest has a lot to account for. My death and resurrection. My lost memories. Poly and all the countless others in the ditch. How many of them did he kill himself? How many were accidents? Were any of them?

Even at a brisk pace, we take a couple hours to walk all the way to Paragon Tower. Once we are within a couple blocks, and the twisting monolith reaches high above us, the density of security has also increased. With fewer alleys to slip through to get from one block to the next, we have to take a more tactical approach. DMA shuttles have blocked off all roads within a one-block radius of the tower itself, and lines of troopers wait mindlessly with weapons and Powers ready.

"I can light it up," Sparky says, nodding toward the nearest DMA shuttle as we crouch behind a parked vehicle. "Then Levi can lob it at their lines."

When Ugene and I made our way through Elpis earlier in the night, he advised caution. *"If we attack, the DMA will figure out where we are. We can't leave a trace."*

I shake my head and place a hand gently on Sparky's forearm. "We can't leave a trace of our passing or we risk exposure."

"*Or* it draws Dr. Pond right where we want him," Sparky counters.

I shake my head more firmly. "No. We want to be on our terms, not his." Besides, if Forrest comes to us, I won't find Ugene. I can tell them he doesn't matter all I want, but he does. What might Forrest, Paragon, the DMA do to him if they keep him in custody long enough?

"Okay, then how do we get in?" Sparky asks.

We fall silent, watching the firm lines and occasional flow of troopers from a nearby building. They only move in groups of two or three.

Levi notices as well, because he nods toward the narrow alley beside the building. "We wait there for one of the smaller groups and I can use my Power to pull them into the alley."

"And we can take their helmets and vests," I say, nodding in agreement. The rest of our clothing is similar to their stiffer uniforms. The vests will make us look more official, as will the helmets—and they will also mask our identity from anyone who might recognize us on sight.

Sparky sighs in disappointment. He must have really wanted to throw a spark shuttle at them.

We wait for an opening, then rush into the mouth of the alley. Only Levi can see out. I wait behind him to knock the troopers out the second they enter the alley. A few minutes later, a trio of troopers drag along the ground toward the alley with Telekinetic power. One of them squeals. Before I pounce, Sparky zaps him in the neck. The man falls deadly quiet and his head sags to the side. A second man pulls his gun and aims at Sparky. I dive at him, breaking his wrist. He screams. I rip off the helmet so it isn't damaged and the Power of my Strength ripples along my arm as I draw back to punch him.

No more killing, Ugene pleaded.

With a grimace, I only hit the man hard enough to knock him out. As I look up, Sparky and Levi have taken care of the third man as well. We bind them all and don their vests and helmets.

"We need to hide them in case anyone else wanders past," Levi says.

I nod, easily hefting one on each shoulder and strolling toward the dumpster, lobbing both limp bodies in. As I return for the third, both Levi and Sparky blink at me, holding their helmets in their hands. I try not to notice as I hoist the third guy and toss him in with his companions.

"They didn't weigh anything to you, did they?" Sparky asks.

I shake my head and check the helmet visor, then adjust the strap. "Helmet up. Let's move."

We exit the alley and encounter another trio headed our direction. My muscles automatically tense for action. If a fight breaks out now, we are seriously outnumbered. All the troopers along the road will see it. Dozens, if not hundreds. Even with our enhanced Powers we can't overpower them all.

"Everything okay?" one man asks. "We thought we heard a shout."

"We heard a disturbance in the alley and went to check it," Levi blurts.

"It was a bunch of rats," I say, then thumb toward Sparky. "Turns out he's terrified of them."

They chuckle and I can feel the energy buzzing from Sparky, but they accept the lie and head back toward the line. We follow on their heels.

The level of security around Paragon Tower is ridiculous. There must be at least a hundred troopers just on this side of the block in lines and marching in patrols. The three of us march in unison toward the wide stairs leading up to the doors of Paragon. My security badge is still in my pocket, and I wonder if it still works. Could it get us where we need to be, or would it just alert Forrest or whoever is watching that we are here? *Maybe that's what we want.*

A group of troopers at the door stops us and scans our vests with a blue-light device, right over the names. Are they genetically coded vests? For our sake, I hope not. As the trooper with the device attempts reading it, the device sparks, then smokes. He smacks it as if that will fix the problem.

"Where are you headed?" he asks at last, giving up on the device.

"Special detail to check in on floor 189," I say. It's the only thing I can remember, thanks to my journal. I have no idea if the lie will work.

They confer for a moment, then wave us through the doors.

The lobby of Paragon Tower is brightly lit for so late at night— or early in the morning; I can't be sure of the time except that it's dark. The ceiling rises through the center of the building five stories, topped by a star-filled illusion of a sky. Glass panel railings line each level. Pristine whites and deep blacks make the slashes of red, blue, yellow, and green stand out in striking contrast. Everything is perfect and clean.

We head toward the far end of the lobby where the employee pass stations bar entrance deeper into the building. Levi pivots to the main lobby elevators, away from the pass stations, but I know that we can't go higher than these five floors without going to the elevators beyond the pass stations.

I freeze near the elevators, unsure what roots me to the spot. Is someone using their Power on me? I glance at Levi and Sparky, who are both turned toward me, waiting. No doubt they are wondering why I don't follow. I can't explain it. Sudden terror grips my chest. A familiarity as if I've been in this exact spot before.

… The cold marble tiles press into my back through my clothing. Derrek

looms over me, a gun pointed at my chest, his face a blank mask devoid of emotion. This is the end. The bullet punches into my gut …

"Steele," Levi hisses. "You're drawing attention."

"This is where it happened," I breathe. "This is where I died."

The two exchange a glance I can't see behind their visors, then Levi steps up beside me and nudges me toward the elevators. "We have to move. Others are watching."

It takes more strength than I have to move my feet one shuffling step at a time. I died right here, in this lobby, yet there is no trace of my passing. It may as well have not happened at all. The elevator doors close in front of us, and a video plays above the number pad immediately.

A video of Directorate Chief Seaduss's strong, confident composure and massive build.

"The city of Elpis has reached a crossroads," Seaduss says. "While Paragon and the Directorate work together to build a better, stronger future of all, radical leader, Ugene Powers, in his jealousy, would oppose us, hijacking our network to spread his message of hate. He attacked your city and filled your heads with lies. He planted the seeds of doubt—a doubt which could destroy what remains of humanity. A doubt which could destroy everything we have build and everything we continue to work for." He leans close to the camera. "My fellow survivors, I implore you. Do not let him win."

A feverish desperation burns in his sharp eyes.

Sparky grunts in disgust and a second later the video display smokes.

"Stop doing that or they will know it's us," Levi says.

"I never liked him," Sparky says. "My parents told me he's little more than a brute with political support."

"Like me?" I snap, not meaning to lose my temper, but the parallel makes me uncomfortable. What more am I that Seaduss is not? A super Somatic with the political backing of the DMA and Paragon—not to mention my brother.

"Time will tell," Spark says with a casual shrug. He still hasn't decided if he should trust me or not. A fair assessment.

The elevator stops on the fifth floor, but before the doors can open, it lurches into motion again, headed upward. Levi's focus is fixed on the ceiling. The gears on the elevator groan in protest, but he is using his Power to lift the entire carriage up the elevator shaft.

"When we stop, you will have to get us out," Levi says through gritted teeth. "The elevator will fall as soon as I let go, but the brakes will catch it before it hits the ground."

I nod.

When the elevator stops, I use my fingertips to pry the doors open. But on the other side is only a solid wall. This elevator was not meant to rise so high. How far up are we, anyway?

"Hurry," Levi growls.

Unsure what he expects me to do, I punch the wall over and over again, creating a hole and likely calling attention to our location.

The moment the plaster and drywall break out into the room on the other side, Sparky slips through. I hold the elevator doors. Levi slips out, and the second he does, the elevator falls. I have only a split second to swing myself into the hole in the wall before the elevator would have crushed my legs.

Breathing hard, I lay on the floor of the office we escaped through, thankful for my luck.

"That was close," Sparky says, and I can hear the thrill of excitement in his tone.

I roll over and hop to my feet. "You could have warned me before letting go."

"I did," Levi says flatly, marching toward the closed office door. He peers out into the hallway and waves us forward. "I don't see anyone. Looks like we are on the sixth floor. From here, we should be able to hitch a ride to your brother's lab. Where might that be?"

I shake my head. They think I know what we're doing? I thought they had a plan here! "I don't know."

"What's on floor 189?" Levi asks.

"I don't know."

"Well, what do you know?" Sparky snaps.

"They have four floors of test subjects."

Levi shifts. "Where?"

Again, I blank.

"She's useless," Sparky grumbles. He stalks into the hallway, headed toward the elevators.

Levi sighs and follows, leaving me to jog to catch up—which I do easily enough.

"They really did a number on you, didn't they?" Levi asks.

"I guess." I rub my neck and pull my hair over my shoulder. "I'm remembering more now, but it's still just pieces, and nothing about my time here at Paragon or anything in connection to how I knew Ugene before."

"Wait, you knew him?" Levi asks, almost in awe.

"Well, according to him, yes. We were friends."

"According to … when did you see him?"

I tell them about what happened. How I convinced Forrest to bring me along on that all hands on deck mission to capture Ugene. How Ugene and his friends captured me instead, and what I've learned since about myself and my past with him.

"I don't really remember anything about him though," I say.

We wait for an elevator that can take us to the upper floors of the tower, and Levi pulls off the helmet and eyes me curiously. "That's all your brother, you know. Whatever he did to you, I would say it's a safe bet that he couldn't let you remember the one person the Directorate wants to capture more than anyone else."

I shrug. "Well, he got his way."

Forrest deleted Ugene from my memory completely. I wish I could remember something. Clearly I cared about him and trusted him before, judging by what my journal told me, but when I try to remember anything for myself, it's like hitting an unbreakable wall. Somehow, I know that memories are there, but I just can't reach them.

The elevator doors slide open. At this hour, only DMA troopers lurk around the building, with maybe a handful of others. Not enough for us to worry about being caught easily. According to the clock in that office, it won't be long before employees show up for work. Maybe an hour.

"Let's go," I say, brushing past both of them into the elevator.

32

SOMEWHERE ON THESE UPPER FLOORS, ALL OF
Paragon's dirty secrets must be just sitting on shelves or servers. I
have no idea what we are looking for as we clear another floor, only
taking down a couple patrols of lower-ranked troopers. Levi seems
to have some specific purpose that he isn't sharing with the class,
and Sparky is more than happy to destroy anything he can along
the way.

"We are running out of time before people come for the
workday," I say as we climb into the elevator.

"What do you suggest?" Levi asks.

"We came here to find Forrest," I say. "So let's draw him out."

"How?" Sparky asks.

"Choose our ground, cause a commotion, let him know
I'm here," I say. "And I know exactly where we can best gain his
attention."

"Where?" Levi asks.

I pass my fingers over the keypad and press numbers 9-9. I
don't know why that stands out to me, but the elevator lurches into
motion.

Something significant is on the ninety-ninth floor. Sparky and
Levi sense it as well, because they tense, prepared to strike out with
their Powers once the doors slide open.

I stride out into the long hallway. Heavily reinforced doors line
either side. We edge along to one of the open doors and Levi is the
first to step through.

"Welcome, Agent Levitator," a soothing female voice says. Her voice emanates from all around the chamber.

Levi nearly jumps out of his skin, thrusting a palm up. The door begins swinging shut, driving me and Sparky into the room before it's too late.

"Welcome Agent Sparks," she says. "Welcome Agent Steele."

"What the—" Sparky mutters.

"Initiating gateway," she says.

The three of us clump together as one wall becomes opalescent, shifting like oil through water before revealing another room with a closed door. All of this is familiar to me, and I tiptoe toward the opening.

Levi seizes my wrist. "Wait. What is going on? We don't know where that leads."

"Gateway to floor 101 open for simulation," the female voice says.

"I've done this before," I say, though I don't know how I'm so certain. I don't remember any of it. I lick my lips. "Initiate sparring sequence."

"Access denied, Agent Steele."

"Have you, now?" Levi teases.

"What do we have access to?" Sparky asks. "It must be something if we can get this far."

"Agent Sparks is authorized to initiate Project Termination Protocol."

"Let's do that then," Sparky says. "Sounds promising."

"No!" I hold out a hand as if that will stop this computer from executing the command. "We have no idea what this protocol is. What if it kills us?"

"Initiating …"

Levi groans. "Way to think things through, Sparkles."

"Shut up."

The door on the other side of the gateway swings wide. My heart hammers in my throat, strong and quick.

Sparky darts through the gateway before either of us can stop him. "Computer, what is the Project Termination Protocol?" he asks as he creeps toward the open door.

"Complete electronic shutdown of the Paragon testing facility," she says as we follow Sparky.

"Not so bad," he comments.

"Including termination of subjects via coordinated link between my command systems and Agent Sparks's Electromagnetic meltdown Power."

"No, no!" Sparky seizes up in the hallway. "Halt initiation."

"Failsafes prevent disruption of initiation," she says.

The three of us stop in a wide hallway lined with doors in regular intervals. All the doors are sealed shut.

"Stop the protocol!" Sparky snaps.

"Failsafes prevent the disruption of Project Termination Protocol."

Sparky drops his helmet on the floor. "What the ...?" His words fail him.

"We have to do something before this protocol finishes initializing," Levi says. He swipes a hand along the first door, then uses all of his Power to work it open. I join him, digging my fingers into the crack and pulling, pushing, but it doesn't budge.

"What is behind all these doors?" Levi mutters.

"Subjects scheduled for termination pending integration of Project Termination Protocol," the female computer says.

Sparky curses and nudges us out of the way, pressing his hand to the door. A buzz emits from the frame, then the door swings inward.

A young girl, perhaps only fourteen or fifteen, scurries back on her bed, trembling violently. *I discovered four floors of test subjects, not just Ugene's floor.* I recall reading that in my journal. At the time it meant little to me, but now, staring at this frightened girl, the truth of just what it could entail hammers against me.

Paragon is experimenting on these people. Ugene told everyone about the experiments, the brutality, the murder.

"We have to get all the doors open and get these people off this floor," Levi says. "Before Project Termination Protocol finishes whatever it's doing." He creeps into the room, holding his hands up to show the girl he is not a threat. "It's okay. We can help you. What's your name?"

The girl's anxious face flits from one of us to the next as she clutches her blanket in quivering hands. "V-violet," she says in the tiniest voice I've ever heard.

"Violet, do you want to leave?" Levi asks soothingly.

She shakes her head and squeezes her back to the wall. "No. No, he will punish me. I can't leave. He is listening!"

"Who is listening?" Levi asks.

I don't need her answer. I already know. "Forrest." I spin on my heel. Anger builds in my chest. "Forrest!"

"What are you doing, Steele?" Sparky hisses.

"Getting his attention."

"Sparky, can you trigger all of these doors open?" Levi asks.

"It'll take a minute, but probably," Sparky says. "I have to identify the right place to do it."

I clench my fists and roar at the ceiling. "Forrest!"

A holographic screen appears in the heart of the hallway, projected from the ceiling, and a woman in her thirties with cropped blonde hair and penetrating eyes stares at me. I turn to face her.

"Bianca Pond," she says. "I cautioned Dr. Pond that you would create more trouble, but he was certain Terry could control it."

"Who are you?" I scoff.

Levi chokes as he joins me in the hallway, gaping at the woman. "That's Dr. Cass. She runs Paragon."

Dr. Cass. I know the name but not the face.

"We were better off with you dead, but your brother is sentimental," Dr. Cass says. "Agent Sparks, please to see you have arrived to conclude your mission."

Sparky hesitates, rising from his crouch. "What?"

"At least Dr. Pond did something right," Dr. Cass says. "Should we risk exposure of our programs, you are programmed to exterminate the evidence."

My stomach sinks and I step away from Sparky. His hands tremble and he rises slowly, shaking his head.

"I'm afraid you are powerless to refuse, Agent Sparks. Your Power will expand until you can no longer contain it, and the electrical burst will fuse with the protocols currently engaging. Paragon and the Directorate thank you for your sacrifice."

Levi and I both edge away from Sparky, holding our eyes trained on him.

"Where is Forrest?" I demand.

"Busy with Ugene, I'm afraid," she says. "Unfortunately, you elected to join Agent Sparks, so you will not have a chance to reconnect." Dr. Cass vanishes into the air.

True to her word, Sparky's Electromancy builds around him, much as it did at the facility. It pulses, increasing as sparks swirl around him in a vortex of light and electricity, gathering from everywhere around him.

"He's an electric bomb," I gasp.

Levi shuffles toward Sparky, whose entire body convulses. Helpless tears roll down Sparky's cheeks. I grab Levi's arm, but he shrugs me off. I shield my eyes from the intense light.

"Sparky, listen to me," Levi says, attempting to coax Sparky. "They don't control us."

The light from the sparks intensifies and pulses around Sparky's terrified form.

"I can't ..." Sparky gulps down a shaky breath. "I can't stop it."

"You can," Levi says resolutely. "Think about why we are doing this. Think about Poly."

"Poly," Sparky breaths her name.

A ball of energy expands around him. Sparky squeezes his eyes tight, reciting her name over and over like a mantra. The overhead lights blink.

"I have seen a ditch filled with bodies outside Elpis," I confess, hoping it will motivate Sparky to battle for domination over his Power. "More bodies than I could ever count alone. Think about what they did to Poly. If you let them win this battle for control of your Power, just think of all the others who will end up like her."

Levi nods.

Sparky sinks to his knees, and I stare as he strives to reach for the floor. Is he struggling to touch it or trying to stop himself?

"This is it, Sparky," Levi says, crouching just outside Sparky's orb of electricity. "This is what you have ranted about for weeks. A chance to punish them, to make them pay for what they did. What better way then releasing these people and destroying their work?"

Sparky's body convulses as he struggles to direct his own Power. His fingers brush along the floor as he bows, pressing his palms flat against the polished floor. The lights strobe. The air charges.

"Sparky, you can do this." Levi says calmly. "You control your own future."

Sparky grinds his teeth as his Power pumps through the floor. I can feel it. The energy drives all the hair on my body stands at attention.

A security guard rounds the corner and aims at Sparky. Levi uses his Levitation to yank the guard off his feet and sends him sailing in my direction. I seize a fistful of the guard's uniform at the collar and punch him square in the jaw, then throw him into the wall where his body embeds, slumped and unconscious.

"He won't be alone," Levi says as he grabs the gun, then the security badge.

I glance toward the elevators. We need those to get these people out, but it will take forever to move as many as there must be on this floor. And what about the other floors? Running down over 100 flights of stairs is out of the question. I might manage it, but I highly doubt anyone else could.

Levi crouches in front of Sparky once more. "Remember what we did in training? I use my Power to contain the burst and you send the electricity out to fry the circuits."

Sparky shakes his head. "It won't … contain this," he says through gritted teeth.

"It will. Trust me, Sparky."

Levi rises, holding his palms toward Sparky's charged orb. Sweat streams down Levi's forehead, along his temples, and drips from his chin. I keep watch so no security can interrupt. Sparks explode outward from around Sparky and pops of electricity fill the air all along the hallway. The impact of the surge hammers against Levi's levitation barrier, flinging him off his feet and shooting him along the hallway. Sparky collapses on the floor, gasping for breath. Locks grind out of place and doors swing open. All the doors.

We have to get these people out of here.

I check on Sparky first, but he waves me off irritably, so I move on to Levi. He accepts my outstretched hand and bumps into me as I jerk him to his feet.

"So how will we get these people out of the building?" I ask.

He stoops over, sucking in air.

"How much can you Levitate at once?" I ask. Maybe I can break a window and he can send massive groups out.

Levi shakes his head as if reading my thoughts. "Not that many. I've spent a lot of my energy and it takes a lot of control to move so many people at once. Much different from a building. Besides, we will just be sending them down into the arms of the DMA troopers lining the street, even if I could. It'll be a massacre."

I huff. This is seriously frustrating. No matter how we get these people out of here, the DMA will be waiting just outside.

"Then we need a massive distraction," I say.

I have an idea. A terrible, dangerous idea. One that could end in me dying … again.

33

IT TAKES THE BETTER PART OF A HALF AN HOUR TO get everyone on this floor herded into one place. The cafeteria with its clean white tables and glass-panel wall leading to the outside. It's crowded and seemingly chaotic. Most of the subjects seem afraid to be here, but also afraid we will leave them behind. Their fear feeds into my anger.

Not everyone is afraid, though. Some test subjects are eager to help get this show on the road. They are outraged by what Paragon has done, not just to them, but to everyone here. These are the leaders in each group we divide out. Their determination is exactly what we need to make sure that everyone is herded out the door.

Levi has used the trash chute to create a Levitation device that will carry everyone down safely to whatever level the trash moves to. Hopefully, near the ground floor where no one will think to look. After all, who wants to escape through the trash. This also allows larger groups to move at once as opposed to the elevator—where surely Paragon or the DMA will have people waiting to scoop up anyone who attempts escaping.

The first group slips in the trash chute one at a time, and Levi shuffles over to stand beside me as I stare out the windows at the city below. The sun is rising. Employees are coming to work now. It will be harder to evade notice.

"This is a terrible idea, Steele," Levi says, pressing his hand to the glass panel and gazing straight down. "What if you don't survive the fall?"

The thought had crossed my mind. Jumping out a window from so high up is a terrifying prospect. But I can't show him my fear. I straighten my back. "That's what I have you for. Remember, break the fall, don't stop my momentum though. I need to hit the ground hard enough to catch everyone's attention."

"Or break your legs."

I wince. "That's happened before. I heal pretty quickly if I can reset it."

"And Dr. Pond?" he asks.

I turn to Levi, placing a hand on his shoulder. "I will make him pay for what he has done to Poly." *And to me.* "He's my brother, and it's my responsibility to deal with him." I dig out Poly's note from my jacket and hand it to him. "Give this to Sparky. I don't need it anymore."

Levi unfolds the letter and skims the page, then nods and holds it in his hand as he glances at the others. Sparky has already moved to the next floor to open the doors. Levi's Levitation chute goes up three more levels. He digs in his pocket and hands me an ear comm.

"Take this so we can contact you," he says. "Sparky and I grabbed a few at the facility and set them to secure channels."

I slip it into my ear with a grateful smile. "I will be sure to share my conversation with Forrest when I find him."

If Forrest was at Paragon, I'm confident we would have heard something from him by now. Freeing so many test subjects surely would have drawn him in.

There is only one place he would be now.

At the Administration Building.

With Ugene.

"Don't die, Steele," Levi says, patting me on the shoulder.

"It's Bianca."

He smiles. "I know."

I stroll to the far wall of the cafeteria, directly across from the windows. A small team of subjects already moved tables and chairs out of the way, leaving me a clear line straight to the window. I pull in a deep breath, crouch in a runner's position, and feel the exhilarating power of my growing muscles. What I am about to do is completely insane and requires so much trust in Levi. He could easily just let me fall to my death. But if he wants the same thing as me—to be free of Paragon and the DMA and the Directorate, to punish Forrest for his part—then it's in his best interest not to let me die. I'm his ticket to freedom and he knows it.

Levi raises his hands, prepared to catch me with his Power and ease my descent. He nods.

I release my anxiety through a slow, careful exhale, then stuff that anxiety and fear into the void, just like I did on missions with my team. Acid churns in my gut even without my emotion attached.

Before I can second-guess this decision, I break into a full speed sprint toward the windows, throwing the full force of my speed, weight, and strength into my shoulder once I'm within a step. The windows shatter into a shower of tempered glass, raining down over 100 stories to the world below. I follow only a heartbeat behind, rolling, flying, diving. I hug my arms against my sides as I free-fall toward the ground. Wind whistles past my ears, and it only takes a few seconds before I feel Levi's Levitation slowing my descent—hopefully, to safe levels. I tuck and roll, preparing to land on my feet.

The fall only lasts a few heartbeats—at most ten seconds—so there is hardly time for the people below to do more than take cover from the falling glass before I slam down into the ground on my knee. Smooth concrete explodes, leaving a shallow crater around me as debris and dirt kick up in the air. *I survived without breaking a bone. Thank you, Levi!*

Using his Power from high above, Levi blasts a Levitation circle around me, throwing the debris, dust, and troopers outward. Screams and shouts of alarm split the air.

Before anyone raises their gun in response, I run. My feet carry me faster than ever before through lines of troopers, punching here, ripping away weapons there, shattering their lines while keeping close enough that none of them can fire at me without risking hitting one of their comrades. The pure Power of my speed and strength is heady.

One trooper gets a hand on me, but my speed rips him off his feet, forcing him to let go. He rolls across the ground as if he just jumped out of a speeding car, hitting several others as he tumbles.

I grin and grab one of the troopers near me by the leg, sweeping his footing out and tossing him like a bowling ball toward others. He impacts hard enough for legs to shatter as others hit the ground.

Despite my efforts to hold the troopers at a distance and use some of them like bowling balls while knocking others out, they still close in around me. Their numbers are significantly higher. In no time, they will overwhelm me.

One of them gets my feet out from under me as another uses chunks of broken concrete to pin me down. But the weight is nothing I can't handle. I wrap my hands around the edges and I thrust it off, then roll aside.

Guns fire and bullets slam into the ground where my body should have been pinned in place. Blue-green fluid oozes out into the ground from the bullets. What is in those?

Two troopers are foolish enough to believe they can grab my arms and hold me back so others can take aim, but I gather the strength in my back and arms and send them sailing toward the men in front of me as they fire guns again. Bullets strike the two troopers. One rolls to the ground, screams, and begins convulsing.

I rush forward, and the ground between me and the troopers expands as if I'm running down a stretching hallway in a nightmare. No matter how fast I run, I can't seem to close the distance. Then my feet slow as the concrete under my feet softens and suctions me with each step. This isn't normal Power. These are agents.

Unable to move fast enough, I reach down and scoop up one of the guns. Not that it will do me any good outnumbered. Dozens of troopers surround me on all sides. More than I can shoot before they get to me first.

The line parts and Stretch leads his team through the gap. Ivy flicks her wrist, and vines shoot up out of the soft ground, wrapping around my legs. I aim the gun at her first.

Unit 12 forms a line in front of me, far enough that I can't reach them. Four bullets. I have that much, at least.

"There she is," Stretch says, grinning at the gun as if it doesn't matter at all. "Dr. Pond's little pet. You've caused quite a bit of trouble."

Somewhere in the distance, a cacophony of voices rises in protest. They solidify into one chant clearly heard even from here. "Unity! Unity!" Over and over again.

"Do you understand what he's done to us?" I ask, glancing around to make sure the troopers don't attack. They seem satisfied by the way the team has contained me. For now. "He has used us all, injected something in us that changed us, erased our memories. All so the Directorate could have its own superpowered army."

Ivy snorts. "You think we care?" She flexes a hand. The vines tighten around my calves. "So much Power. I would do it all again. And when we return you to him, he will reward us."

Their line spreads in an arc around me. I'm losing time. But the distraction should help Levi and Sparky get people out of Paragon Tower. And now all the agents are standing right in front of me.

All but one.

"Where is Nevermore?" I ask.

"He has his own mission," Stretch says.

I lower the gun and relax, hoping to put their guard down. "Then claim your reward."

"Dyspnea," Stretch nods to the leggy girl beside him.

My lungs squeeze. All the air escapes and no matter how hard I try to suck in breaths, I can't seem to collect any. Why take my breath away? My vision darkens, and the answer becomes apparent. Without breath, I will lose consciousness. Then I can't fight back at all. The gun slips from my limp hand and clatters against the ground.

I've lost.

Again.

34

AIR RUSHES BACK TO MY LUNGS AS DYSPNEA SOARS backward through the sky, high above the heads of everyone else. She screams and fights the force propelling her, then her screams cut off abruptly somewhere in the distance.

Unit 12 has turned away from me, staring upward. I follow their gaze as I climb back to my feet. When did I fall over?

Levi hovers high above the crowd. He winds up like a pitcher and lobs nothing from his fist. A DMA shuttle flies at the crowd of troopers. Ivy and Stretch scramble in opposite directions to get out its path. Their last team member isn't so lucky.

I duck, unable to move, and hold my arms over my head as if that will make a difference. The shuttle sails over me by inches and crashes through the crowd of troopers behind me. I grab the gun and launch to my feet as Ivy's vines release my calves and she turns her attention to Levi. Her vines shoot up into the sky toward him like leafy projectiles, but they all bounce off a barrier that shimmers around him like a globe. I gape in awe, but only for a moment.

Stretch has his limbs extended, reaching high into the air unnaturally. He can do more than just stretch the ground. He can use the Power on his own body as well. Ivy can't reach Levi, but Stretch could. I aim. They made their choice. They are not mindless drones, like Ugene warned me to believe.

"Unless I have no choice," I say, remembering my promise to Ugene as I release a calming breath as I pull the trigger. The bullet slams into Stretch's shoulder and sends him spinning. The extended arms retract back into his body as he convulses and screams like something is burning him alive.

I spin to Ivy, who gapes at Stretch in abject horror. The rest of her team is gone. She is the last agent standing. Her against us.

An earthquake shakes the ground. I stumble, fumbling the gun and nearly losing my footing. Screams in the distance rip through the air, sending pulsing shivers down my spine. What is happening?

"Go!" Levi calls down to me. "I got this!"

I want to shoot Ivy for him, but the sounds of battle in the distance draws my gaze east. The Administration Building is that direction. I break into a sprint, vaulting over vehicles and slamming my way through the mass of troopers too stunned to respond.

The ground beneath my feet groans. Buildings around me shake and sway. An intense, high-pitch whistle screams overhead. The thunderous tinkling of glass falling fills the air. A gust of wind licks at my heels. I glance back and gape at the rolling cloud of dust chasing me. It's the only thing I can see. I tuck my arms tighter and run as fast as I can, but it isn't fast enough even at my top speed. Something slices at my leg, and I throw my weight sideways through the window of an office building, then rolling across the floor as the windows explode inward all along the walls, and the whole building quivers like it might collapse.

I duck behind a door, pressing my weight against it to hold it shut as the force of the dust cloud rattles the frame. Dust clogs my throat and I cough, gag, spit. The thunderous crash from the world outside continues for far too long, and the building around me groans. *Please don't collapse on me!* I squeeze my eyes shut and wait for the sound to stop.

Cries from outside, wails of grief or pain, fill the air outside. I ease the door open, staring at the mass of debris and the hole in the side of the building. My heartbeat quickens as I cover my mouth with my jacket and pick my way out into the street.

Everything is coated in layers of dust and debris. Bodies lay unmoving in the street, some at odd angles. Others drag toward me, crying for help. One woman leaves a trail of blood in her wake from a missing leg.

What just happened?

I turn toward the direction the cloud had chased me from.

As the dust settles, a hole in the skyline reveals the complete collapse of Paragon Tower. *Levi. Sparky.* I stumble toward the wreckage.

Remembering the comm device Levi gave me, I call to both of them and get no response. "Levi! Answer me!"

Nothing.

For a moment, I stare at the gap in the skyline, too stunned to move.

There is only one place to go. Clenching my hands into fists, I spin on my heels and race toward the Administration Building a few blocks east. Forrest must be there. He has to be there. And with any luck, Ugene will be with him and safe from the destruction of the Tower.

I break out across the massive square in front of the Administration Building, scanning the front of it for any weak points or signs of life. Bodies litter the courtyard, and people fall over, some of them weeping openly. I pass them all as I race toward the building, spotting Ugene just as he disappears back into the building on the fourth floor. The front of the building is ripped open as if some giant beast took a bite out of it. A massive stone pillar lays at an odd angle on from the ground up toward the third story. If I time it right, I can run up the pillar and jump to the 4th floor balcony where Ugene just disappeared.

Vehicles race into the square from another intersection. Ignoring them as they squeal to a stop near to the pillar and the people within begin filing out with purpose, I jump onto the pillar and race toward the top, spotting a few of Ugene's friends among those storming the building, launching their own attack. I have to reach him before they do. I need to reach Forrest. He will either be with Ugene, or he died in the Tower. The latter isn't an option. Not if I want a chance to avenge what Forrest has done.

A heartbeat before my feet reach the top end of the pillar, I leap, pushing off hard enough to make the pillar shift and grind as if about to fall. I vault through the air. Someone screams above. I sail over the rail of the balcony and land with a thunderous thud that makes the whole balcony quiver.

Ugene is frozen in place in the middle of the room, and Forrest faces him with a hateful snarl on his face.

"Forrest!" I step up beside Ugene, giving him a once over to try to figure out what is going on. Forrest must be using his Power on him. Sweat rolls in rivers down Ugene's body, as if he stands beside a massive fire. I clench my fists and I turn my attention on my brother. "Enough."

Forrest bares his teeth, and he looks feral, not at all like my brother. "Do you understand what he's done?"

There will be no peaceful way to do this. Forrest wants a fight. I will give it to him. I flex my muscles and plant my feet into the floor, cracking the tiles as I dig in the balls of my feet, preparing to launch. As I tighten my fists, the heady Power of my Strength courses through me, engorging my muscles.

"What about what you've done?" I snap, fury burning in my chest. "You lied to me, to our parents. You killed me!"

Forrest flicks his gaze in my direction, and for just a moment he seems lost. I would feel bad for him if he hadn't killed me and used me, then lied to me with every breath since I woke in his care.

He shakes his head ever so slightly. "I didn't pull the trigger."

Ugene remains stiff. Whatever Forrest is doing to him, it keeps Ugene from moving at all.

"You didn't stop the guards either," I say, remembering the video I watched at the facility. "You were my brother. Does that mean nothing to you?"

Forrest holds his hand toward Ugene. Somehow I have to get him to release that Power grip. "It won't matter if Elpis falls," he says with fevered conviction.

I shiver. "Let him go. This is between us."

Forrest rotates his hand as if turning a dial while he says, "No."

Ugene groans in pain, powerless to stop this.

There's only one way to break his hold. I lunge at my brother, turning away at the last second to snatch the arm he holds out, and twist it behind his back, then use my other hand to throw several measured punches into his ribs. The bones crack under my fist.

Ugene falls to the floor in a heap, but I can't trouble myself with him. This is between me and Forrest now. I sweep my leg out to knock Forrest off his feet. His back drives into the floor with a thud and he gasps, but recovers quickly. He sends a hand in Ugene's direction again, and I peek over just long enough to see Ugene pressed down against the floor, clawing at the tiles.

The building shakes as lightning and thunder outside moved in rumbles and flashes. I don't know what's taking place out there. If the building falls on our heads, I will take my brother with me.

I strike my fist into Forrest's jaw, strong enough to emit a satisfying crunch. But stone rolls across his skin from the point of impact—no, his skin becomes stone from that point, rippling away as it absorbs the brunt of my punch, though it does still separate us. He's stronger than I remember.

As my brother glares at me, my heart aches. I can no longer shove my emotions into a void. This is my brother. He's supposed to protect me. He's not supposed to hurt me. The betrayal is worse than anything I can recall. Worse than Hound lying to me and betraying my trust. Worse than the lies of everybody who has been around me these past weeks. Forrest was supposed to be on my side, in my corner.

I don't cry. I won't cry over him. But my throat still constricts with grief over a loss I can't even begin to understand. "Why did you let them steal my memories?" I ask, dismayed that the words fall out strangled. I've already revealed too much emotion.

Forrest pushes himself to his feet, lifting his chin in arrogance that looks all too recognizable. He holds distance between us, as if he doesn't wish for a fight. Too bad.

"I brought you back from the dead." He sets a hand proudly

against his chest. "I did that, but you aren't thanking me for that, are you?"

Thanking him? Is he serious? No. I won't ever thank him for what he's done to me.

I run with lightning speed toward him, summoning one of the movements from a video he forced me to watch after waking in that facility. Muscles move with instinct, as if realizing what I am doing before even I do. It all passes instantaneously. My arm around his neck, swinging my body around behind him hard enough for the momentum to fling both of us onto the floor. Tiles crack. The floor shakes.

Forrest rolls to his side and hacks up blood.

I roll away from him before he gains a chance to recuperate, striking my leg down into his chest with a half-scissor kick. The sweet harmony of more of his ribs cracking rips across the open office. I kick back on my hands and spring to my feet to charge again as Forrest scrapes at the floor for leverage to rise.

He betrayed my trust.

Punch to the jaw.

He killed innocent people.

Punch to the skull.

He stole my memories.

Punch to the ribs.

Forrest tries to thwart my blows with his stone-skin, and each impact quivers up my arm. He deserves this. Why is he refusing to grant me this moment of vengeance? I clamp my jaw. My fingernails bite into my palms, and I can feel the blood from my nails breaking the skin. But I can't stop myself. Forrest did this to me. He hacked away the valuable parts and left me this shell. He created a monster, and now he won't let me punish him. It isn't fair!

I snarl in frustration and jump to my feet, planting a boot over his back. "Why did you steal my memories?" My voice is shrill, swollen with rage and grief and despair.

Forrest squirms and my lips peel back in contentment. *Good.*

Squirm. Then he flips over onto his back and snatches my ankle. Sudden cold rushes through me and my muscles seize. I grunt and stumble to the side, breaking Forrest's contact with my skin.

Whatever he just did to me, the agony of it slows my muscles down as if tearing them out of blocks of ice. I try to close the distance between us again as he climbs to his feet with labored breathing. He sidesteps me with ease.

My muscles refuse further movement. Everything freezes in places as if my body has turned to stone. Unable to thrust my hands out to break my fall, I pitch forward and thump against the floor. What did he do to me?

Despite my attempts to keep my emotions in check, tears roll down my cheeks and drip from the tip of my nose.

"Your loyalty to him was a weakness," Forrest says. His shoes scuff the filthy floor toward me, and he wrenches my hand, twisting my body over onto my back. I'm powerless to do anything about it. His Power continues to hold me hostage.

Forrest drops my arm and squats over me, rotating his hands in a circle away from each other. "I removed that weakness. To protect you. As I've always done." His passionate, mad gaze penetrates me, and I can't bear to witness this savage monster. What did he do with my brother?

My throat tightens. Every cell in my body weakens as if ripped out one at a time. I can sense the excruciating flow of my life-force ebbing away into Forrest, as if he is collecting the fragments of me in a roil of never-ending agony, only to suck them out. My body is no longer my own to command. Muscles pop and strain in protest. My bones dissolve, generating a burning hot, blinding pain through every nerve. A high-pitched scream rolls off the walls of the room, and I don't realize it's me until my throat becomes raw.

I rolled my head to the side, powerless to stop the tears from escaping, and meet Ugene's gaze. He stares at me in abject horror, digging at the tiles in a lame attempt at reaching me.

Forrest speaks, and his voice is thick with frantic grief. "I tried to help you."

I strive for some form of control, despite the blinding agony, tugging and bucking. Then blazing pressure crushes my organs. My back arches and I howl, but no sound escapes my spent lungs. The tang of blood fills my mouth and dribbles from the edge of my lips like drool.

I can't beat him. I can't defeat Forrest. I don't even know if I will survive this assault. *I'm sorry, Levi and Sparky. Ugene… I've failed again.*

Forrest's Power lessens, yet he never surrenders it. I moan in relief, back sagging against the floor as I weep, inhaling in shallow breaths. If I have any chance at defeating him, there is only one choice. I don't want to execute him. I don't even know if I have the energy anymore. "Don't … don't make me … please …" It's all I can say.

Forrest sags beside me, tears rolling down his own cheeks. "It isn't supposed to be like this." He is mourning. Either he can't kill me, or he knows he has to and is bracing himself.

I pinch my eyes shut, incapable of witnessing the torment on his face. "Fo-Forrest …"

Forrest weeps. Not aloud, but he acts as if I'm already dead. I gaze past him, gasping for breath as I feel the Power in my body slowly rebuild the damages. Hunger gnaws at my belly.

Ugene brushes his fingers over an already bloody spike and he strains to snag it. He means to kill Forrest, but I can't let him. Not for Forrest's benefit, but for Ugene's. Killing strips away a piece of the soul. I will never forgive myself for my part in the death of innocent people. I can't let Ugene suffer. I shake my head, knowing the Power returns to me.

I have to stop Forrest before Ugene does anything he will regret. I can't save myself, but I can save him.

With a wail, I draw my Strength and punch my legs out as hard as I can. My boots plant against Forrest's side, and he sails through the air into a wall where his limp form lodges in the stone. All the pain and pressure from Forrest's Power disappears as he slumps.

I gasp out and roll to my feet, then stalk toward Forrest. This isn't over yet.

"We need to go," Ugene says as he gulps down breaths of air. "The building is under attack."

I crack my neck and roll my shoulders in front of Forrest, still planted in the wall. My blood runs cold. I can't kill Forrest. I have to somehow remove his Power. Without that, he's nothing more than a big brain. "You go. I have unfinished business with my brother."

Ugene hesitates, though. Why can't he leave me alone?

"Why did you come back for me?" he asks.

Just go! "I came back for answers. You just happened to be here." I don't mean to upset him, but I need him to leave me. I can't have him witness what I am about to do, the monster within. I can't even look at him as he hovers nearby. My back stiffens. "Go."

Ugene shifts closer. "Come with me."

I clamp my jaw, gather my courage, and whirl around to glower at him with all the anger I can muster. I need him to leave me. I don't deserve his support. "I need to do this. Please. Go."

Ugene flinches. I may as well have slapped him. But he says nothing else as he picks his path warily to the balcony.

I gaze at my brother, realizing what I must do, not possessing the strength to follow through. Forrest is as much a monster as I am. We both deserve to suffer. I shouldn't even be here in the first place. The two of us are abominations in our own fashion.

I pluck the collar of Forrest's shirt and rip him out of the wall.

Thunder rumbles. The building rocks. The floor shifts, ripples, and everything comes toppling down. I thrust my body over Forrest and a support beam slams against my chest, knocking me out cold.

35

INTENSE PRESSURE CRUSHES DOWN ON MY CHEST. I TRY gulping down breaths only to have all of my internal organs scream at me in pain. Dirt clogs my mouth and I cough, which only intensifies the crushing injury in my chest. With quivering hands, I grasp around my body, unable to see in the darkness. Chunks of concrete. A steel girder. A steel support rod gouged my side, leaving behind a bleeding gash I can feel but can't see. My hands scratch back, touching Forrest's still-limp form beneath me.

"Bianca!" Ugene's voice is muffled by layers of collapsed building. Is he trapped like me?

I suck in a careful breath, fighting off a cough and trying to ignore the burning and stabbing pain shooting throughout my body. "Ugene!" It takes everything to call back.

I have to get out of here. If he is trapped, we will both likely die beneath the rubble. I place my trembling hands against the beam crushing my chest and gather all the Strength my crippled body can handle. Pure molten fire courses through every nerve as if threatening to burn me alive while I drive the beam up off my chest.

A ray of light breaks through the darkness, creating a halo of dust still tumbling around me.

Ugene's face appears at the gap, grabbing the beam and attempting to help. It doesn't offer much extra aid. Already, the muscles and skin of my body stretch tight, the bones stitch back together like a blade sliding along them. My body attempts fixing the damage, but the hunger from the last few hours of using my Power has chewed away at me. My arms quake, promising collapse. My Strength is failing me. With a roar, I focus all of my remaining energy into forcing the beam out of the way.

"Are you hurt?" Ugene asks, examining me like a distressed parent. It would be endearing if it wasn't such a stupid question.

I grunt, shifting the beam an inch to the side where another mound of debris can support the weight. My body sags against Forrest beneath me. "Broken ribs, and I think I dislocated my shoulder."

I'm a bigger mess than that, but I don't need to worry him over anything he can't fix. I'm pretty confident my leg is fractured. That will mend itself. Blood mats my hair to my head, and I brush the gash in my side only to discover the wound is already closed. Hopefully he won't notice. I cling to the remains of my Power, afraid that if I let go, it will slip away for good.

"I'll be fine. You go. Find your friends." My damaged lungs are already getting better without the crushing weight against my chest. I can breathe a little smoother.

"I can reset your shoulder first," Ugene offers.

Broken bones I can readjust, but getting his help with my shoulder would make things easier. I glance at Forrest to be assured he isn't waking up—we don't need his Power interrupting us—then nod in agreement and sit up straighter, hoping Ugene can't see me cringe. My foot is pinned, and I'm pretty sure my ankle has shattered.

Ugene's touch is delicate as he raises my arm into position. I clamp my jaw as heat shoots out of my shoulder, but I don't complain.

"Ready?" he asks.

No. I'm not ready for this. But it has to be done. "Do it," I say, gritting my teeth in preparation.

Ugene moves the arm rapidly, and there's a flash of stabbing agony in the joint, then it fades gradually. My eyes water and I glance away so he can't witness the tears in my eyes. I test the shoulder, satisfied that it's fixed.

"I can help you out of here," he offers.

If Ugene stays, he will discover the monster my brother has

created. It's better that he leaves me now. I don't want him to see what I aim to do next. I shake my head. "Time is wasting. Find your friends. I'll deal with Forrest."

Ugene hesitates, and I'm glad I'm not watching at him. I don't want to see his disappointment. He sighs heavily, as if I've requested the worst, then picks his path out of the remnants of the office.

I whimper the moment I'm positive he's gone, then lift the slab of concrete off my leg and clench my jaw as tight as possible to reset the bone. A sob of pain slips out, but my foot is already rebuilding. I shift off Forrest and press my back against a cracked beam, gulping down breaths as tears spill from my eyes.

When will this end? Can I even die? The bones stitch back together, a sensation that feels a lot like pins and needles in the bones themselves. The pain is dimmer, but agonizing sorrow clenches my heart. Forrest has betrayed and manipulated everyone. There is only one means to stop him. I can determine no alternative.

I brush bloody, grimy hands across my face to clean away the tears. It's time to take care of my brother myself.

Steeling myself against what I must do, I crawl over Forrest, turning away any remaining debris to create a clear route. Something in Forrest's jacket budges. I dig in the pocket and first pluck out his tablet. The screen is shattered. I attempt powering it on, but nothing happens. It's worthless now. I thrust my hand into the pocket again and my fingertips brush something cool, familiar. A gun. I draw it out and study the cylinder. One bullet remains, and the green-blue liquid in it casts an eerie light on Forrest's unconscious face as the sunshine catches it. I shove the cartridge back in and cock the gun, shifting to my feet.

My stance is wide. I aim straight for his chest. Tears blur my vision and I growl in annoyance as the floor of the building hums with life. It will give way soon. I have to settle this before it's too late.

But I can't seem to pull the trigger.

My stomach turns to stone. My head throbs. The image of Forrest aiming a gun at me wielding the same firm posture reinforces my intention. This has to be done. He has to be stopped.

I flex my fingers and wrap my index finger around the trigger again, but regardless of how often I try to squeeze, I can't seem to shoot. I howl in frustration, tempted to hurl the gun at his head. But that won't do any good.

Forrest stirs. There isn't time for this reluctance.

His eyes drift open.

I stiffen, aiming deliberately at his chest again.

Seeing the gun in my hand, Forrest freezes, staring at it. "Don't do this, B." His voice sounds like someone rubbed it over gravel. He coughs, but never once removes his eyes from me.

"Use your Power on me again, and I won't hesitate to pull the trigger," I say, praying my tone sounds serious enough for him to believe me.

It must work, because Forrest remains statue still, watching the gun. Watching my finger on the trigger. "He got to you again," he says. "Why do you follow that boy so blindly?"

I shake my head as tears roll down my cheeks. "This isn't about him. This is about you. It's always about you, isn't it? Nevermind what anyone else wants if it doesn't align with Forrest's ambitions. I remember what it was like living in your shadow. The perfect, gifted son." I jeer. "They were all mistaken."

"I'm working to *save* Elpis from ruin," Forrest says. "I need you to see that, B. I'm doing this for the city, for our *family*."

"How long before you finally revealed the truth?" I snap. "How long would you have waited before telling Mom and Dad that I was still alive, or before you told me they were? How long would you have used me for your own gain?" I'm growling now, seething in anger.

Forrest's gaze flicks to my arms. The muscles swell as I tense more and more. I want to pull the trigger. *That's the only way to stop him.* But I don't believe the words as they punch through my mind.

"I am your *sister*, Forrest. You are supposed to help me, defend me, support me, not use me." Grief makes my voice thick, and spittle flies from the corner of my mouth. "Why did you kill me?"

"Like I said before, I didn't pull the trigger," Forrest snaps. His mouth turns downward, and he slumps back against the rubble.

"Not the first time." I test my finger on the trigger.

Forrest holds up a palm. "Wait, B. I didn't the second time either. I couldn't. When I raised that gun, I couldn't squeeze the trigger. Just like you can't now. Because we're family. Because, despite what you might assume, I *do* love you." His Adam's apple bobs and his chin quivers almost as briskly as his hand. Tears well in his eyes, but I recall the tears he conjured for our parents. It was all a show. I can't believe this either.

I let out a shaky breath, correcting my aim. "I want to believe you, but I can't. You've fooled me too many times, Forrest."

"Let me help!" Forrest pleads as I prepare to fire. "I can get your memories back."

The offer makes me falter. It's another lie. It must be. But if there's a chance, shouldn't I accept it?

No. I can't. I can't be that girl. I can't give him a chance to do this all over again. I sniffle and swing my head. My voice breaks as I say, "You can't fix me, Forrest. You broke me. You created a monster. I can't let you create another."

"I just wanted you back," he stammers, strangling out the words. He closes his eyes. "I'm sorry."

But an apology won't reverse what he has done to me. I want to pull the trigger. A head shot will still kill, Sims said. I need to pull the trigger, but Ugene's plea rings out in my head. *No more killing.*

I deserve justice. I deserve the right to judge Forrest's fate, just as he undertook choosing mine.

"I'm sorry," Forrest asserts repeatedly.

No more killing.

I howl in frustration and smash the butt of the gun against Forrest's skull, knocking him unconscious.

But I won't cry anymore. Not for Forrest. Not for the girl I used to be. Not for the memories lost.

36

FORREST'S BODY IS WEIGHTIER THAN I PREDICTED, but it's nothing I can't handle. He slumps over my shoulder as I amble down the corridor. Ugene leans over at the far end, toiling with a body. Nevermore.

"Did you find anyone?" I inquire, electing a casual tone, hoping Ugene can't identify the misery I've just suffered. I jam my grief into the void. This level of suppression can't be healthy for me, but I don't see how else to handle the trauma when the entire building still hums around me.

"Just Enid," Ugene says, grunting as he grapples with Nevermore's frame. "The others are in the building somewhere."

I nudge Ugene aside and grab Nevermore with my open hand, slinging his body into the air.

Ugene stumbles out of my path. "In there." He points at an open office door.

I trudge into the office with both Nevermore and Forrest, dropping the former on the floor in the corner before easing Forrest down beside him. Forrest retains his Power. If he wakes, he can employ it against us before we even realize he's conscious. But I don't have any means to interrupt him anymore, short of keeping him unconscious. The least I can do is restrain him with a pair of zip-cuffs Ugene offers.

"Paragon used a Telepath to alter your memories," Ugene says, regarding me with his hands jammed in his pockets.

My back stiffens, but I continue binding Forrest as if it doesn't matter. "How do you know?"

Not that we didn't previously suspect, but Ugene sounds so positive this time.

"Because he confessed."

Confessed? I spin around and follow Ugene's gaze.

Nevermore.

All this time, he has been fooling with my mind! *I will snap his scrawny little neck!*

In a few strides, I cut across the office, ready to extract my vengeance, but Ugene jumps between us. "Wait," he says, bearing a palm out to me. "I know you're angry, and I would love nothing as much as watching you beat him to a pulp, but if you hurt him, we may not get your memories back."

Hate burns through my veins. Nevermore did this to me. But could I truly get those memories back? I peer at Ugene. If I could remember what I read in those journal entries …

"Is that possible?" I ask.

Ugene chews his lip as he rubs his neck. "I don't know. But is it worth the risk?"

Is it? I don't know. Bianca before death was weak-willed, keen to trust and listen to the people she cared about. That girl ended up dead and violated. But, at the same time, the affection that girl knew for Ugene was so deep. If I could have just a fraction of that.

Then I notice the girl on the couch, unconscious. Enid. My heart plummets.

It's too late. Those memories will only hurt me. I want to tell Ugene it doesn't matter anymore. That girl is dead. But I can't bear the notion of eliminating that hope from his eyes. Instead, I huff and stalk over to Forrest, double checking to be positive he is still out and securely bound.

Others join us, but I don't grant them much consideration. I center all my focus on ensuring that my brother doesn't wake up, a diversion from the disappointment balling up and turning to lead in my gut.

That girl is dead.

But is there a chance that maybe, just maybe, a fragment of her still lives?

No. She's gone. I have to accept that. It's time to push forward.

"Willow is an Empath," Ugene is explaining to Miller and Jayme.

I remain huddled in front of Forrest, pondering alternatives to punish him. Maybe I can get Nevermore to erase some of his memories? How would Forrest like to forget all of his precious research?

"She can Influence people to do her bidding," Ugene continues explaining. "If you helped, it isn't really your fault."

Influence. Like Theus? I rise, turning to the rest of the office.

"We did what needed to be done," Jayme says, crossing his arms defensively.

Ugene's face lights up as he takes an eager step toward his friends. "No. You did what she wanted."

Back in that house, while Ugene's friends held me captive, Willow tried forcing me to talk. It makes simple sense now. I edge toward Ugene. "I felt it."

He spins around, alarmed to spot me so close behind him.

"Back at the safehouse, she tried to do it to me when we were alone," I clarify. "But I didn't fall for it. I let her think she did though."

Ugene's eyebrows shoot up his forehead. "How?"

I shrug. "Just acted like I was obeying her wishes when she tried to Influence me to stay put and not speak a word."

He shakes his head. His face positively lights up when he is excited.

My heart jumps into my throat.

"No," he says. "I mean, how did you resist?"

Again, I shrug. Probably Nevermore's responsibility. "It just didn't work. Terry tried to read me at training." I nod toward his prone form. "And that failed, too."

Ugene nods resolutely. "Good. I need you to do that again if she tries."

He assumes I can control it like a Power? "It isn't something I consciously do. It just happens."

Willow storms into the office as if summoned, with her obedient

Somatic dog on her heels. Sho, another boy I recognize from the safehouse, stands behind her as well.

A dispute breaks out between Ugene and Willow almost instantly. It's tedious. Their drama is their own. I don't care about it. All I care about is seeing Forrest pay for what he has done.

Willow stalks across the office toward Forrest and I tense. I shouldn't care if she does anything to harm him, but somehow he feels like my burden. If anyone will punish him, it's me. Willow crouches beside him, and I observe her as she caresses his face. Her back is to the room, but I can just see the way her features turn downward. Then she smiles marginally. Any hesitation I might have had that this is the same Willow from the fern is gone. Whatever happened between her and my brother, they loved each other once. Forrest isn't the nostalgic type to keep a plant someone gave him.

Ugene must notice as well. He inches closer and asks, "Do you know him?"

"A long time ago," Willow says, her voice remote and her gaze almost tender. Realizing we are all staring at her, Willow stiffens and checks his zip-cuffs, nodding once in satisfaction. "How did Seaduss die?"

Ugene's scowl makes it obvious just what he thinks of his testimony. "You killed him."

Willow smirks. "I think I would remember that."

I have no concept of how I feel about this announcement. Sparky said Seaduss was nothing more than a brute with political support. Maybe the world is better off without him.

"When you destroyed the Tower," Ugene says.

The revelation brings me back to my senses and I whirl around. Sparky was in that Tower. Levi was levitating outside of it. Both of them are dead now. And it was her crime. I clamp my hands into fists at my sides as fury fills my blood. Rage blocks out all my other senses. Willow is guilty of their deaths. She and Forrest really must have created a pair in their day.

The rest of their exchange is wasted on me. All I can think about are Sparky and Levi, and the innocent people they were working to rescue. Others join us in the office, dragging people bound and gagged along. The space becomes cramped, and I don't recognize half of them, or identify who any of these people are, and I don't care. What I do care about is punishing Willow.

Her minions line up at her command, holding guns that look remarkably like the one I still carry under my jacket. The last bullet remains in the chamber.

Ugene edges toward Willow. "What are you doing with them?"

Willow turns slowly, and I prepare to pounce. If she plants a finger on Ugene …

"Giving them a taste of their own medicine," Willow says. Her tone is recognizable, the same as the pure hate Forrest showed Ugene earlier. "Bring them over to the line." Willow motions toward Nevermore and Forrest.

No. Forrest is mine.

I plant myself between Forrest and the rest of the office. "He is my brother. He is my problem."

Willow narrows her gaze at me. "Move out of the way if you don't want to join them."

I coil my muscles.

Ugene jumps up beside me. "Willow, stop. The fight is over. Seaduss is dead, the Directorate is finished. Let's find Ds. Cass and call this victory."

Does he truly see this as a victory? Levi and Sparky are dead! No, he doesn't believe what he claims. The dip of his thick lips, the sorrow in his dark eyes. He is grieving. "Enough people have died today," he says.

"Move or be moved," Willow snaps.

Ugene tenses, clenching his fists at his sides, bracing for a confrontation. But he's Powerless. He won't stand a chance in this throw-down.

Willow scowls. "So be it."

Everything happens instantaneously. Chase tries to move Ugene as he goes on arguing and petitioning to Willow's humanity. But if she is anything like Forrest, his words will fall on deaf ears. Willow's

Power slams against the block in my mind, freezing me in place. Sweat rolls down her temples.

"This can't be what Doc wanted," Ugene protests as Chase pulls him aside.

I still don't move. Forrest is my burden to bear.

"He wanted this to end," she says, drawing out her gun and directing it at Forrest.

I can't hear the rest, stupefied, as I glare at the barrel of Willow's gun. *She won't, will she? Not if they sincerely loved each other before.* She can't actually be so jaded that she would remove his Power or shoot him. Her finger tightens on the trigger and I snap out of my stupor, shoving my weight against her as she shoots. Her gunshot is followed by an echo of guns in the office.

Our backs drive into the floor, strong enough to split it but not break it. I draw back a fist to strike straight into her pretty face, but Chase grabs my wrist and wrenches my arm back before I can stop him. And in one deft, fluid movement, Willow swings around me, her arm wrapped around my throat and crushing in a remarkably powerful grip. I rise and shuffle back, suddenly thrusting my body against the wall behind us to attempt dislodging Willow's hold. Fists slam into my ribs, cracking bones as Chase hammers at me. Pain momentarily blinds me. I dig fingers into Willow's arm as her stranglehold robs me of air.

I only have a few moments.

Bright light shocks the office. I work it to my advantage, swinging my arms backward to grab Willow by the neck and fling her off my back. She flies into her Somatic dog, sending them both across the floor in a heap. Air floods my lungs and I suck it down, then I catch Chase before he can recover. His burden is higher than most of the others I've fought before, but I have just enough leverage and momentum to toss him across the office.

Lightning flashes.

Chase's back skips along the floor, and before he skids to a stop, I plunge forward, landing on him and hammering my fists into his ribs.

He kicks and bucks to dislodge me, but my fingers have dug into his vest. He isn't running anywhere before I defeat him.

With a snarl, I wind up and crack my fist against his jaw hard enough to watch his bones break.

"Stop!" A wail is accompanied instantly by a burst of air that blows across my back, knocking me off balance.

A bullet rips the sleeve of my jacket but doesn't break skin. I draw my own gun. Snarling, I lift the gun at Willow as she lies on the floor. She is provoking this rebellion with her Influence, just like Theus destroyed Unit 14. I squeeze the trigger.

No one else moves, as if all are suspended in time.

"Bianca." Ugene edges toward me. "What did you do?"

What I had to. "She's in charge, right?" I say, and even to my own ears my voice sounds cold, distant. "Without her Influence, this is over."

Chase rushes over to Willow and brushes her hair affectionately, then probes for the bullet wound.

I observe with icy detachment. She isn't dead. It's just a leg wound. But her Influence is gone. And we are all better off for it.

Chase surges to his feet, but before he takes a step, lightning comes out of nowhere around both him and Willow like a jail. I peer to my left, where Miller stands clutching his ribs, grimacing.

Willow trembles, clutching her leg and flinching in pain. Good. She deserves worse. "I told you, we ..." She sucks in a shuddering breath. "We can't affect change without some nec-necessary loses."

Ugene looks fit to vomit. "People aren't expendables." He turns to me, and the grief in his eyes cracks my hardened heart. "Bianca."

He is awaiting an explanation, or maybe even remorse. He won't find it.

I hold the gun out to him. "I would do it again."

His lips part as if I just punched him in the gut. I can't bear to watch the sorrow in his eyes a moment longer. The second he accepts the gun from my hands, I hunch down and scoop up my brother, then head toward the door.

No one moves to stop me.

37

THERE ISN'T ENOUGH FOOD IN THE WORLD TO SATE my hunger. I perch on the edge of a broken wall near the capital square with Forrest unconscious under my boots and a platter of hamburgers balanced on my knees. Some big fellow named Harvey seemed to understand I needed a snack. I don't think he expected me to take the full platter. Blood still mars my arms and dirt clings to everything, but my hands are washed, at least.

In the square, people mill around, checking for survivors and collecting their dead. So many people died today. Yet I live. Do I deserve life? I've never witnessed so much carnage in one place. Not even in the ditch outside the city.

The ditch. I need to tell someone where to find it.

Levi. Sparky. Poly. Vortex. Hound. Their deaths rest on my shoulders. Hound may have had it coming, to some extent, but did Vortex? I should have saved her. And Poly ... I know her death was my fault. She tried to help me, warn me. Forrest punished her. *The Directorate and Paragon punished her*, I remind myself. Forrest played his part, but he worked for someone else on their orders. I cannot absolve him of his guilt, but I can accept that he didn't act alone.

Levi and Sparky's deaths hit me the heaviest. Sparky distrusted me, and with excellent reason, but deep down he was a decent person working to make up for his own mistakes. And Levi. Just thinking of the way he grinned at me before I dove out that window breaks my heart. If any of us deserved better, undoubtedly it was him. Tears blur my vision as I polish off another burger and choke it down, setting the empty platter aside.

"Levi?" I say, hoping the comm will come alive and his voice will call back. A hope I have maintained several times since leaving the Administration Building.

But there's still nobody.

"I've watched you eat before, but this is a whole new level," Ugene says as he strolls over and perches on the wall beside me. The grin on his face is lighthearted, but I can't bring myself to match his gaze. He must notice my reluctance, because he shifts gears. "I'm sorry about what happened to you, Bianca."

"It isn't your fault," I mutter, briskly brushing away my tears before he can see them.

"It sort of is," he admits, fidgeting. "I tried to carry you out of Paragon that night, but I wasn't strong enough or fast enough. Rosie might have saved you and you wouldn't have …" He swallows and peers down at Forrest. "But I left you there."

I can't fault him for leaving dead weight behind. Tears prick my eyes and I bow my head to let my matted hair cover my face.

"I know you don't really remember me," he says, and I can hear the sorrow bleeding through. "And that you've changed, but I'm still your friend if you need to talk."

My throat swells shut. It takes several attempts to speak. "I don't know what he did to me, and I'm not sure I want to. But I'm a monster, Ugene. And people like you don't make friends with monsters."

Ugene leans forward, propping his elbows on his knees, and peers out at the square. "You aren't a monster, Bianca."

"Theus is dead," I snap, not intending to lose my temper but powerless to contain the truth any longer.

"I know."

"Because of me."

Ugene frowns as he transfers his gaze to me. He isn't angry, like I expect him to be—like I need him to be. "Did you pull the trigger?"

"I may as well have." My grief rips at my throat, making me croak out the confession.

"But you didn't," he says immediately. "The DMA did. Not you. Bianca, I don't care what you've done. We have all done terrible things these past few months." For a flash, his face is haunted, but it passes swiftly. "And often at the bidding of someone else. You are not a monster. You are extraordinary."

"All these people died because of a problem I helped create," I cry, ashamed of my tears. "And when I shot Willow, I felt no remorse. I meant what I said. I would do it again without regret."

Ugene twists to confront me, grabbing my hand. "A monster doesn't grieve the loss of others. I know you. I know your heart. And it's full of compassion, even if you need to dig a little to find it."

I sniffle and scrub away more tears.

Ugene nods at Forrest. "What will you do with him?"

I gaze at Forrest, then withdraw my boots from his chest. "I think it's better if you choose." I can't trust myself with this decision. I don't even know where to start.

"Dying is easy," Ugene says. "Living with his guilt is harder. I will see that he is brought to justice."

I nod stiffly.

My ear comm crackles and I reach up to pluck it out, but freeze when I hear a voice.

"Bi—ca?"

I surge to my feet, pressing against the comm.

"Hel—nyone there?"

"What is it?" Ugene asks, sitting upright and attentive.

"Levi?" I call back.

"Bia—a!" Levi's voice breaks over the signal, but it's him. He's alive!

"Where are you?" I ask.

Static. "—trapped. I—another building."

I gaze down at Forrest.

Ugene rises. "Go. I'll make sure your brother is properly cared for."

I meet Ugene's gaze, intimate and unfamiliar, inviting and

frightening. Then he smirks and waves me off.

And I run.

"I'm coming, Levi, but I need a location. Where are you?" I ask as I sprint toward the last place I saw him alive—outside Paragon Tower.

Now, only the heaped rubble remains. Crew of people already mill around, probing for survivors in the wreckage. I skid to a stop roughly where I recall standing last time I saw him and examine the sky.

"Levi?"

"Bianca." Levi's voice reaches out to me and I turn in place, seeking some clue. It's so hard to identify when everything has been damaged by the collapsing Tower.

"Across—st—"

Across the street. He must be across the street. It makes sense if the blast from the Tower thrust him forward. It probably tossed him into another building while he was in the air.

I sprint to the building across the street with several gaping holes and shattered windows, and a collapsed roof. He's trapped in there somewhere. I dig, hurling chunks of concrete out behind me. After a few minutes, citizens join me, burrowing into the building for survivors.

"I can see you!" Levi calls through the comm. "Left. My left. Sorry."

I stare right and see the second floor collapsed into the first, allowing a narrow crater. Through that hole, Levi's hand waves at me. I gap and charge to him, excavating careful of the others now as I dig him out. His arm. His dumb grinning face, bleeding and bruised. His torso is damaged from the impact. I hoist beams with no effort and toss aside chunks of concrete like stones.

"I thought you died!" I breathe out as I drag him to his feet.

Levi yelps and collapses against me. "I thought everyone did. Where is Forrest?"

"He won't be a problem anymore," I say. "They shot him with a bullet that removed his Power."

"But he's alive?"

I nod. "The Protectorate will decide what to do with him now."

Levi pulls back, blanching and clasping his ribs. "I feel like everything is broken."

"Let's get you a healer."

"Sparky?" Mourning in his eyes makes it evident he already knows what happened.

I shake my head.

Levi nods, slumping a little more against me. "So, what now, then? What do we do? Turn ourselves in?"

I slip my arm under his and help him out of the building. "I don't think they care much about us anymore."

"Who?"

"Anyone." If Ugene's judgments were any indication, he has no intention of punishing me for my crimes—even if I deserve it. That must extend to Levi as well.

Still, my stomach twists painfully. No one cares about me, except maybe my parents.

Levi stares at me with such energy it makes my cheeks heat. Then he says, "I care."

He draws a careful breath as we break out into the street, tipping his head back and basking in the sunlight. "I don't remember the sun being this warm."

"I don't remember the sun at all," I say honestly.

We both laugh, which makes him wince once again. I'm not sure what it is about the comment that's so funny. Surely I've felt the warmth of the sun and have some memory of it in some form. But I don't remember it. That shouldn't be so amusing.

Levi gasps. "Don't make me laugh. It hurts."

"Sorry."

We shuffle along the street to a tent set up for injuries. Recovery and rescue are in full swing all over downtown. Hundreds of people mill around caked in dirt, blood, powdered concrete. Some are entirely clean, helping tidy up the mess and search for survivors.

"So what do we do now? The DMA is toast, right? Which means

we are both out of a job," Levi says.

I glance up the street. At the far end of the block, Ugene stands over Forrest with an older man, engaged into serious discussion. "There will always be need for people like us. Maybe instead of being part of a cruel system, we can help others build a better one."

Levi grins. "I like the sound of that."

Inside the tent, the physician attempts taking Levi off my hands. I cling to him, escorting him to a bed myself and easing him down. The physician tries to usher me away, but I cross my arms and refuse to budge. How could I ever trust a physician again?

"Bianca!" Dad runs over, winded, concern etched all over his face. "You could have died! What were you thinking running off like that?"

His tone should affront me. I'm stronger than anyone else, and this assuredly was my war. Instead, I fling my arms around him and press my face into his shoulder. Startled, he embraces me, rubbing at my back.

"My baby girl. I'm so sorry about everything."

I wish people would stop apologizing.

"Forrest is in custody," I tell Dad, my voice muffled against his shirt.

Dad stiffens, but his hold doesn't relax. "That's probably for the best." He draws back and grasps my face in both of his hands. Tears redden his eyes. I don't remember seeing him cry before. Then again, I remember little. Still, witnessing so much relief and love and knowing it's directed toward me helps fill the void in my soul.

Levi watches us from his bed, smirking.

Maybe I'm not entirely lost.

Epilogue

LIBERATION DAY, THEY NOW CALL THAT DREADFUL day. The day when we all rose together and freed ourselves from an unjust system.

If they only knew. Some things cannot be liberated.

A couple weeks after Liberation Day, Levi and I approached Ugene and Dr. Finnias—an older fellow whom Ugene trusted to help build a new government. We confessed our part in everything, serving the DMA as agents. I could not have admitted most of what I did without Levi beside me. His presence provided me courage. It continues to provide me strength my enhanced Power could never affect. Levi was first to extend his services to help defend those who worked toward establishing a new government from any potential resistance. Ugene observed me the entire time, waiting.

"What about you?" he asked. "A Powerless idiot like me sure could use a strong bodyguard."

How could I say no when he grinned at me like a boob?

I've memorized my old journal. Every word committed to memory. But those are the words of a girl who no longer exists. No amount of Psionic therapy can restore what I lost. Nevermore—or Terry Poe, as everyone else calls him now—lost his Power in the office on Liberation Day. No one else even comes close to what he was capable of with his enhanced Telepathy. As much as anyone else can surmise, those memories are completely erased from my mind. Every piece of my former self that had any association to Ugene before I woke up in that facility is gone permanently. Nevermore was exceedingly thorough.

At first, I wanted to reclaim those memories, at least some of them. But Ugene has moved on. Whatever might have been is long gone. It's time for me to move on as well.

So I quit going to the therapy sessions my parents arranged and moved into a two-bedroom apartment with Levi downtown. I couldn't stand the disappointment on my parents' faces every time my sessions failed.

Ugene asked me why I elected to quit the therapy. I told him the plain truth. I don't want to remember what they did to me. I've wasted enough of my life looking backward and chasing the past. It's time to accept what and who I am now and proceed forward.

"Maybe some things are best left in the past," I told him. "But right now I just need to find myself."

Whoever that is.

Ugene agreed, even though he sounded a bit disappointed that I wouldn't try to recover memories of our time together before all of this. I would rather build fresh memories than cling to old ones.

I admire this version of Ugene. Whether it's a new him or the same old one, it doesn't matter. He is confident and intelligent and compassionate. People follow him precisely because he doesn't have a Power to use people, because he genuinely has their best interests at heart.

Today, Levi and I will escort Ugene and Enid to the commencement of Tribute Park.

And tomorrow, for once, is my own to decide.

Dying to know how these dangerous
experiments began?

Get a free copy of Superior and find out.

Just visit: www.starrzdavies.com

Read the Powers Series

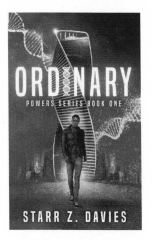

Ordinary (Powers Book 1)

Ugene only wanted a Power. What he got was something far more dangerous.

Read how it all began.

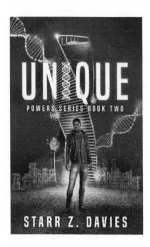

Unique (Powers Book 2)

Ugene and the other test subjects escaped Paragon. They thought they were finally safe. But the battle for freedom is far from over.

Did you enjoy this book?
Don't forget to leave a review on Amazon and
Goodreads! It's like street cred for authors.

ABOUT STARR Z. DAVIES

STARR is a Midwesterner at heart. While pursuing her Creative Writing degree, Starr gained a reputation as the "Character Assassin" because she had a habit of utterly destroying her characters emotionally and physically -- a habit she steadfastly maintains. From a young age, she has been obsessed with superheroes like Batman and Spiderman, which continues to inspire her work.

Follow Starr:

Web: WWW.STARRZDAVIES.COM
Facebook: @SZDavies
Twitter: @SZDavies
Instagram: @S.Z.Davies

Get Dr. Joyce Cass's prequel short story FREE!

Visit: subscribepage.com/starrzdavies_webform